Hauntingly beautiful, Alcina Cove lures many into its lovely port. But these days, the coastal New England town's allure could be deadly....

Drawn back to Alcina Cove by an ominous dream, Maris Granger hopes to reconcile with her beloved but long-estranged Aunt Alva. Sadly, Maris discovers Alva has died under mysterious circumstances, destroying any hope for closure. Bereft and vulnerable, Maris finds shelter in the arms of the sexy, stalwart cop handling the case. But loving Detective Dan Stauffer feels like a betrayal of Aunt Alva's memory, especially when the stubborn lawman denies her sinister suspicions about her aunt's death.

Falling for Maris is easy. Believing in the "clues" the dark-haired beauty swears will solve her aunt's murder is another story. Dan isn't about to let go of reason when it comes to solving the biggest case of his career. But when Maris is suddenly pegged as the prime suspect, Dan is ready to do anything to keep her safe, no matter what dark truths emerge....

Books by Celia Ashley

Dark Tides Series
Dark Tides
Storm Surge
Comes the Dark

Published by Kensington Publishing Corporation

Comes the Dark

A Dark Tides Romance

Celia Ashley

LYRICAL PRESS
Kensington Publishing Corp.
www.kensingtonbooks.com

To the believers in this world

Author's Foreword

I know readers have wondered why I write what I do. In my other existence (well, under my other pen name) I write sweet romance, wholesome and, at this point in time, centered around small town life and the holiday season. Readers wonder where the darkness in this world of Alcina Cove comes from. I freely admit, at the risk of sounding dramatic, it comes from experience. I have witnessed the paranormal—the first time as a very young child—and I have had premonitions of events that have come to pass, both while dreaming and when awake and staring with open eyes at something I could not possibly be seeing. None of these events have been, perhaps, as mysterious and dark as the situations in which I place my characters, but we as writers all draw on experience somewhere and expound on that hard-won knowledge to create mood and tale. I know a few of you have questioned with digital frowns the flights of dark fancy my stories take, but not all paranormal is werewolves and vampires, shape shifters and demons. Some of it comes much closer to real life. And some of it moves clearly to the other side of life…

Acknowledgements

Once again, I would like to thank the sisters in my writers group. When the going gets tough, they are always quick with a well-aimed kick to the inspiration. Thanks again to my editor, Corinne, who is not only great at her job but provides an excellent sounding board for all things.

And as always, thank you dear readers for keeping your faith in me and making me remember the reason I write.

Chapter 1

"The Sun's rim dips; the stars rush out:
At one stride comes the dark."
Samuel Taylor Coleridge – *The Rime of the Ancient Mariner*

No one got a second chance. Not really. There were no reconstructed moments, no opportunities to make a different decision, because all the time between could not be erased. The consequences of choice remained. All one could hope for was a chance to start again.

Maris finished packing her bag. She zipped it shut, clutching the zipper tag between thumb and forefinger so tightly the raised letters on metal imprinted themselves into her flesh.

Time to go.

To her right, white curtains fluttered with a song's rhythm, rising in a pale, curling billow and falling back again, the delicate rasp of lace against the window screen like sand settling over paper. Cold, the air—colder than it had been for more than a week. Too early. September was the month for embedding one's fingernails into the last of summer, unwilling to let it go. Instead, the temperature felt like winter's onset, as if the season was rushing toward bone-chill and long nights. When she'd first climbed into bed, the air had been refreshing. Now she hastened to shut and lock the casement before adding her wool coat to the items on the bed.

Maris glanced at the clock. Midnight. Yes. Time to go.

It would be hard driving on two hours sleep, but the weighted urgency would carry her through, keep her eyes wide and her thoughts alert. She hadn't dreamed in a very long time. Not of that place. Not of the woman who waited for her there.

Reaching for the switch on the bedside lamp, Maris paused in contemplation of the brown plastic bottle she'd told herself to leave behind. The sleeping pills kept the dreams at bay, held the haunting down to a minimum. She didn't take them every night. Last night she hadn't, and the past had broken through. Perhaps it would all be too much. Perhaps... yes, perhaps she should bring the pills with her.

She grabbed the medicine bottle—and the diary, too—shoving both items into her purse. Before turning off the light, Maris gave herself a final look in the mirror, finger-fluffing her short, dark hair as she stared into the eyes looking back at her. Black-lashed, gray as smoke. *Her* eyes.

Outside, she stowed the canvas satchel, her laptop, and an insulated lunch bag on the passenger side floor. She tossed her coat over the seat with her purse and went back around to the driver's side where she spent a moment studying the sky. Earlier clouds had been ushered to the sidelines by the cold front. Stars shone in velvety blackness, barely dimmed by the lights of the strip mall in the distance. Before the intervention of modern technology, sailors navigated by the stars. She supposed many still did. The last sailor she'd known had died nine years past. She hadn't let his stories die with him, though. In those final days, she'd written down by hand into a notebook every word her father had spoken, then transferred the narratives to her laptop. One day she would see those marvelous tales of the sea published. That was her plan. But like many other plans, there were no assurances.

One hundred miles into her drive and the pavement of the interstate awash in the glow of her headlights, a pair of blue eyes flashed into her mind's eye with such clarity her gut wrenched. She had no idea whose they were, but a name had come with them. A first name only. No one she knew. Maris pulled her car off onto the shoulder of the highway and stopped. Gripping the wheel with tightly curled fingers, she leaned toward the glow of the dashboard lights, bile churning in her stomach.

I'm sorry, my dear. So very sorry...

No one got a second chance.

Chapter 2

Dan slapped across the surface of the nightstand in search of the buzzing cell phone, head pounding with each vibration of his palm against wood. Locating the instrument, he snatched it up to his ear, smacking himself in the temple. Ow.

"Dan Stauffer here." Dan cleared his throat before speaking again. "What's up?" He glanced at the clock. "At three forty-five in the damned morning."

His head hurt. Sometimes one more beer could be the one that caused the damage. He hadn't been drunk, but for some reason he felt like he had one hell of a hangover. Maybe it was a cold coming on. This damned, indecisive weather didn't help. "Hello?"

"We've got a body."

"Where?" Groaning, Dan swung his legs over the side of the bed. He leaned forward, squinting at the bright rays of the streetlight burning through the slats of the blinds. He crossed the floor, and with an aching stretch of his arm, he reached up and shut them, dimming the room to near-darkness. What the heck had he been doing? Sure, he'd spent some time at the gym before heading out with the guys, but being hit by a truck hadn't been in his exercise regimen.

"Alva Mabry's."

Rubbing his eyes, Dan scanned the floor through his fingers for the clothes he'd discarded earlier. Paler than the dark rug beneath them, they lay in a shadowed, crumpled heap. "Is it Alva herself?"

"Looks to be."

Dan massaged the back of his neck, turning his head from side to side. "You don't know for sure?"

"Whitley's here. He says it's her. I've never met the woman."

"Never had the hankering to get your fortune told?" His joke met by silence, Dan straightened. "Signs of foul play?"

Dan heard a voice in the background—presumably Whitley—speaking in an undertone. Officer Green spoke once the other officer had finished.

"Not really," he said without inflection.

Dan paused as he reached for his pants. "Not really or no? You need to be more specific when I'm asking questions."

Green inhaled and then hesitated before speaking. "Then the answer would be no."

"Alva has to be more than ninety years old. I'm willing to lay odds on natural causes."

"I don't want to make that call, Detective. That would...that would be your job."

Dan didn't need the reminder. He didn't like the reminder. Since his advancement to detective several months ago, he'd noted some of the younger officers were miffed. He didn't understand why. He had seniority over them all, and the position was based on experience. He'd worked hard for it. The promotion certainly hadn't been handed to him as matter of favoritism. Far from it.

"All right," Dan said. "I'll be there in ten minutes."

"Look, Detective Stauffer, I apologize if it seems I'm out of line. It's just...well, there's something off about her. The dead lady."

Jonathan Green was fairly young. Maybe this was his first dead body and his reaction one of nerves. "Okay," Dan said in an attempt at reassurance, "I'll be heading out in a sec."

"You need the address?"

"Nope. I know the place."

Dan hung up and pulled on his pants. His button-down shirt had been slung crookedly over the back of the desk chair, and he pulled it free. He held the fabric to his face to breathe in the scent of perfume clinging to the soft folds. Nice. Trouble was he couldn't even remember the woman's name. He hadn't had *that* much to drink tonight. His inability to recall the identity of the perfume owner had nothing to do with inebriation, only lack of interest.

God, was he that much of a bastard? He didn't want to be. As he slipped his arms into his shirtsleeves, he gave brief consideration to his defunct marriage. Funny, everyone figured he'd caused the demise of that relationship. He had a reputation. Not a particularly good one. Not unfounded. But for the time he'd been married, he'd been an honest husband. It had been his wife who'd strayed, who eventually left him for some guy she hooked up with in the grocery store after discussing the cost of chicken with him. Dan had spent the years since making sure he didn't get hurt again. Maybe he'd gotten too good at it.

Shoving his feet into his shoes, he snorted. Hell, the issues between him and his ex had begun long before she found a lover in the packaged meat aisle. And that was something for which they both were to blame.

Dan dropped his cell phone into his pants pocket, grabbed his keys, ID, and wallet, and jogged down the stairs, body protesting. He snagged his jacket from the banister as he passed. As he put on the garment, he noticed lipstick on the lapel. The marking appeared deliberately placed to form a full set of lips. Dan pulled a tissue out of the box by the door and scrubbed the oily substance off. "Sorry, Miss Nameless, but I don't need the guys seeing that."

Not at an investigation. Not in front of men who resented him enough already.

As he backed out of the garage, he glanced in the rearview mirror and stopped short, the force of the brakes jerking him in the seat. A feminine silhouette blocked the driveway behind his car, a shawl on her shoulders blowing like a flag in the breeze. He started to get out, then paused. He could see through her to the post of the streetlight across the road. Tightening his fingers on the inside handle, he pulled the door shut.

"Not tonight. I don't need this type of shit tonight."

The figure didn't move. Dan held a silent debate with himself regarding the difference between reality and the effects of sleep deprivation. "Get away from me. I mean it."

Good God, if anyone at the station could hear him now he'd be up for a psych evaluation. He couldn't deny, though, that he'd seen his share of strange, but he had hoped to go the rest of his lifetime without a repeat. He opted to wait, keeping the figure in sight in his rearview. After a moment, the apparition turned and vanished like smoke in the wind.

With a great deal of profanity, Dan backed the car from the driveway and sped down the street in the direction of Alva Mabry's house, pushing the hair at his nape down with an open palm. A few years back, he'd learned rather horrifically that more existed in this world than logic could explain. But what did a person do with that type of knowledge? It wasn't something a man imparted to others as the wisdom of experience. No, it was the kind of information a man kept to himself, mouth shut, teeth clenched against the yell that always wanted to escape at the memory.

When Dan reached Alva Mabry's two-story, nineteenth-century house at the edge of the commercial district of Alcina Cove, two marked cars were already parked out front. The nearest partially blocked the purple sign that read in large, block letters *Alva Mabry, Psychic - Palmistry and Tarot Card Readings*. Dan managed to prevent rolling his eyes at the last second. A little respect for the dead might be in order. No matter what her occupation, Alva had been a resident of Alcina Cove for nearly a century. And if a man believed he'd seen ghosts, who the heck was he to question a woman's claim to clairvoyance or an ability to speak with those very spirits? Even so, the notion made him far from comfortable. He wanted to deny all of it outright, but lying had its own costs.

Dan closed the car door with a quiet *click*. As he strode across the sidewalk and up the steps to the front door, he shoved his hands into his pockets in a search for the notepad and pen he'd clearly forgotten to grab from his desk. Green and the other officer, Whitley, stood together in the foyer of the antiquated white house, not doing much of anything. Dan nodded at the man who'd phoned him. "Green. Where's the body?"

The two uniformed men stepped back, parting in opposite directions like a pair of double doors. Dan looked past them into the parlor Alva utilized for her business and sucked a breath in through his teeth. He resisted the urge to smooth the fine hairs on his neck again. "Shit."

"See what I mean?" Green said.

Dan walked into the room in silence. His contact with the dead wasn't the same as what this woman had claimed when alive, but in the corporeal sense. In a harbor town, there were plenty of drowning victims. Accident victims, too, and the occasional murder, as well as those who had died from whatever natural cause had taken them. Even so, Dan's heart had skipped a beat at the sight of Alva Mabry sitting bolt upright in the red upholstered wing-back chair behind the draped table. Her thin arms lay along the tabletop. Clouded eyes in a wrinkled face slanted at an angle that made them appear to be watching Dan and the officers behind him.

"Shit," Dan said again and hastened forward. "Did either of you think to take her damned pulse?"

He reached for the woman's arm as the two men protested—of course they had. Dan closed his fingers on chilled flesh. Pressing his middle finger against the inside of Alva's narrow wrist, he found no evidence of life. He watched her chest for movement, bent his cheek to her face to feel for breath, pressed the flesh beneath her jaw. Alva was definitely gone.

Dropping his hand to his thigh with a small slap against fabric, Dan sighed. "Did you call the medical examiner's office?"

"Yep." This from Whitley.

"What have you touched in here?" When neither of them answered, Dan glanced back.

"Nothing," said Green. "I called you first."

"All right."

Dan stared at the body in the chair, a fringed shawl draped across the shoulders in folds, as if blown by a current of air. The memory of the silhouette, shawl fluttering in the wind behind his car, came back to him. "Bloody hell."

"What's up, Detective?"

Dan raised his hand in dismissal of his own brief expletive and moved forward, making a careful stroll around the table's circumference, looking for anything that might be lying on the floor. He settled each foot one step at a time, eyes downcast. No scuff marks on the carpet, no debris. With the exception of the uncanny positioning of Alva's body, all appeared in order. "Who called this in?"

"A neighbor noticed the parlor lights on. Figured it was late for that, so asked us to check on her."

He shot a glance at Whitley. "And what was this neighbor doing out at this hour?"

"Walking his dog," Whitley informed him. "Seemed straight up."

Dan nodded and completed his circuit around the table, pausing once again at the woman's right side. He bent and studied Alva's neck, her face. He looked over her clothing, her hands resting on the table, the right turned up, a single card gripped in the fingers. Beyond them, a series of illustrated cards lay in a pattern on the table. Dan assumed the card in Alva's hand coincided with the one empty space. He didn't know anything about Tarot reading, although he had heard that people sometimes performed their own. Across from Alva, the guest chair remained pushed against the table and the rug beneath undisturbed. He felt safe in concluding the presence of the cards didn't necessarily mean someone had been there.

Dan's gaze strayed back to the card in Alva's hand. He wondered what the picture on it signified and supposed each card held a meaning. Perhaps the pattern in which they ended up on the table did, as well. Quackery, if you asked him. The pictures, however, were quite beautiful, especially the one in Alva's hand. What he could see of it appeared to be a woman in ceremonial garb, dark hair curling down her shoulders but partially concealed by some type of headdress.

He heard the voice of the local ME outside at the bottom of the short flight of steps leading to the front door. God, he'd forgotten to close it. He glanced at Alva apologetically, but stopped at the realization she was beyond caring. He turned back to the two officers. "I always heard Alva didn't have any family. Did you locate any signs of her people? Photos?"

Green stirred. "Not in here, but we'll check around the house. Hello, Dr. Rankin."

Charlie Rankin lumbered into the room carrying a folded black bag. He nodded. "Jonathan. Dick. Dan, congratulations on the promotion."

"Thanks," Dan said. The young officers exchanged a glance. Dan ignored them. Rankin's assistant arrived dragging a rattling gurney.

Rankin cleared his throat. Beside him, the younger man, eyes wide, glanced at Alva, then around the decorated parlor. Rankin's face wrinkled in amusement. "Ed here thinks Alva's ghost is going to follow him home."

Dan frowned. "And why would he think that?"

Ed's voice squeaked like a dry hinge as he answered, "The things she's done. You know, seeing the future, talking to the dead. All of it."

Grunting, Dan stepped out of their way. "Ed, that's a load of bullshit. She was good at fooling people, that's all."

Rankin chuckled and started his cursory exam. Dan backed to the corner, instructing Whitley and Green to check the house for photos or paperwork that might help with notification. "You see any evidence someone else has been searching the place before you, give me a shout."

"No family?" Rankin asked.

"Not that I'm aware. Never heard of any, and it's always been rumored she was the last Mabry."

"A shame."

Dan released a breath as Ed unzipped the bag and laid it on the floor. Rankin removed the card from Alva's fingers, placing it on the vibrant tablecloth. Dan lifted the card to the light fixture centered over the table. The corners were worn with use, the sheen gone, yet the blue of the woman's dress remained strong, shimmering in the bulb's illumination against a background yellowed with age. The woman's eyes stared out from the picture in an enigmatic gaze. Other symbols lurked in the illustrated scenery. Yes, really quite beautiful. Dan was about to toss the card down when Ed spoke beside him.

"The Priestess card," he said.

Dan frowned. "The what?"

"The Priestess."

"What is that? And how do you know?"

Ed shrugged. "Been around it some growing up. The women in my family fancied themselves touched by the Sight or something. Hate all of it."

"Hate's a pretty strong word. Some reason for that?"

"Don't mind him," Rankin said with a jerk of his head toward Ed. "He's a superstitious youngster."

"Oh, because superstition is something you outgrow," Ed shot back at him. "I've seen you cross yourself before moving a body."

"That's religion. There's a difference." With that, he raised his hand and did precisely what Ed had said.

Funny, Dan had never noticed that ritual of Rankin's before. Ed grunted without further reply and turned to assist with moving Alva's body into the bag. Dan watched dispassionately, noting how Alva remained somewhat pliable. Less than three hours since she'd died then. "Look natural to you?" he asked Rankin.

"Given her age and some of the indications, probably a heart attack. I'll do a few tests back at the morgue. Not a full-out autopsy, but just something to tell her next of kin, if she has any. And for the death certificate."

Dan nodded. Whitley and Green returned, the latter shaking his head. "No photos," he said. "Not a one. A basket full of bills, some marked paid, others…well, not. Could be something in the attic. We didn't go up there. The house didn't look disturbed. How much do you want us to dig?"

Dan's gaze followed the slow pull of the zipper on the heavy black bag. "Before we tear the house apart, I'll ask questions of the neighbors in the morning. Thanks."

"Kinda sad, having no one," Green added.

Dan gave the junior officer a curious look. "Agreed."

"What do you know about her? Alva Mabry," Green persisted.

Cocking an eyebrow, Dan shrugged. "To most of the residents, Alva was a harmless fortune teller relying more on a practiced formula than any psychic ability. That is, if you believe in that sort of thing."

From the floor on his knees beside the body bag, Ed raised a hand with forefinger and pinkie extended like a pair of horns. When he saw Dan watching, he muttered, "To ward off the evil eye."

"Oh, for crying out loud," Rankin said. "Enough already."

"It doesn't matter anyway," Dan said. "She's not going to make any more predictions, no matter how inaccurate."

"I wouldn't joke," Ed said in a warning tone.

"I wasn't joking."

Rankin stood and stretched. "I'd bet on natural causes without blinking an eye."

Before Dan could make a suitable reply, his cell buzzed in his pocket. He pulled out the phone. "Stauffer."

"Detective, there's a woman here at the station asking for you."

Dan's mind jumped to the owner of the perfume still scenting his shirt. For the sake of propriety, he suppressed a grin. "Who is it, Mac? What's her name?"

"She won't give me her name. But I wouldn't keep her waiting."

Had to be the perfume owner, but why the hell she'd shown up at the station, he had no idea. Especially at this hour. "Hot?"

"In so many strange but perfect ways," Mac said.

Snorting, Dan hung up, his heart doing a little dance in his chest. He issued last minute instructions to Green and Whitley and returned to his car with deliberate nonchalance. Once inside, he checked his hair in the rearview mirror. Since making detective, he'd let his hair grow out a little from the close-cropped style he'd worn for years. Sometimes strands stuck out at ridiculous angles, but it all looked reasonably placed for the moment.

Putting the car in gear, he headed for the station. Halfway there, he remembered picking up the Priestess card and his hand flew to his breast pocket. "Crap-freaking-tastic."

He knew better. Damn it, he knew better. Crime scene or not, no one walked out with material from the location, but Dan had slipped the blasted Tarot card into his shirt. Without conscious thought, sure, but still he'd done something that stupid.

He considered turning the car around but rejected the idea. No point now. It wasn't like anyone was going to miss it. He'd restore the oversize card to the deck tomorrow.

At the station, he parked and hopped out, feeling somewhat rejuvenated by anticipation of a pleasant interlude with the woman from the bar. He locked the vehicle on the fly as he raced up the steps. Despite the fact he couldn't remember the scented woman's name, he found himself recalling certain promising attributes. And if the woman was that anxious to hook up with him that she tracked him down, well, so be it.

Dan let himself in the back door. He slowed his steps in the hallway that led toward the front desk. No need to act like a fool. He rounded the corner at a stroll with his hand in his coat, nodding at the officer on duty. "Mac. Where'd you put her?"

"In your office."

"Thanks." Dan strode inside, pretending an intense study of the car keys he'd removed from his pocket. A rustle of cloth greeted him as the woman in question stood. He paused, arranging his features into a look of mild curiosity prior to facing her. When he turned, his heart gave a sharp jolt at the sight of the woman before him. Short, dark hair framed an amazing face and the most striking eyes he had ever seen.

He met her gaze. "Who the hell are you?"

Chapter 3

Maris focused all her annoyance into the hand gripping her purse and then discharged the emotion with a single, long breath from her nostrils. Better. After all, this man looked to have had a hard night. No need to judge him on his opening statement. Obviously, he had been expecting someone else. "Dan, is it?"

"Yes, yes, Dan Stauffer," he replied impatiently. "Detective Dan Stauffer. Why don't you go ahead and sit back down. You can tell me who you are and why you demanded I return to the station."

As he was speaking, he had stridden to the chair behind the desk and dropped into it like a lead weight. The chair squeaked, rolling back a few inches across the plastic mat beneath. Yes, aggravated and disappointed. He had been expecting another woman. Maris wondered who as she resumed her seat and crossed her legs at the knee with a flip of the long skirt over her boots. Not his wife. Not with that kind of reaction. No ring on his finger anyway. She had noticed when Detective Stauffer yanked open a drawer in his desk from which he pulled a yellow legal pad and a ballpoint pen. No thinning of the flesh on the ring finger either. If he'd been married, must have been a while ago. Some men didn't wear rings, though…

Dan Stauffer cleared his throat. Maris straightened.

"Detective Stauffer, I did not demand your return."

The man clicked the pen twice with the ball of his thumb. "That wasn't the impression I got."

Maris shrugged. "I cannot help the impression you received. I can only tell you that I did not demand anything."

"Except to speak to me."

"I was adamant," Maris clarified. "Not demanding."

The man gave the pen another click and wrote something at the top of the lined page. "Name?"

"Mine?"

He squinted at her. "Who else?"

"Maris. M-a-r-i-s. Granger. G-r-a-n-g-e-r."

His lips quirked at one corner as he applied pen to paper again, gaze intent on the pad balanced across his cocked knee. Maris took advantage of his preoccupation to study his face. The annoyance had left it, leaving his features relaxed, the vivid blue eyes she had glimpsed shuttered now by thick, short lashes and downturned lids. A cowlick in his sandy hair stuck up at a point to the right of his forehead. He lifted his gaze and looked at her. She lowered hers, avoiding his eyes, to concentrate on pulling a piece of lint from the sleeve of her jacket.

"Why did you ask for me, Ms. Granger?"

"I asked for Dan."

"And that's me. No other Dans or Daniels in this station. Once again, why did you ask for me?"

Maris's fingers shook. She shoved them beneath the hem of her coat. "I was…I was told to."

"Who told you?"

This wasn't going to be easy. She didn't like lying, but she'd spent so long skirting certain truths that to tell a falsehood in these matters had become second nature. She never really felt they were lies, only misleading statements in avoidance of ridicule and disaster. Besides, second nature or not, she wasn't much good at it. She always wanted to preface her words with "I'm a good person," and even though she didn't, she figured the sentiment often showed on her face because it had been very hard to keep friends as a child. As an adult, well, she continued the loner pattern with resigned acceptance.

"Ms. Granger?"

"I'd rather not say, Detective."

"That's not really acceptable. Not in my line of work. What is it you want?"

Maris let her breath out in a long, silent release. She reached into her purse, pulled out her wallet, and flipped through the old-fashioned protective pages until she reached a certain photograph at the very back. She wriggled the photo free and slid it across the desk to the man. Frowning, he picked up the picture, turning it toward the bulb in the lamp at his side. His attention snapped back to Maris.

"Is your child missing?"

"I have no children. The baby is my father. And the woman holding him is his aunt."

"You look exactly like her."

"Check the clothing and the condition of the photo. The woman is not me."

Brow wrinkling in further study of the photograph, Dan Stauffer's lips thinned in displeasure, possibly at being directed to see the obvious. Maris nodded at the picture in his hand. "My great-aunt, to be precise. Alva Mabry. And I believe she has died. This very night, in fact."

He said nothing.

"Tell me," Maris persisted, "am I right?"

He turned the pen and tapped it several times on the top end of the pad. His left hand lifted to the pocket on his shirt and hovered there briefly before returning to lie flat on the desktop.

"Yes." He clicked the pen again twice. Point in. Point out. Thoughts flew across the man's face more swiftly than he could possibly have realized. "I'm sorry for your loss. I wasn't aware Alva had any family left. No one at her house tonight was either. Someone at the station contact you?"

"No."

He leaned toward her. "I'd be interested in knowing who did call you, then. Was it the neighbor who contacted the department? We would have gotten around to the neighbors later today regarding family."

Maris drew a steadying breath. "No one called me, Detective. I drove straight here from my home."

"I'm not following."

"I...I had a dream."

"I'm sorry, what?"

She'd been hiding this—gift? curse?—for so many years now she'd forgotten what it felt like to witness the derision. Except in him, it wasn't quite that. He'd known someone like her in his past and didn't want to admit it. She felt sure of it. "I had a dream my aunt wanted me here, that I needed to come right away, after all these years. And then, on the way, I knew she had died and that you were at her home."

Stauffer's eyes narrowed. "You'll forgive me if I'm a little skeptical about what you're saying. Do you, by chance, have access to a police scanner?"

"A police scanner? I live a hundred and fifty miles away. Even if I did have such a thing as a police scanner, I certainly wouldn't hear about anything in Alcina Cove. It took me more than three hours to get here."

"Address?" he asked in a gruff tone, shooting a look at the clock on the wall above his desk.

"Pardon me?"

He shook the pen poised above the pad. "What is your address? Also, some identification if you wouldn't mind?"

With a lift of her brow, Maris took out her license and slid it across the desk to lie beside the photo. "There. You can copy my information from that. The address is current."

He took his time in doing so, writing everything out with deliberation. After studying the license a moment longer, he held it out to her. "You don't have to prove to me you were related to Alva. That would be an issue for her estate attorney, although if that really is a picture of your great-aunt, I would say there is no question. Did she have a large estate? She didn't live like she did, but you never know."

She bristled, snatching back both items. "Of course it's Aunt Alva. And I resent your implication. I really do." She dropped the wallet into her purse and followed with a pull to the zipper that broke it. Maris swore under her breath. She dropped her hands to her lap. "There was an estrangement in the family years ago. I...I was too young to understand the reasons why." Yes, another lie. Damn it, would she ever be permitted to stop? "I haven't seen or spoken to my great-aunt since, I'm ashamed to say. All I know is that she came to me in a dream, and that alone brought me here." Maris blinked back tears of frustration and—even after all this time—grief. "I only want to know what happened."

"What happened? She died, Ms. Granger. I'm still curious as to how you knew."

"I told you—"

"I know. You had a dream." He sighed. "Where does your aunt live?"

"What? You were there, weren't you? You didn't deny it."

"Oh, yes, I certainly was there. But I'm asking you the question. Where does—did she live?"

For some reason, Maris had been foolish enough not to expect this type of interrogation. She frowned. "Here. In your town. After all this time, I don't remember her exact address, or I would have driven straight there. An old white house, tiny, with a fence, and there used to be a small business sign out front, too."

"Right. Well, it's a big sign now, purple with gold letters. I have another question."

"Go ahead."

"What made you ask for me? I need a real answer to that."

Maris bent her head. She moved her fingers across the supple surface of her purse. She wanted to grab her keys from the front pocket, walk out the door, and not look back. But she couldn't run away. Not this time.

Clearing her throat, she met his eyes, the stunning blue that made her think of the sky. "Because Alva told me to. She said you were the one."

"In your dream."

"No. After the dream. While I was driving. The dead do speak, you know."

He didn't respond, but after a moment, he set the pen down on the desk as if dismissing the need for its use. The discussion clearly over, she gathered her purse against her chest, readying to rise from her seat. She was halfway up when he spoke again.

"Forensically, yes, they do speak. Outside of that, I have experienced some...unexplained incidents here in Alcina Cove. It's not called 'haunted Alcina Cove' for nothing, I suppose." He snorted, more in self-derision than amusement.

Maris sat back down.

"And I'd like to believe you—"

"Except you don't," Maris whispered.

"Except I don't," he agreed.

"I thought...my aunt—well, that you would find out everything about tonight."

Once more she met his gaze. Something moved in his eyes, a knowledge of darkness, fear. He blinked, banishing the ghosts in his life back to where he kept them hidden. He picked up the pen again. Click.

"There's another problem with what you're saying. There's nothing to discover. It would appear Alva Mabry passed from the most natural of causes—old age."

With a twist deep in her abdomen, Maris stood. "I don't understand."

"The ME believes it to be the case. As I do. I don't like having my time wasted, Ms. Granger. Especially at this hour."

"I'm not trying to waste your time. I'm trying to get answers."

"There aren't any answers to get. I suggest you go to wherever you're staying for the night, and tomorrow I'll take you to the house. If the estrangement you spoke of really exists, you may need an address book in order to make funeral arrangements."

"Fine. But I'd rather go now."

"Now?"

"Right now."

He beat a rolling rhythm across the desktop with his fingertips, the pen in his other hand keeping time in counterpoint. She had a sudden urge to take the pen from him and throw it across the room.

"All right."

Maris's shoulders relaxed. "Thank you."

Dan Stauffer heaved himself up from the chair. He wasn't a big man. Less than six feet with a natural build. Not the sort of man who tended to muscular bulk, even if he worked at it. But not weak. Not for one moment. He moved as if the man inside of him, inside his head, was huge. He probably lived his life with the same attitude, fearless but for the darkness he had known. She might wrestle the information of his experience out of him, but she doubted it. He'd never give her the time… or reveal that weakness.

Chapter 4

Dan felt himself hunching over the steering wheel in a defensive position. He tried to settle down, sit back, but found he couldn't. The knuckles of his hand shone white beneath the skin in the streetlights' glow. In the passenger seat, Maris sat with her own hands folded in her lap.

"Detective."

"Yeah?"

"Relax. I'm not the big bad wolf. I'm not scary."

The hell you aren't. He thought of another woman he had known, a woman with dreams who'd allowed an evil into her life, and into his, too.

"Take deep breaths. In through your nose, out through your mouth."

Part of him wanted to lash out at her words, but the less primal portion of his brain recognized the sense in them. He breathed in, let the air out.

"Once more."

He did so, loosening his grip on the wheel. With a release of the curve in his spine, he settled back against the seat, filling his lungs again.

"What are you afraid of? Psychic ability isn't a malevolent gift."

His breath left him in an audible rush. "I'm not afraid, least of all of you. It's been a very long day, starting at about five o'clock yesterday morning with less than two hours of sleep in between."

"But that's not my fault." She glanced at him. "Is it?"

"I didn't say it was. I'm just explaining—"

"Okay."

His molars ground together. "I don't believe there's any such thing as clairvoyance either. Sorry." God, when had he become such a bald-faced liar? When necessity had made him one, he supposed.

"Were you out celebrating something last night?"

He glanced at her and away, back to the road. "Yes. My promotion to detective several months ago. Finally got the chance. Why? Did you 'see' that, too?"

"No." She shifted in the seat, turning her attention to the street outside the window. "You smell a bit like alcohol. You know, when it's been in your system a while."

Dan shook his head. If she could smell it, Whitley and Green and even Rankin and his assistant had probably gotten a good whiff, too. "Today was supposed to be my day off. I never would have picked last night if I'd known I'd be working." Why was he explaining himself to her?

"And perfume."

"What?" He bent his head, sniffing at his shirt collar.

"Very nice scent, actually. I couldn't smell any of this in the office, but now that we're confined in your car, well…"

He suppressed a groan of frustration. Like her great-aunt, Maris Granger noticed a damned sight too much, a talent that made people susceptible to their load of crap. They weren't reading anything, "seeing" anything. They paid attention. Period.

"Was that who you were expecting?" Maris went on, relentless. "When you came in and saw me, I mean. The woman whose perfume is clinging to your clothes?"

Jaw clenched, Dan applied the turn signal. "Would you mind not talking, please?"

In the light thrown from the dashboard, he witnessed her deadpan expression broaden into a grin. The volcanic eruption of his blood at the sight of her surprisingly sexy smile burned the inclination to snap at her to ashes.

Oh no you don't, Danny boy. That's about as screwed up as you could get.

He pulled the car to the curb. "Well, Ms. Granger, here we are."

"Maris."

Nope. He wasn't going to allow himself that familiarity. Not after the heat that had whipped through him. He turned off the ignition and climbed out of the car. Maris followed a moment later. She stood beside him on the sidewalk, her gaze straying to the one patrol unit still parked out front.

"Finishing up, I expect," he said.

"With what?"

"Securing the place."

"You can ask the neighbors about me if you need to. Don't think they'll remember." She took a long moment in consideration of Alva Mabry's house, brow creased in an attitude he couldn't read. The bangs of her short dark hair drifted over her smoke-colored eyes in a current of air. What had Mac said? *Hot in so many strange but perfect ways.* Dan could see that. Yeah, he could see that.

He cleared his throat. "How long ago did you move away?"

"Twenty years? Long time. Long enough for no one around here to remember anymore, I'm sure."

Dan shoved his hands into his jacket pockets, giving her a minute. She took a step closer to the lawn and paused. He eyed her clothing, the black, laced-up boots, the mid-calf skirt that looked as if it had been manufactured in another century, the coat, too, fitted and flared in an old-fashioned design. Not a style he would have picked out in a crowd except maybe to gawk at, but something about it suited her. Marched to her own drummer, Maris Granger did.

"Did the people of this town come to respect my aunt before she died? For…for what she practiced?"

He hesitated before answering. He didn't want to tell her the truth because he knew the truth would hurt her. And why should that matter?

"I'm sure they did," he found himself saying. "Maybe not all, but I know she did a good business."

Maris nodded. He contemplated her profile, the petite features almost elfin in character. He pictured her in a red Santa hat and almost laughed.

"What you're thinking, Detective Stauffer? Not funny."

He sucked in a breath. "Okay. That was just creepy."

"Sorry." She spun to face him again. "Can we go inside now?"

God, yes. Anything but standing outside staring at a strange woman while besotted school boy thoughts ran through his brain. Once he got himself under control, he would chalk it up to lack of sleep and whatever trace of alcohol might still be in his bloodstream. For now, though, he hastened ahead of her and held open the door. She stepped inside and stopped.

"I remember this," she said quietly. Officer Whitley paused in reaching for the light switch nearest the door. He looked from Maris to Dan, his eyes as wide as a shying horse.

"Detective?"

"Sorry. Maris Granger, Officer Dick Whitley. Ms. Granger came to the station to speak with me about the death of Alva Mabry. Her great-aunt."

"But how did she even know Mabry had died?"

"A very good question to have answered," Dan said. From the corner of his eye, he saw the arched wings of Maris's eyebrows lift. She opened her mouth, probably to voice her objection to being spoken about as if she wasn't present, or worse, to tell Whitley what she had told him, about the nonsense of her "dreams." Dan forestalled the mention of either. "We'll lock up. Thanks, Whitley."

Whitley gave Dan an uncertain nod. "Nice to meet you, Ms. Granger. I'm sorry about your aunt." He left, pulling the door closed behind him.

Maris headed into the darkened parlor and paused on the threshold. She ran her hand over the wall in search of the switch and turned on the fixture over the table.

"Don't touch anything," Dan instructed.

"You said you believed her death was natural."

"I did. I do. But until there's definite confirmation, we're going to keep our hands in our pockets, got it?"

"Got it."

Dan resisted the urge to grab his shirt where the Priestess card lay tucked away. Too late to sneak it back onto the table. Damn it. How could he have done something so idiotic? Especially fresh into his newly promoted position. Fuck.

"Something wrong, Detective?"

He narrowed his eyes. "Did I curse out loud? I'm sorry."

"Nope. You didn't."

Intuition. A long study of body language. Something. She was *not* reading his mind. Not. No freaking way.

She walked around the table much as he had done earlier, her hands clasped together behind her back. Instead of looking at the floor, though, her gaze was on the papered walls, taking in the few paintings. She came fully round to the chair and nodded at it. "Is this where you found her?"

He cleared his throat with a brief cough. "Yes."

"Sitting up?"

A chill danced along his nape. "Yes."

She studied the layout of the cards, her dark hair swinging forward along her neck. He did his best not to follow the movement but the dark, silky strands against the paleness of her skin fascinated him.

"She was performing a reading for someone."

"No, I don't think so." He jerked his chin toward the opposite side of the table. "The other chair was pushed up. The carpet was unmarked. There would have been indentations had anyone been sitting in the chair and moved it back. She, your aunt, hadn't been gone very long when she was found."

Maris lifted her head, gazing toward the far side of the room. "How long?"

"I'm not a medical professional, but I'd wager a few hours only."

Maris closed her eyes, tipped back her head, her neck slender, long, and graceful. He pictured his mouth against it and looked away. Fantasies like these could land him in deep trouble. He didn't even know the woman. He hadn't known the woman in the bar either, yet off he'd run to the station imagining she'd come looking for him. Imagining a good deal more than that. He needed a grip on reality.

"There's a card missing."

Dan started guiltily. "Is there?" The Priestess flashed into his mind's eye in her blue garment, dark hair long and curling. He mentally shoved it away, apprehensive that she would see it, too. An absurd notion he couldn't shake.

"Right here. From the formation." She pointed at the empty space on the cloth. "Of course, she might have been in the process of laying them out when she died." She turned and looked at him directly, her eyes almond-shaped, long-lashed, and so very pale. There was no denying the familial relationship between her and Alva Mabry. Strange how much they looked alike. He couldn't imagine a generation lay between them based on the photo.

Scanning the table again, Maris's gaze flickered over the surface, then seemed to linger on the empty place among the Tarot cards. He had a feeling she knew exactly where the missing card had ended up. The sensation of her knowledge troubled him more than if she had accused him outright, called him out on a mistake, a momentary lapse of awareness. But to pull the stupid thing from his pocket now would make him look like an ass. Dishonest even. And yet he wanted to. Wanted to ask her to tell him what the card meant, explain its significance. As if he'd ever really given a crap about something like that.

"Detective."

He released a breath. "What?"

"Someone was here. Aunt Alva was not alone when she died. She's telling me that."

"No."

"What?"

"No. In no way am I going to believe your deceased aunt is giving you information from beyond." And yet he'd known others who'd experienced the unexplained—people with whom he shared more than the acquaintance of a mere half an hour. God, he'd seen things himself that sometimes caused him to wake out of a sound sleep soaked in sweat and reaching for the light. The vanishing figure behind his car tonight paled in comparison. Had strangeness become so commonplace that he rejected and mocked it?

"Believe what you want. As her only surviving blood relative, I am asking you to check. Do not dismiss my aunt's death so easily. I don't care how old she was. I think she deserves a few hours of your time. I'm not denying her death was natural, but whoever was here with her might be able to tell me something about her last moments."

"Ms. Granger…"

"Maris. Call me Maris, will you? Calling me 'Ms' anything isn't going to make a difference in what you feel about everything I've said."

Dan scratched his head, observing Maris across the room as she tucked her hair behind her ear. Multiple earrings glittered in the light, a feather dangling from her lobe drifting in the current of air created by her hand. How had he missed *that*? She was…outlandish, not his type at all. And yet…and yet nothing. "I think it's time for me to bring you back to your car. You can get on to wherever it is you're staying for the night, and we can discuss this further tomorrow after I've had a few more hours of sleep."

"May I go upstairs first?"

"No."

"I'd really like—"

"No."

She cocked a hip. In another woman, there might have been something sexy about it. In her, the movement looked like an issued challenge. He shrugged. "Tomorrow. Take it or leave it. I want sleep and the opportunity to think about what you're saying. I mean, look at the place. Nothing disturbed, no signs of anything amiss. Your aunt was ninety-three, Maris. She lived a good long life." He moved toward the light switch. "Let's go."

Maris hesitated. "Someone was here with her when she died. Maybe it was natural causes, maybe not. But someone was here."

With a sigh, Dan snapped off the light, plunging the room into darkness. Only the porch fixture shining through glass cast a dim illumination over Maris's features. Dan indicated the front door with a jerk of his head.

"Then why doesn't she just tell you who the hell it was and save me the trouble?"

Maris strode past him and yanked open the door. "It doesn't work that way. I wish to God it did."

Dan followed. "You wouldn't happen to have a key?"

"Of course not."

Dan pulled the door shut after locking it in order to secure the house overnight. Tomorrow they'd have to get a locksmith out here to make a key. "Give me your number. I'll call. We'll take it from there."

With a nod, she strode to his car, walking with a provocative but baffling elemental grace. He hit the key fob to unlock the door. She'd gotten into his vehicle and yanked the seat belt into place before he'd reached the driver's side.

They rode in silence back in the direction of the station. He tried to think of something to say. An apology worked its way to his lips as he tapped the steering wheel in indecision. Finally, he bit the words back. What the hell did he need to apologize for? What he needed to do was double-check Maris's claims of estrangement, her whereabouts for the evening. Without all the mumbo jumbo she had thrown at him, her knowledge of her aunt's demise was suspicious. Maybe the woman really hadn't died of natural causes and her supposed grandniece was merely trying to throw him off.

"I'm not guilty of anything but responding to a call for help."

Dan snorted. "Is my face that easy to read?"

"Everyone's is."

"So you admit that's how you and others like your aunt fool people?"

"Having no idea what others do, I don't admit to anything."

"That's not an answer."

"Yes, it is." She reached into the console and drew out a pen in order to write on a narrow slip of paper, a receipt maybe. "Here's my number."

He tucked the paper into his breast pocket, a small shock running through his body when he felt the surface of the Tarot card beneath his fingertips. Driving the rest of the way in silence, he only spoke again when he'd pulled into the department lot beside a car with out-of-state plates. "This yours?"

"Yep." Before he'd put his own car in park, she flung open the door and climbed out with a nod. "We'll talk later?"

"Yeah. Later."

Through the rearview mirror, he watched her pull out of the lot and turn left. He'd gotten most of the numbers from her plate, but not all. He was curious if the registered address would match up to her license. Hell, he was curious about anything related to Maris Granger. She intrigued him. That wasn't an easy thing to do.

It also felt distinctly dangerous.

Chapter 5

She'd lied. Then again, so had he. Did that make them well-matched? She doubted it. Survival. Preservation. These alone made liars and hypocrites of most men and women in this world. Dan Stauffer had his own secrets to protect, and she had hers. So be it.

Even so, the key lay heavy on her palm with the weight of another untruth. She flipped it around in her fingers until it faced the correct way for insertion into the knob. With a glance over her shoulder in both directions, Maris pushed the key into the lock and turned it, the sound of grinding tumblers loud in the predawn hour. When she'd rushed from her home, she'd made no plan, had no place to stay. All these years, the key tucked away safe in her diary now opened a refuge from the chill September night.

Inside, she leaned her back against the door until she felt the plunger catch. She turned the latch on the knob and waited in the darkness until her eyes had grown accustomed, lingering still longer as she listened to the not-quite silence. People always referred to an empty house as silent, but it wasn't. It couldn't be. Fluctuations in temperature made floors creak, wind against loosened frames rattled glass. A clock's second hand ticked quietly, shifting papers whispered in a draft, even the stubborn drop of water clinging on a faucet's lip might suddenly succumb to gravity to splatter in a sink. She'd been living alone for far too long to jump at every little sound. But then there were the others, from a world beyond her own. It was those she listened for now, breath held, eyes wide and staring into a blackness growing ever brighter as her vision adjusted.

Nothing.

Surprised, she made her way across the foyer and through the parlor, skirting Aunt Alva's table. She climbed the stairs to the second floor and paused outside the room she remembered as being her Aunt Alva's bedroom. She studied the dim shapes of the bed with its ruffled coverlet, the curtains, the curved edges of the ornate, period furnishings. Not antiques to Aunt Alva, of course. To Aunt Alva this was all she'd ever known, as familiar and comfortable as a pair of well-worn shoes. Standing in the doorway, Maris drew a long, slow breath through her nose. She closed her eyes. After all these years, the smell of the room was exactly the same. Memory rushed in on the mingled scents of lavender and the oil of some sweet and resinous fruitwood.

She took a single step over the threshold and brought her other foot to rest beside the first as she contemplated the shadows. Empty, the shadows. Nothing waited for her here.

"Aunt Alva, where have you gone? I thought to find you here still."

Maris's voice echoed along the smooth, polished surfaces, across the walls covered in watered silk paper. Age undisturbed held a special magic all its own. Barriers to the past were thin indeed.

The carefully made bed looked soft and comfortable. Alva had been the type of woman to make her bed every morning. The fact she had continued to do so, climbing up and down the stairs daily at her venerable age, amazed Maris. A spunky lady, Alva Mabry. Maris remembered that much, too.

Of course, Alva might have had paid help at this point, or a kind and conscientious neighbor stopping by to lend a hand. Maris knew nothing of her great-aunt's life since the schism twenty years ago. She herself had been entering puberty at that time, an important period for a girl with her heritage, a time of change and growing power, a transformation from the sparse gifts of youth.

You will know your art soon, Maris. You have only to listen to what is inside of you.

But she'd never gotten the chance. At least not with the guidance Alva had promised her. Maris's mother, fearful of the gifts of the women in her husband's family, had insisted he take a job far away. God, what a battle had ensued. The family had scattered and stayed apart. All of them.

Yet, she'd gotten the impression tonight from Dan Stauffer that Alva was considered something of a quack these days. Women like her often were by those who didn't believe or who had interacted with a charlatan and judged all by that experience. However, the sign out front was evidence, at least, of a successful business, no matter what Dan had said.

Understanding she had waited too long to renew her relationship with her elderly aunt pained her, and the strange energy she felt from Dan Stauffer still clung to her like the perfume to his shirt and caused a churning in her stomach. That man definitely had secrets. They circled around him like half-seen vultures awaiting a meal. For someone like that to so adamantly deny the *otherness* in this world confounded her. But he wasn't her problem. He couldn't be. Not a problem, not an interest, but a means to an end. Alva had pointed her in his direction for a reason. Maris hoped for more than warmth and rest in her aunt's home. She hoped to find out why.

Abandoning Alva's bedroom, Maris continued down the hall. Years ago, the two rooms on the opposite side of the corridor had been used for sewing and for guests, respectively. That guest had usually been Maris, in a room made special for her. No one else caught on to the fact that Alva had created the space to celebrate Maris's gifts, but Maris and Alva knew. Most likely the room had been given over to storage as time went by. It didn't seem probable that Alva had many guests come to visit, and certainly not family.

Guilt cut through Maris like a knife to the soul. How could she have let this happen? In the beginning, Maris had written letters to Alva, but one day Alva had written back to her *No more.* The woman may as well have cut out her heart. After that, Maris had nearly hated her aunt for abandoning her with a skill that seared her like fire.

Popping into the bathroom, Maris took a moment to wash her face and rinse her mouth using her cell phone for illumination. Morning would come soon enough, and she would need to be out of the house before Dan returned. No time for sleep, really. She hadn't been looking to rest, anyway, only a few minutes of meditation to open herself up to whatever was meant to come to her.

Maris dried her face on her sleeve, not wishing to dampen Alva's towels. Twofold, that caution. The first reason was out of a sense of respect, and the second had to do with a certain police officer noticing the wet condition of a towel that should have been long dried since its owner's use. She crossed the hall to the former guestroom and turned the handle. Maris sucked in a breath and held it as the first glimmer of day revealed a room that looked the same as it had in her childhood. A room designed to educate and comfort, but had ended up a prison. The woman who had created this so-called sanctuary for her was gone forever now, as was the child who had spent so many days and nights there alone.

* * * *

Dan sat upright, a series of profanities rolling off his tongue. The sunlight made him squint. He tossed himself out of bed and toward the desk where his gun lay holstered and hanging from the back of the chair.

"Who the fuck is that?" he demanded and then stopped, his heart hammering in his chest. He listened hard for the noise that had awakened him. Knocking. He'd heard knocking on the door to his room. Or had that merely been a dream?

Disgusted for even entertaining the thought someone would break into his house and then politely knock at the bedroom door, Dan removed the gun from the holster anyway and strode quietly across the carpeted floor. Weapon raised, he paused to listen before turning the knob. The sunshine through the window revealed an empty hall. He hadn't expected anything else. Still, he went through the house from top to bottom, assuring himself his residence was secure. No one had a key, and if one of the guys from work wanted him, they knew his number.

The hour was barely past nine according to the clock on the kitchen wall. He normally didn't sleep past six whether working or not, but last night's lack of shut-eye had pretty much knocked him out. Deciding he might squeeze in a couple more hours before starting his day, Dan headed back up the stairs. Outside the bedroom door, he stopped and stared at the thick carpet in front of his bare feet. How the hell did that get there?

With a snort, Dan bent and picked up the Priestess card from the floor. No doubt he had knocked it out of his shirt pocket when he grabbed the gun and kicked it out the door without noticing as he hurried across the room. Today he would return the card to Alva's residence. It would be a good idea to meet Maris there later with the locksmith so he could accompany her around the house while she looked for some kind of contact list or address book in order to start arrangements. Hopefully she could locate the name of her aunt's attorney in order to ascertain the woman's final wishes since he'd gotten the impression from Maris there wasn't any other family left to ask. Still, should he take her word for that? For any of it? Of course not.

He tossed the Tarot card onto the desk and re-holstered his gun, wondering when he had decided definitively to ignore Maris's drivel and treat the incident like any other. He hadn't. Not really. God, his mind kept jumping back and forth between suspicion and acceptance. But unless he received word of something irregular from Rankin regarding Alva Mabry's death, he would give the all clear to Maris and hopefully see her on her way soon.

Rolling himself in the blankets until he faced the wall, Dan shut his eyes against the glare of daylight. And what seemed only a moment later, he opened them again. Flailing himself free of the covers, he managed to turn around, staring wide-eyed into the room. Nothing. No one calling his name, no one knocking at the door, nothing but a disruption of his slumber caused by his consumption of alcohol and interrupted sleep the night before.

"And if not, just go the hell away. I'm not dealing with that crap ever again, you understand?" He thought of the silhouette behind his car and pushed the image away. "Kiss my ass. This is the real world." And in the real world, cops who talked to themselves ended up spending time away from duty warming up a psych's couch.

With a groan, Dan got back out of bed and headed for the shower. No point in wasting time seeking oblivion. Another freaking day had begun.

An hour later, Dan dialed Maris's number. "I'll come pick you up now if you're ready," he said without preamble.

"I assume this is Dan."

"Oh, yes. Sorry."

"I'm standing out front."

Dan hurried to the door and peered out the sidelight, turning to view the steps and the street in both directions. "How the hell do you know where I live? Wait, I don't see you."

"I'm in front of my aunt's house. Alva's place. Why would I be at your door?"

Dan straightened. "What are you doing there?"

"Waiting for you."

"How did you know—"

"Lucky guess. Besides, didn't you say we would discuss this further?"

"Did I say at the house?"

"I don't know. Did you?"

He honestly didn't recall, and the lack of recollection bothered him. She might tell him she'd known in advance through some hocus-pocus manner—that she had a vision of meeting him there or some such nonsense. If she did, he'd probably lose his patience once and for all.

"Feel like getting a cup of coffee or something?"

That stopped him dead. He stared a moment at a slow-moving vehicle making its way up the street. "Sure."

"Pick me up here then." She rang off.

Ordering him around like he was some kind of errand boy. He hastened to put on his shoes and slip into a sweatshirt. But he would drive slowly. Yep, he would do that.

* * * *

Maris sat on the step with eyes closed, her face turned to the sun. The light was red through the skin of her lids. Warm, too, and on her cheeks a delicious contrast to the cool, gentle breeze that ruffled her hair.

Why had she done that? Why had she asked him to have coffee with her? For one, she needed some, but she could have gone on her own. For another, the longer she kept him away from certain truths, the better off they both would be. She wanted him to unearth the mystery relative to her aunt, but to unearth all her secrets might be extremely unpleasant for her. As for Dan himself…well, he wasn't ready. Anyone could tell that by looking in his eyes.

He had lovely eyes. Most people didn't trust a man with eyes that color, but she'd always found the color beautiful. When she was very young, she sometimes fantasized about an imaginary friend with eyes like that, pale and clear and deep as the striated coloration of a blue marble. In fact, if the man she sought at the police station had walked in with eyes of any other shade, she would have decided she hadn't had a vision at all, but had reverted to that old companion in her loneliness.

Yes, loneliness made one strange and fey. For a time, Maris had blamed her aunt for that, and later her parents, but really, it was who she was. She discovered as an adult her *otherness* made her different, and her difference kept her apart from the people around her. The stories went back generation after generation about the women in her family. They had their own community of people who understood. Once Maris and her parents left Alcina Cove, Maris had no one. In fact, if Maris never had a girl child, she'd be the last in a long line of gifted females.

At thirty-two, having a child wasn't beyond imagining, but she'd never found anyone with whom she'd consider that kind of relationship. Maybe, like Alva, she was destined to be alone.

Maris leaned back onto her elbows, tilting her face toward the sky, the step above pressed into the ridge of her spine through her sweater. She began to breathe in a deliberate cadence, willing herself to relax, to accept the present state of her life. She heard a car door open and close quietly, almost as if he didn't want her to know he was there. Her lips curled. The step beneath her hips reverberated slightly with the lowering of a booted foot onto the concrete.

"Wake up. I thought you wanted a cup of coffee."

She opened her eyes and squinted at his silhouette, his head highlighted by the sun at his back. "I'm not asleep. And I do."

He held out his hand. She hesitated and then slipped her fingers into his, allowing him to pull her to her feet. Standing on the step above him, she nearly matched his height, head to head. He looked amused. She wondered what had gotten into him.

"Did you have someplace in mind?"

She shook her head. "It's been twenty years. The places I remember might not even exist anymore."

"There's a diner on the edge of town. I haven't had breakfast yet. You?"

"Nope."

"Good. Let's go."

Releasing her hand, he started toward the car. Maris lingered on the steps to the porch, something about his behavior throwing her off balance. He opened the passenger side door for her like an actual gentleman, then cocked his head to the side as he looked back in her direction. "Are you coming?"

Wordlessly, she descended the steps to the sidewalk where she ducked under his arm and into the seat. He shut the door as soon as she drew her leg inside. Suddenly she felt as nervous as a kid in school awaiting the outcome of a test.

He slid behind the wheel. "You never did say where you were staying."

"No," she agreed, "I didn't." Her stomach flipped beneath her diaphragm.

He arched an eyebrow but kept silent regarding her reply. Pulling away from the curb, he gave the front door of the house a quick glance. "That's strange."

"What?"

"I'm just remembering something incorrectly. I thought those curtains on the front door were closed."

Maris turned to check. "They are closed."

Dan slammed on the brakes. "They are. What the hell. Is somebody in there? I could have sworn they were just open."

"Nope. They've been closed. I think you're imagining things." Still, Maris stared at the front door through narrowed eyes, waiting to see movement again. Nothing. What had Stauffer seen? She was beginning to think the man had a hidden talent he would have despised had he recognized it.

After a moment, Dan continued driving. Maris relaxed against the seat. "Have you given any further thought to what I was saying last night?"

"Nope."

Maris frowned. "None at all?"

"It wasn't last night. It was this morning, and I've spent the rest of it trying to catch up on my interrupted sleep. We'll talk about things after I've had something to eat."

With a snort, Maris focused on the passing vista. In the light of day, she recognized the landmark of the sailors' cross beyond the far end of the main street and certain houses on either side as they headed through town. "Stop!"

Dan jerked the wheel, bringing his car up against the curb. "What's wrong?"

"That's...that's my house."

"Right there?"

Maris nodded at the house he pointed out. "Yes. Right there."

"It can't be."

"It is." The home where she'd spent her early childhood had been converted to a bed and breakfast. The Timeless Inn, it was called. Someone had planted a beautiful English-style garden out front behind a white picket fence. Because of that, she almost hadn't recognized the house itself. But the bones of it remained, the once silvered wooden siding painted a pristine white now. The narrow window of her old bedroom faced the huge Victorian mansion across the street.

"Friends of mine own the place," Dan said beside her.

"Well that's quite the coincidence. Or don't you believe in coincidence either?"

He didn't answer.

Of course he did, whether he admitted it or not. He believed in the power of coincidence, of meant-to-be. She knew he had to. If he didn't, he'd say so. So far, he hadn't been a man to hold back on his opinions. "Do you think they'd let me in?"

"I'm not asking them to let you in for a look around. They have a business to run."

"Right."

"I'm sorry. I shouldn't have—"

"Nope, it's fine." Maris swiveled front in her seat. Goodness, they sounded like an old married couple, half-bickering, and they'd barely met. And like the denizen of a fifty-year marriage, she found herself trying to reassure him. "I understand, really. It would be rude to ask your friends. Let's go eat, though, I'm starving."

He, in like form, started to backpedal. "It's only that I'm not sure what type of thing they might have going this week. Sometimes they have business clients—"

"Don't."

"Don't what?"

"Don't go back on your original statement. You said it for a reason. And don't try to appease me. I don't need appeasing. I don't need coddling. I don't need…anything." God, was that true? Had she designed herself around acceptance to the point of not needing anything from anybody? What a sad state of affairs, if true. "Except coffee," she amended. "And a couple of eggs on toast. I do need that."

He laughed. The sound of it startled her, yet warmed her through and through. She managed to stop herself squirming on the seat in response, but she couldn't prevent grinning in return.

"Your wish is my command," he said, pulling back out into the street.

Now he was flirting with her. There was something so not right about their exchanges, as if neither one of them could figure out where they stood. And why should they? This was business. He was a police officer—a detective—and she was a citizen looking for assurance about a death. Period. What else need there be?

As Dan Stauffer pulled his car into the lot of the diner, she thought— what else, indeed.

* * * *

Watching Maris surreptitiously from the corner of his eye as she sipped from her second mug of coffee, Dan mopped up the remnants of his eggs with the last piece of toast. She looked tired. Not haggard, only sleepy. He speculated about the reason the death of an aunt she claimed not to have spoken with in years might have affected her more than she admitted.

"So, Maris means 'by the sea,' doesn't it?"

She appeared startled at the sound of his voice. Small wonder. They'd consumed their entire meal without speaking.

"It means 'of the sea' actually. There's a difference."

"Okay." He drank a mouthful of orange juice. Since their conversation outside of the Timeless, she'd withdrawn, become less talkative. Why, because she hadn't gotten her way? And yet she said she understood. Typical woman.

"There's a reason I was named Maris. A rather interesting story, I think."

Oh, so now she was willing to chat. He found his thoughts wandering to the nameless woman in the slinky dress exuding the overdose of perfume. That woman hadn't wanted to chat either. Had something else in mind entirely.

"Do you want to hear it?"

Recalled from his musing, he lowered his glass to the table. "Sure."

"I was born in the ocean."

He straightened against the booth cushion. "On the ocean, you mean?"

"No. In."

"Okay, I'm listening. Let's hear it."

"My mother has a high tolerance for pain. She'd been in labor for hours without realizing it. Thought she was having some intestinal issues from something she ate. I wasn't quite due yet, you see."

Dan propped his elbow up on the table, leaning his chin on his palm. He couldn't help the smile forming on his lips. "And then?"

"She decided to go ahead with her daily swim even though her obstetrician had warned her she was too far along. And out I came."

"Just like that?"

"Not quite like that. There was a bit more drama. She realized what was going on at nearly the last minute and struggled to make it back to shore. Gave birth to me on the tide line. A couple walking along the beach found us and called for an ambulance."

"Good God."

Maris laughed—no, giggled really. He'd never been one for giggling women, but the sound of hers was less a giddy twittering than a deep, bubbling of water. "That's quite the story," he said. "Got any more?"

"What? Don't you believe me?"

"I do believe you. And it seems to me that someone whose life started out in that fashion probably has a good deal more to tell." Across from him, she stilled, her expression settling into one of soft consideration when she met his gaze dead-on. Oh. Right. She had tried to tell him about her "abilities," and he had scoffed them off.

"What about you?" she asked. "I'm sure you have some stories to share."

"No. Not really."

"None? I can see them, waiting at the back of your eyes." She lifted her hand and pointed from one to the other on his face.

He frowned. "Nope. Lived a pretty boring life, all things considered."

"But you're a cop."

"In a boring town."

"Not true. Even I remember that much."

Dan shifted in his seat, reaching for the dregs of his orange juice. "Perhaps things have changed."

"And perhaps not. The reputation of this town goes back beyond our combined ages times four. I can't see what might have changed so drastically. Modernization really doesn't make a difference."

"You don't know how old I am." Dan drained his glass.

"I can make a good guess."

"Don't bother."

Maris turned her head in search of the waitress. Spotting the woman, she lifted her hand to draw the woman closer. "Could I have the check please?"

"I've got it," Dan growled.

"I asked you. I've got it."

"You're driving me crazy."

"In a matter of hours? Goodness, I'm slipping. I should have driven you there within moments of our meeting."

"Maris."

That got her attention, stopped her rambling repartee. She folded her hands on the table, the wing of her brows lifting slowly.

Dan leaned forward. "Are you flirting with me? Because you shouldn't—"

"No."

"You're not?"

"Flirting? No. I don't do that. I don't know how to do that. I can connect to a person's thoughts sometimes, but I can't always tell the truth of them, you know? So flirting is a risky game I don't play."

Dan sat back again, contemplating the woman before him. What female didn't flirt? Yet, he believed what she said, or at least that she believed it. So did that mean this effervescent, mysterious, exasperating personality was truly her own? He didn't know whether to get up and run or bask in it awhile.

He folded his arms over his chest. "What's the point of the feather?"

She reached up and fingered the white plume hanging from her lobe. "It's the feather of a dove. I found it on the ground and made it into an earring to remind me to maintain peace in my life. It feels good against my neck, too."

He bit his tongue at what he could only assume was an unconscious sensuality in her last statement. Either that or she was an accomplished liar, fooling him into trusting that she wasn't a flirt. God, she confused the hell out of him.

"Peace is something you need in your life, is it? What do you do for a living?"

The waitress had returned with the check, and Maris reached into her purse for the cash to pay the bill. "I'm a librarian."

"A—a librarian?" Laughter erupted from his lips.

"Yes, that's the old-fashioned term, but I prefer it. Keep the change." This to the waitress. "What's so funny?"

"Just trying to picture you in a room full of books, that's all. And why the need for peace with a job like that."

"There's more to my job than returning books to their proper place. Besides, it's the assistants who do that. Students mostly. I like books. I like being around them. Better than people, if I must be honest."

"I see. So you're not a people-person?"

"No."

"Could have fooled me," he said.

"What's that supposed to mean?" Maris gathered her purse, dropping her napkin onto her empty plate.

"I don't know." Dan grabbed his sunglasses from the table. "I don't. But you don't strike me as a loner."

"Well, that's exactly what I am."

Dan followed Maris out, observing the way she moved. What did a woman do with all that sexuality when she spent her days avoiding people? A quick picture flashed into his mind that he swiftly dismissed. He didn't need to go there. He was trying his best not to be enticed by Maris Granger. He really was.

He unlocked the car, and she climbed into the passenger side without waiting for him. As he approached the driver's door, his phone chirped in his pocket. He yanked it out. "Stauffer."

Opening the door, he stood outside the car, the phone against his ear. Maris leaned across the seats, peering up at him. He ignored the concern on her face.

"Dan, it's Rankin. Glad I didn't place a bet on that Mabry woman. Not natural at all. Looks like somebody poisoned her."

Chapter 6

Maris frowned at Dan, blinking with each smack of his hand against the steering wheel, her stomach sinking into her ankles at his reaction.

"I never should have let you into your aunt's house. Stupid mistake. A rookie mistake. The kind of thing that'll get your ass handed to you."

"What's happened?" Maris asked for the third time. "Tell me."

"You mean you don't already know?"

"Sarcasm? Lovely."

Dan inhaled and released a slow, steady stream of air. "I'm not being sarcastic. Your great-aunt didn't die of natural causes. The ME is thinking poison and testing for the type and how it was administered. I'm sorry. And I've screwed up by bringing you to her house. It's a crime scene, and now it's been compromised."

"You didn't know."

"No, but you did. Or at least you hinted that you did. That opens up a whole different can of worms."

"You don't think—"

"I don't know what I think."

Maris bit her lip, staring out the window. Dan leaned closer to the wheel, yanking his right hand off it and curling the fingers into a fist, which he smacked once in the middle of his forehead.

"What? Dan, what?" Calling him by his first name appeared to calm him in some fashion. Jaw set, he leaned back in his seat.

"I remembered something. No big deal. I'm going to take you back to your car, and you'll head over to your hotel and stay put, got it? Where are you staying, by the way?"

Rubbing her eyes, Maris shook her head. "Nearby. I don't remember what it's called. Some little place." God, she hoped there was a motel matching that description in the vicinity. "I'll call you from my room when I get there to give you the exact name and the main phone number."

"Okay, fine. Wait a second. Where did you get my number?"

Maris pulled her cell phone out and waved it a couple of times in the air. "You called me, remember? It's in my phone."

"Oh for the love of—right. I forgot."

"You need to stop being so suspicious." She turned in the seat to get a better look at him. "And jumpy. And skeptical. And secretive."

"Secretive? What does that mean?"

He knew exactly what she meant. His eyes told all, as did the fact he'd zeroed in on that comment above the others. He'd never admit to it, of course, but he understood the secrets she referenced. She decided to drop it, though. Now was not the time to address those things he kept hidden. Nor was it any of her business. She had no right to the knowledge she received, whether intuitive or clairvoyant, and no duty to impart it. That was one of the problems of being gifted in this fashion. It was very difficult to decipher when to open your mouth or when you were better off stuffing what you had seen into some deep, dark corner.

Dan pulled alongside her car, his vehicle facing the wrong way on the street. She got out, bending to look in at him, her fingers curled over the doorframe. "Thanks for the company at breakfast."

"Thanks for asking…and buying. Do not, and I repeat, do not leave the area. Go back to where you're staying and dig in. You might be there for a while. You call me, or I'll call you. There are going to be questions, I'm sure."

Maris nodded and straightened, noticing two police cars parked in front of her aunt's house. She pulled her car key from her purse and pressed the button to unlock the driver's door while shutting the passenger side of Dan's. He pulled away slowly and up against the curb, still facing the wrong way. He'd climbed out before she'd gotten into her vehicle. She hovered outside to observe his energetic stride as he took the steps two at a time, stretching an arm out and yanking the door open before he'd reached the top of the stairs.

Maris slid down into the seat and shut the door. She clutched the cross bar of the steering wheel with both hands. *Poison.* Was this, then, why Alva had reached out to her at the very end of her life? To insist on the truth? But no, there had to be more. The results of testing would have been the same whether Maris had insisted on further investigation or not. Apparently, the medical examiner had made the discovery in the process of doing his job despite the belief held that Alva had died of old age.

"Who did this to you?"

But no answers came to her out of the air. If only it were that easy.

Knuckles rapped on the passenger side window. Maris jerked and turned, finding Dan's eyes gazing in at her through the glass. She rolled the window down.

"You're still here."

"I know. I'm leaving. I was just thinking about Aunt Alva."

"Understandable. Since you didn't leave yet, would you mind coming inside for a couple of minutes? Hands in your pockets, like I said before."

Maris's heart began a faster rhythm in her breast. Without a word, she disconnected her seatbelt and got back out. She stood a moment in the street with her hand on the roof, steadying herself. "What is it? What's wrong?"

"Come with me, please. I need to show you something."

Oh, God, oh God.

"Maris, are you all right?"

She nodded, her breath refusing to enter her lungs. She sucked in a gulp of air that sounded like a gasp in the sudden stillness. Dan shot her a look but said nothing and stepped around the back of the car to take her elbow. Maris let him, his grip strong and warm through the woven knit of her sweater. As they neared the porch steps, Maris removed her arm from his hand, climbing unaided to the front door.

What had they found? She'd been so careful.

"In here."

Maris allowed Dan to take her arm again, steering her toward the parlor. Once there, she pushed both hands down into the pockets of her skirt, balling them into fists. Beside her, Dan nodded his head toward the table. The tiny hairs on her nape danced like a field in the wind.

Aunt Alva's cards, in the family for at least two, if not three generations, lay in an entirely different pattern across the paisley tablecloth.

* * * *

"Head between your knees. Don't get up yet. What the fuck just happened?"

He had a mouth, Dan Stauffer did. Maris might have laughed if the shifting blackness wasn't still threatening her. That and the nausea. She really didn't want to throw up in front of this man. Not in front of any of them. From the corner of her eye, she could see the officers' gazes focused on her, some concerned, others speculative. She bent her head forward again, burying her brow into the sling of her skirt between her parted knees.

Breathe. Breathe, child. The Sight will sometimes do this to you, but it will pass.

She did, in and out, hampered by her position on the floor. Fingers kneaded the back of her neck. Dan's. He couldn't have had any awareness of what he was doing. She hoped none of the others noticed his ministrations. She was quite aware of the intimacy of his actions, but perhaps the men around him would view his touch as merely functional.

"You all right now? Let me help you up."

"Sure. Just…"

"Give me your hand."

Did he not hear his own voice? He sounded like someone who cared. He had no business using that tone with her. Not here. Not in front of men who would wonder. Ignoring the fingers he held out to her, she pressed her palm to the wall for balance and stood without assistance. The room spun a little and settled.

"There we go," he said. "Right as rain."

He sounded jovial now, distant. *Good. Stay there.* The other officers muttered a few words as they moved away, good-natured on the surface as if thankful she had recovered, but she sensed their underlying confusion. Maris drew several more breaths until the nausea abated. Dan stepped closer.

"What the hell just happened? I'm not kidding."

Wow. The man was all over the place, his emotions bouncing like a ping-pong ball. Maris looked him in the eye, held his gaze, tried her best to steady him. After a moment, the tempo of his respiration began to match hers. He took a step back.

"Well?" Gentle now, but official.

How could she tell him the impressions swirling in her brain? If they made no sense to her, they certainly wouldn't to him. She jerked her chin toward the table. "I didn't do that. Is that why you brought me in here, because you thought I did?"

He frowned. "Damn it, I know you didn't. I had my eyes on you the whole time you were in here last night…this morning. But somebody did it."

That somebody could have been her. He didn't know that. She could never let him know that. But when she left the house this morning, the cards were where they had been.

Alva?

Nothing.

Maris wiped the back of a hand across her mouth. "Why did you want me to see this? I don't understand."

Dan came in close again, brushing her cheek with breath scented with juice and the smoky smell of bacon. "Does it mean something, the layout?

I'm trying to figure out if someone might have left this as a message. A taunt, perhaps. You're into this type of thing, aren't you? Tarot reading?"

The condescension, the skepticism, had returned. Maris tucked her hair behind her ear, running her index finger along the length of the small white feather. *Peace, Maris. Peace.*

She nodded at the table once more. "May I go closer?"

"Don't touch anything."

"I think I got that message already, Detective."

He made a noise in his throat. Shock, disapproval, amusement? She couldn't follow him anymore. Better to leave her thoughts away from his and concentrate on what was being shown to her.

Through narrowed eyes, she studied the array of cards. Her fingers tingled, longing to reach out and handle them. She could sense the energy even with her hands tucked deep into her pockets.

That's right, Maris, you extraordinary child. Close your eyes and feel the narrative unfold...

"What are you doing?"

Maris jumped, eyes flying wide. She pulled her open hands back from the static-filled air above the table, forcing their return to the warm folds of her skirt. "Sorry. I wasn't touching."

"You were pretty damned close."

"Right." When Maris had seen the spread before, the layout had been somewhat confusing to her, but now ten cards were positioned in the most common form of the Celtic cross. She chewed her lower lip as she again studied the cards. Her heart rate slowed, her respiration evened out. "What is it you want me to tell you?"

"Is there any significance to what's on the table?"

There's always significance, she wanted to say. "If you're trying to determine some message left for you, I have no idea."

"That card there is fairly obvious," Dan said, pointing. "A confession, perhaps?"

Maris curled her lips at his words. "The Death card? You think someone is saying 'I killed her' with that card? There are many meanings to the Death card. It could mean something as positive as becoming a new person." One of the officers standing nearby snorted. She ignored him. "This one here, the Hangman, could imply the suspension of disbelief." She gave a significant look first to the amused officer and then Dan. "Here, the Seven of Wands, one of the Minor Arcana, could be interpreted as being true to yourself, your principles, despite the pressure of others to make you see differently. This, taken alone? Possibly a truce of sorts.

This one? Despair. However, these cards together tell a story I cannot see because I didn't lay them out. The psychic connection is missing."

This time the officer laughed out loud. Dan turned to him with a word of dismissal, sending him away. "What about that one?"

Maris sighed, pushing down the image that came to mind. "Desire."

She heard his breath catch behind her. "That card means desire? It looks like—I don't know what it looks like."

"That is the impression I get from it." Heightened, of course, by the fact he had pointed it out. She couldn't control the visualization. "Of course, it could mean many things. Like I said, I didn't have any command over the cards. This is a cold reading. All I can tell you is that I don't think someone sat here and thought to lay out a confession to a crime with pictures."

Even so, there was more to what she saw on the table, what had crashed through her, leaving her staggered and breathless and sprawled on the floor, but she would hold that close. Now was not the time. All of it related in some fashion to the man standing beside her, and she needed to sort through what she had seen. Part of what she had witnessed burst out, however, almost of its own accord. "If the High Priestess card were lying here, I'd say the entire spread had to do with secrets and the choices we make." She closed her eyes. *Maris, just shut up.*

"The Priestess card?" Dan cleared his throat. "What is the significance of that card?"

She fisted her hands in her pockets. "In what I see before me, I would say a prediction of an event that could disrupt everything in your world."

A floorboard creaked as Dan moved closer. "*My* world? What the hell do you mean?"

Maris turned her face from him. "I didn't mean your world in particular. I meant in a general sense. And it's not in the spread, anyway. It just came to me for a moment, an image of the card in my mind's eye. And now, if you're through with me, I'd really like to go lie down. My head is hurting."

He touched her arm. At the charge that radiated along her skin, she wanted to shake him off, to yell, but she managed to remain still.

"Maybe you should get checked out," he said, for her ears alone.

"No."

"Maris."

She frowned. He needed to stop that tone of tenderness in his voice. It popped up in ways it shouldn't, indicating an emotion that did not—could not—exist. There was no caring here. There was suspicion and mistrust and a vague, undefined attraction they both felt and she knew made no sense to him. She could put a stop to the latter with a single word, but somehow, she didn't want to.

She turned without speaking and headed out the door. He accompanied her as far as the sidewalk, dogging her steps. "Are you sure you're all right to drive?"

"Yes, I'm fine. An aspirin, and I'll be perfect." She spoke with deliberate detachment. "You'll keep me posted about my aunt?"

He took a step back, sensing the space she was putting between them. The crease between his brows indicated his inability to discern why, the stern set of his jaw his willingness to accept it nevertheless. "We won't be able to release the body for burial just yet, of course. And there will be questions for you later."

"Understood."

"And like I said, don't leave town."

"I didn't plan on it."

He nodded and turned away. At the top of the porch steps he looked back at her. A shadow aligned itself with him, almost like an aura of smoke. His shoulders jerked as if trying to shake off his sense of the shadow enfolding him. Then he raised his hand in a quick wave and went back inside.

Maris hurried into her car. Clutching the wheel, tears of dread and deep, chilling sorrow ran down her cheeks.

Chapter 7

Dan let the curtain hooked by his finger fall back into place against the glass in Alva Mabry's front door. His skin shifted between his shoulder blades in a brief shiver, the kind that made people pass comments about a soul walking over one's grave. He blew a breath from his lips with a small noise.

"A strange bird, that one."

Dan turned to see who had uttered the remark. He couldn't distinguish which of the officers gathered in the house had spoken. Better to let the quiet statement pass without comment rather than call attention to his displeasure at hearing it. He couldn't even be sure why the sentiment bothered him. Maris was a strange woman, but the observation had seemed particularly disparaging.

"All right. Let's dust the place for prints. Upstairs and down since we don't have any idea where the perp might have been. You'll find mine on the door, the knob, the light switch plates, possibly elsewhere. Green's and Whitley's, too. Rankin. His assistant. We'll need to get comparison prints off the deceased."

And Maris. Shit, and Maris. He'd have to bring her in for elimination purposes. She hadn't touched anything but the plate and switch for the light over the table in the parlor, if he remembered right. Yes, she'd been walking with her hands behind her back, and today they'd been in her pockets.

"Gather any hair, fibers, grab the trash. Somebody check outside for footprints, cigarette butts, smudges on the windows. Poison seems a personal means of killing someone, but it could have been a random act. The front door was intact, but we didn't check for signs of break-in. Shit." Two of the men turned his way, Henderson with a look of sympathy, Whitley smug. Yeah, they knew he'd fucked up. Times like these would tell whether a man could be trusted to stand by him or turn him on his ear.

His cell phone rang in his pocket. "Rankin, what have you got?"

"Small puncture wound in the side of her neck. If I hadn't been looking, might have mistaken it for a freckle. Don't know what kind of poison yet."

Dan glanced toward the chair in the parlor where Alva had been found. "So what are you thinking? Whoever did it was standing behind her, to the side? It didn't look like there was any struggle, so it must've been quick. Of course, she was nearly a century old. How much of a struggle could she have put up? The guy didn't even have to be big."

"Or the woman."

Dan's stomach did a slow roll beneath his diaphragm. "Or the woman," he agreed with massive reluctance. He didn't like where his mind was going, to the one person who had claimed she'd known Alva Mabry was dead. No *way* it was Maris. No freaking way. She just…No. The woman had come to the station looking for answers. Was that the action of a guilty person? Shit, sure it was, if they were trying to make themselves look innocent. Damn it, it could be Maris. He swore again, softly this time. Only Rankin heard him.

"You got an idea, Stauffer?"

"I don't know."

Rankin breathed heavily into the phone. "I've got prints. Figured you'd need 'em."

"Right. Thanks."

Dan hung up. So much for days off.

Hours later, everything bagged, tagged, and heading back to the station, Dan locked the door and descended the porch steps, looking back toward the yellow police tape crossed over the door. He considered the purpose behind the crime. Revenge for a fortune that hadn't turned out quite as predicted? Not funny. The place didn't appear to have been rummaged through, so if robbery was the motive, the murderer had something particular in mind and knew where to find it. An old woman like this could have had funds stashed around the house. He'd seen it before. And any of the neighbors could have known about the money, or anyone in town, really. Word of mouth, especially among criminals, could spread and grow at even the smallest hint of cash unprotected except by a ninety-three-year-old soothsayer.

He pulled out his phone and called Maris's number, but received no reply. After four rings, he left a vague message for her on voicemail. She'd have to come in, of course, but he didn't want to leave anything she would view as accusatory. He merely reminded her she hadn't called him with the information about where she was staying and left it at that.

And if she didn't call him back? What then?

He shoved the phone back in his pocket without answering that question. He didn't want to go there. Not yet. Yes, the crime seemed personal, but if Maris's story was true, she'd had no contact with her aunt for years. Certainly no one harbored a grudge that long, and what type of offense would burrow in like that from the time of childhood? Well, he could think of several, but he set those aside as well. In addition to canvassing the neighbors for anything they'd seen or suspicious behavior, he'd check out Maris's story about the estrangement, seek proof of her whereabouts the past couple of days, and clear her from whatever list of suspects was formulated. She hadn't killed her aunt. No way could she commit a cold-blooded crime like that.

Yet, how well did he know her? Not at all, really. Gut feeling counted for something, but people could put on a convincing show, good enough to mislead. He'd seen it before. Deceptive prevaricators who kept a straight face or broke down in what he could swear were honest-to-God tears and lying all the while.

His stomach twisted anew, to the point of making him want to vomit. He fought the sensation down with a few deep breaths, realizing he hadn't eaten anything since his impromptu breakfast with Maris.

Am I a fool?

No. Only once, and he'd never let it happen again.

His phone rang. "Maris?"

"I'm sorry, who? Is this Detective Stauffer?"

"Yes. Who's this?"

"It's Ed. We met last night—this morning. Dr. Rankin wanted to know if you're coming by for those prints tonight or if he should just store them until tomorrow."

"Tomorrow's good enough. I need something to eat and a good night's freaking sleep."

When he hung up, Dan tried Maris again, cutting the call as soon as her voicemail came on. Son of a bitch, she wasn't making this easy.

Deciding he would give her half a chance to call him back, he went to grab dinner before heading home.

* * * *

Maris ran her fingers over the scarred, wooden table, digging her thumbnail into the letters someone had carved there. *A name*, she thought, interrupted before completion, possibly by an irate barman. Defacing property in this place, however, didn't seem to be doing the table any disservice. A point of interest in an otherwise clichéd sort of establishment, somewhere to focus one's attention, curlicues and smiley faces and half-formed words with their own story, their own mystery. The rest of the bar impressed her as a beige and brown amalgam of aged wood, old nicotine stains from when smoking was still allowed, and the prerequisite, faded posters on the wall advertising various types of beer with the assistance of scantily clad women or dogs. The type of bar where working men came to relax and enjoy masculine company, not a family restaurant. The sign outside had been misleading.

But the little motel next door had matched the description she'd given Dan, and she didn't want to be caught in a lie.

Funny thing, though, she hadn't called him as promised with the information and had ignored both of his calls when they came in. A chill had settled into her bones she couldn't shake, and she didn't want him to hear it in her voice. Because he would. She knew he would. Around him, the cloak concealing her soul became insubstantial, making her feel naked and vulnerable and very much afraid. Afraid he would hurt her, she supposed. Not physically, but in a way no one had because she'd never allowed it. With him, she would. And that could invoke a perilous chain of events.

"Oh, stop feeling sorry for yourself, you idiot," she said.

"Pardon me?"

Maris glanced up at the waitress, a woman in her twenties with blond hair pulled up into a ponytail and a sweatshirt stretched across her bosom emblazoned with the words *Can't Touch This*. A mixed message, that one.

"I was talking to myself."

"Are you eating?" the woman asked.

Maris lifted the menu. She hadn't even looked at it.

"What's good here?"

"The meatloaf special is tasty. Comes with mashed potatoes. From scratch, not instant. And peas. Sorry, we don't give a choice of sides with our specials."

"That's fine. I'll take it."

A handful of men sat on high stools at the bar, trying not to look in her direction. Maris appreciated their efforts. She tried not to look at them in turn. She didn't want them to know how out of place she felt in an establishment that obviously gave them comfort and possibly a sense of bravado to go with their camaraderie. She went back to deciphering the hieroglyphs on the table.

For the first time in a good many years, loneliness had breached her solitude. True loneliness, not the type one felt when one realized one's friends could be counted on five digits. A loneliness enhanced by the constant interruption of strangeness in her life, stealing away the time people normally devoted to friendships. Those relationships had been a changing collage, and only one or two were longstanding and true. Her own fault, she knew, but once upon a time she had blamed her Aunt Alva for exposing her to her supposed gifts and the barrier they made to a normal life.

Yet, Aunt Alva hadn't given her the family aptitude. Not like a wrapped present. Maris had been born to it and once realized, it couldn't be forsaken. No matter how hard she tried.

"Mind if I join you?"

Maris closed her eyes. "Are you following me?"

Metal feet scraped across the floor as Dan pulled out the chair next to hers. He flopped onto the seat. "Hardly. I like to come here when I'm looking for, I don't know…"

"Anonymity?"

He scoffed. "I was going to say good company, but it's not even that."

"No pretenses."

"What?"

Maris moved her head to encompass the entire bar. "No pretenses. You are who you are here."

"Yeah, I guess that's it. And the food's good." He waved at the waitress, asking her to bring him a glass of water and the meatloaf special.

"Water?" Maris said.

"Something wrong with water?"

"Nope."

For several seconds, Maris silently toyed with her sweating glass of beer, twirling it back and forth in the ring of condensation on the table. It was more than two-thirds full. She didn't know why she'd ordered it except that's what people did in a bar. Although Dan hadn't. Water. Perhaps he was still dehydrated from his night out. Or he could be normally abstemious. She knew nothing about him,

As she shot a quick glance in his direction, expecting him to be gazing at the television muted across the room, she found him watching her instead.

"I honestly didn't follow you. I apologize if I'm disturbing your solitude."

Maris shrugged. "I would have told you not to sit if I had a problem. It's okay."

"Good."

The waitress brought his water, and he indicated with a raised finger that she should wait while he gulped it down, then he asked for another. "I'll take my time with this one," he promised with a smile. A rather charming smile reserved for every woman from the quick ease of it. He hadn't smiled at her. Not once.

The waitress tapped the table in front of Maris's hand. "I'll bring out both dinners together. I didn't realize you were waiting on company."

"I wasn't. But I have company now. Thanks." Maris delayed until the server had departed before swinging around in her chair to face Dan. "I was hungry. I don't normally hang around in bars."

"I'm not questioning your judgment. You can pick anywhere you want to eat. And the food is good here, so…"

Maris returned her attention to the table, picking at what appeared to be an old-fashioned Kilroy. She hadn't seen one of those since she was a kid and found the character drawn in the back of her mother's old school book in the attic. *Kilroy was here.* Evidently it meant something back then. What it meant now was that these tables hadn't been replaced in forty years.

"Why would someone want to kill your aunt, Maris?"

With a frown, Maris lifted her head. "Couldn't this wait until we're done eating?"

"I figured the topic would be uppermost in your mind."

"I…it is. Of course, it is." It hadn't been, not until he'd spoken, but the mystery of her great-aunt's demise took a momentary backseat to the flare of shadow licking suddenly around Dan like dark flame. Maris's heart contracted in her chest. *Please, please, no.*

"Are you not feeling well?" she asked, trying to sound casual but knowing she hadn't succeeded.

His eyes narrowed. "Don't even go there."

"I…You just look tired, that's all."

His eyes went to mere slits and then opened, almost as if he were trying to disprove her point as he stretched them wide. "I ought to be tired, but I'm not. It has been a long day, though."

Maris nodded, taking a swig of beer. She lowered the glass slowly, licking a drop off the side of her lip. Dan observed the latter action with a pained expression. Damn it, she wasn't doing it deliberately to entice him.

"I'm going to have to ask you to come in tomorrow," he said, "for elimination prints."

Maris agreed too fast. She should have acted confused or indignant or something other than guilty.

"And to ask you some questions about your whereabouts," he added.

Maris rubbed her eyelids. "*Did* you follow me here? Why are you bringing this up now? Shouldn't you have just waited until you were ready to haul me down to the station?"

Shifting in his seat, Dan reached to take the second glass of water from the blond server. He swallowed a mouthful before setting the glass down. "Maris, it's routine. And I'm done poking at you. Let's eat and chat about other things."

Like what? The fact that death surrounds you, clinging like a second skin?

Tears pricked at her lids, shocking her. She turned away, pretending rapt interest in the descending plate of steaming food. Her stomach growled. She slapped her hand to her abdomen.

Beside her, Dan chuckled. "You kill me."

Don't. Don't use words like that. Don't pretend they don't matter. Not with me. Not with someone who sees your doom as clearly as you see that fork in your hand.

"Maris, you okay?"

"Yes." She shoved a forkful of mashed potato into her mouth, and her next words slid around it. "Hungry, like I said."

"I think I'm getting that. And I'm not even psychic."

She shot him a look from beneath lowered lids, glad to see the aura of shadow had retreated to the thinnest outline, as if it were an illustration in a coloring book and filled in with life. She studied him, storing the images of his sandy hair and his thick, brown lashes, watched the way he cut his food, spreading pieces across his plate and then eating them one by one, because one day what she remembered of him would matter.

"You're staring at me, Maris Granger. What on earth are you looking for?"

"I'm not looking for anything." She speared a piece of meatloaf and popped it into her mouth.

"What is it you see, then? You talk about seeing things. What are you seeing when you look at me? I realize I just told you not to go there when you asked me how I was feeling, but now I want to know."

She swallowed. "Nothing."

"At all?"

"I see you." She placed another mouthful of meat on her tongue.

He laid his knife and fork on the edge of his plate. She lifted her gaze to his face.

"You're not exactly lying, Maris, but you speak in half-truths, don't you? Is that all part of the presentation? The fortune-teller performance?"

The little bit of food she'd eaten turned in her stomach. His words were designed to ridicule, perhaps even to hurt, but he spoke them softly, gently, as if trying to provoke candor rather than anger. Maris sighed, lowering her utensils as well. "It's not a performance. This isn't a sideshow act."

"Then what is it?"

"Life. My life. My reality. It's not a show, not a trick. It's both gift and curse, and I've tried for years to disown it, but it won't let me. I was born with a cowl over my face. Right there in the ocean tide. Do you know what that means?"

He shook his head, his inner energy stilled and listening.

"I can see things, as you said. I have the Sight. And that ability has shaped me. It's who I am. What I am."

Dan shoved his plate aside, signaling to the waitress with his other hand. "May I have the check, please? And box the food to go. We'll be back for it."

Maris looked from her meal to Dan. "Back for it?"

"You and I are taking a walk."

Chapter 8

Maris walked with her hands shoved into the pockets of her wooly sweater, the hood pulled up over her head. The weight pressed her dark bangs against her forehead. She kept blinking to chase the hair out of her lashes.

Dan had never known a woman like Maris, and he'd been acquainted with many. Enamored of a few, sure, and in love once. With the exception of his former wife, he'd never felt as connected as he did right now to Maris. And without exception, he'd never felt the nearness of a woman fire his blood the way Maris did. Yeah, she was hot, but it was something else, too. Stupid, foolish nonsense, all of it, but even nonsense had its place in a person's life.

"I don't even know you."

She glanced aside at him through fine, black strands. "What?"

"Sorry. Thinking out loud."

She went back to looking ahead along the road. He slowed his pace in order to watch her stride, the sensual tendency of her movements. She didn't walk with the conscious aggression of a model's runway saunter, but with the pacing of a feral cat. After a moment she looked back over her shoulder, her smoke-gray eyes dark in the growing gloom. "Am I walking too fast for you?"

"Of course not." He hastened his step, falling in beside her again.

"So, Dan, why exactly are we taking this stroll?"

"I needed to clear my head"—which was becoming more befuddled by the minute—"and I wanted to talk to you alone."

"About?"

"About what you said back there."

"Oh." Her breath plumed in the air. The temperature had dropped since he'd gone into the bar for dinner. Perhaps a walk outside hadn't been the best choice since neither of them wore a coat. But he had no desire to turn around and go back. The sensation of being locked inside a bubble with her, separate from the world, was strong, and he didn't want to give that up just yet.

"Not about your aunt and not about..." About the fact he should be considering her a suspect. He couldn't say that. Not right now. "I want to talk about this thing you call 'the sight.' You really believe it."

"I believe it because it's true."

With no sidewalks on the outskirts of town, they had been walking along the shoulder of the roadway. Through the trees, he saw the gleam of headlights approaching the curve and took Maris's arm, tugging her into the grass. She stood next to him, her shoulder against his bicep. The car sped past, tires growling on the blacktop.

"How you do you know it's true? What definitive proof do you have?"

She stared across the street at the burgundy sign marking the entrance to Alcina Cove's nature preserve. "A lifetime's worth. Can we go in there? It's not dark yet. Don't those types of places close at sundown?"

Amused by her abrupt and somewhat childlike distraction, he took her hand and pulled her across the road to the lane leading into the preserve. Once on the gravel, he released her. Their footsteps crunched on stone.

"Give me some examples," he said.

"I knew my aunt was gone."

Ah, yes, but there could be other reasons for that knowledge. He didn't want to think about that, though. "Something else."

Maris bowed her head, looking at the ground in front of her feet as she moved along. "Sometimes they're little things, relatively unimportant things. Like I'll wake up with a newspaper headline in my head, and when I retrieve the paper from the front steps, it's there."

"But couldn't that be some trick your mind plays on you? Where you think you thought of it before, but you really hadn't?"

Her lips compressed. She shook her head.

"I want to believe you, Maris. I really think I *do* want to."

"You didn't before. What's changed?"

He released a breath through his nostrils. "I don't know."

Maris lifted her head and looked across the long parking lot they'd reached. "I had a breast cancer scare a few years back. I hadn't even gone to my yearly appointment yet, didn't know the doctor would send me for an ultrasound because she felt something in her exam. I had a vision of the entire visit as I was waking up, though. I knew the doctor's exact words. I told my mother about it in advance, and she came with me to the appointment, stood by as the doctor told me her concerns. My mother knows what I can do, and she doesn't like it. She asked me to never tell her anything like that again."

The catch in Maris's voice, the evident pain, twisted Dan's guts into a knot. But it could all be an act. It could. "Everything turned out all right?"

"Oh yeah, I was fine." She smiled, the turn of her lips visible through her blowing hair, the white feather in her right ear entwined in the black strands.

He reached out and stroked the tiny plume, pulling the hair away. "Peace, Maris."

Her hand shot up and grasped the feather between thumb and forefinger, pushing his hand away in the process.

"I'm sorry," he said. "I didn't mean—"

"Don't apologize. You didn't do anything wrong. I was surprised, that's all."

She picked up her pace, scurrying toward the sign of the park's layout several dozen feet away. Dan joined her a moment later, observing her finger pressed to a point on the map.

"I didn't think I remembered this place. According to that over there"— she nodded at the park's history charted out on the sign—"this park was created a while after I left with my family. I want to go see this."

Dan leaned forward for a better look. He hadn't needed to. Of course Maris would gravitate toward that particular landmark. He straightened. "The sun's nearly down. I don't think we should be hiking in the dark."

"Why? You think somebody's going to arrest us? You're a cop. You should have some leverage."

"No, it's the dark that worries me. The terrain isn't all that level." And he had no desire to test the validity of the tales that had been circulating for years regarding the stone circle—the Circle of Alcina, from which the town had gotten its name. Buried for a century or more beneath the encroaching forest, some of the stones tumbled flat long ago, the whole monument had been unearthed and resurrected as a project of some professor who had finally located it after years of searching. The preserve was created around the circle with the monolithic stones as the focal point.

Maris fumbled through her purse and pulled out a flashlight a few seconds later. She flicked it on. "Not dark. We're good."

"Great."

"I'll lead the way. It says the path is marked."

"Even better."

Dan followed close behind, looking from side to side beyond the light's beam into the deep shadows beneath the trees. The park was a perfect place for an attack, if someone was so inclined. Dark, secluded, and a good five hundred feet away was the nearest neighbor liable to hear a cry for help . The naturalist, Felicia Woodward, lived in that house all by herself. She never gave an impression she had any fear of this place. She was a lot like Maris in her beliefs and her attitude. Maybe he should introduce the two of them. Maybe Maris wouldn't feel so alone.

As that final sentiment circled through his brain, he had a strong urge to take the woman marching in front of him into his arms. That would be a mistake, one he couldn't come back from.

Maris stopped abruptly and spun to face him.

"Shit," he said. "Are you going to tell me you know what I'm thinking?"

She cocked her head to the side, flipping the flashlight up to his face and back down toward the ground again. "Why? Is it bad? I was just going to say we're here." Turning around, she raised the beam. Twenty feet away the stones rose out of the earth like the silvered bones of giants. A chill danced down his spine. He'd been here once or twice in recent years to roust out unruly teenagers drinking inside the circle. In the atmosphere of a silent night without commotion, he could understand why people made up stories about the stones.

"Come on, Detective. I'll race you."

"I'm not—" But she was gone, and the light with her.

* * * *

Maris stood in the center of the circle with the dark flashlight held against her thigh. Enough ambient light existed from above for Dan to pick his way in after her. She'd sensed his hesitation when she insisted they come to the stones and had wondered why he faltered. She had no regrets. It was amazing and beautiful. Tonight, she would describe this in her diary. She'd been writing down her thoughts since she was a teenager, most of them intimate and not the type of thing she'd share. But the act of writing helped her to cope. Her therapist had suggested the exercise to help with healing, but she had chosen to keep it going.

Raising her arms toward the sky, head tipped back, she turned in a slow circle. Energy reflected off the stones' surfaces like radiant heat on a sunny day. Even through her sweater, the hairs on her arms lifted with the fizzing of power. She felt welcomed here, as if encircled by old friends. She understood the force encased in a configuration of stones such as this, had learned of it in her lessons with Aunt Alva long ago. A strength existed within the circles, often called upon by many to enhance their gifts.

Maris stopped turning, lowering her arms to her sides. She'd been told her family had lived for generations in this area, nearly four hundred years of connection. Had the females of her bloodline met here, communing beneath the stars, before the stones had fallen?

And I am the last.

A sound welled up in her throat like a howl. She clamped her teeth together to keep the noise contained, refusing to let it loose into the night. All around her whispers began to flutter like leaves in the wind. Or was it the wind? Confused and unsteady, she began to turn again, arms outstretched for balance.

"Maris!"

"Dan, I'm he—" Holy Mother of God, what the hell was that?

Tall and thin and nearly in the shape of a man, a shadow flitted from stone to stone with no source of illumination strong enough to create it. Maris sucked in a breath, lifting the flashlight, thumb fumbling for the switch.

"Who are you?" she hissed through her teeth.

You know who I am.

"No. I don't." Maris depressed the round button on the flashlight's plastic casing. The bulb remained dark.

Yes. You do.

"Maris!"

"I don't. I swear I don't."

Think. Think hard...

"Maris!" Dan burst between the stones into the circle. The flashlight in Maris's fist flared into life. Dan hurried to her side and grabbed her arm. "Who were you talking to?"

Maris swung the light around to illuminate the stones one by one. "Nobody. There...there was no one here."

Dan pulled her close. She let him, turning her head against his sweatshirt, the scent of rank fear rising from both of them mildly offensive as well as reassuring. Even if Dan didn't understand what had just happened, hadn't been close enough to witness it, at least he'd *felt* it. Maris burrowed her face against his chest.

"I think we'll come back another day," she said. "A sunny mid-afternoon."

A sound rumbled through him, a kind of laughing growl. Not because he thought what she'd said was funny, but in defiance—a deliberate insolence to counter the unease. With his fingers tight on her upper arm, he led the way out of the stone circle and back across the parking lot to the main road. By the time they reached it, Maris was breathless from trotting alongside him.

"I didn't see your car when I came into the bar. Are you staying at the Hideaway?"

She nodded.

"Let's collect our food, and I'll walk you back, okay?"

"Okay."

Maris kept an eye on him as they made their way to the bar, marking his mood in the lines of his profile. By the time they reached the parking lot, he'd calmed down considerably. Once they'd claimed their boxes of leftovers, they continued on to the quaint motel, walking with enough distance between them they could have driven a small vehicle through. It had to be that way.

Maris fished in her purse for the motel key. "This is my room. So now you know. Sorry I didn't call you earlier with that information."

"This is your room?"

"Yes. Why?"

"Nothing. May I come in for a minute?"

Maris lifted her gaze to blue eyes shielded by the downward turn of his lashes. Somewhere inside, in some unexplored place, she knew him. Had to be the eyes, the same as the friend she used to talk to in the night as a child. Imaginary, sure, but the impact of the memory remained.

"Sure," she said as she inserted the key into the door, her back to him. She gave the room a quick onceover, speculating what he would think when he walked in. As a police officer, he might wonder why her unpacked suitcase lay in the middle of a bed she should have slept in the night before.

He entered behind her and shut the door while she placed her leftovers in a dorm-sized refrigerator. She couldn't decide whether she should offer to put his in there, too, as that might imply she expected him to stick around a while.

She indicated the desk chair. "Have a seat." He remained standing. "Or not." Maris yanked her suitcase off the bed, stowing it in the open cupboard. Let him think she was the type who lived out of it rather than utilizing the dresser in the room. She then went into the bathroom and returned a few minutes later to find he hadn't moved.

With a snort of impatience, she crossed the floor. She grabbed the take-out container from him and shoved it into the refrigerator. "Would you sit down? You make me nervous standing there. I assume you want to finish the conversation we started?"

"I…First, I want to know what happened in that damned stone circle."

Maris pointed at the chair. "Sit."

He complied, straddling it backward, his arms crossed over the curved back. Maris sat opposite him on the edge of the mattress.

"I don't know what happened, Dan. I really don't."

"You were talking to someone."

"There was no one there."

"I heard you talking, and there was this...this..." He lapsed into silence, staring at the floor.

"I don't know what happened," Maris repeated. "I don't know what I saw. There's no one I can ask, either, now that Aunt Alva is gone. I could have spoken with my father about it, once upon a time, but he's gone now, too."

He frowned, scrubbing at a worn place on the carpet with the toe of his boot. "Is this the type of thing you deal with because of this...this 'gift' you have?"

Maris shook her head. "No."

"But when you look at me, you see something, don't you? Something you are familiar with. Something you recognize. And it's bad, isn't it?"

Maris curled the ring finger of her right hand until the nail dug deep into her palm. "I don't fully understand what I'm getting from you yet. I'm working through it."

Dan nodded. "Okay. Fine. And what happened in the preserve, that'll leave me eventually, right? Because I feel like I need a really hot shower to wash the sensation from my skin."

Odd, she hadn't perceived the episode in that way at all. She'd been frightened, yes, but she didn't feel sullied. "Do you want to hang out here for a while? We could watch television. A mundane occupation might be just the thing."

He lifted his head and met her gaze. "Yeah. I think I would."

Chapter 9

Had he actually agreed to watch television with a woman in her motel room? Maris stood up from the corner of the mattress and turned on the set with the remote. She switched to the guide and began scrolling through the options with a running commentary on each one. When he didn't respond, she finally picked a sitcom and settled on it.

"A laugh will do you good," she said before striding to the bed and yanking the pillows from beneath the bedspread, which she then piled against the headboard. "You may as well be comfortable."

"What about you?"

"I'll sit next to you. No big deal. I'm pretty damned resistible so I'm not worried."

She was dead wrong about that one, but he wasn't going to argue. Dan pushed up from the chair and stood. "You don't know me."

"You don't know me either. We just shared a rather disturbing experience together, so I think we can cut the cop and suspect bit for a while at least."

Dan slid the chair back beneath the desk. "I didn't say you were a suspect."

"And I'd say I'm all you have right now."

Perched on the edge of the mattress, Dan loosened the laces on his boots. "I told you the fingerprints are routine. The questions are routine. Family members are always questioned first in order to eliminate them. Do you mind if I kick these off?"

"Suit yourself."

Dan arranged himself comfortably on one side of the bed as Maris tossed the remote his way. "Is that door locked?"

In two strides, she was at the door and turning the dead bolt. "Whatever that was, I think it belongs to those stones, and it certainly didn't have substance. It's not going to follow you."

Dan started flipping through the channels. "I thought you said you didn't see anything."

"What I said was that no one was there and I didn't know what I had seen. There's a big difference." Maris pulled her food back out of the refrigerator and forked a huge dollop of potatoes into a mug from the kitchenette counter. "Want some?"

"Thank you, no. Not hungry. I can't imagine how you are."

She didn't answer, but put the mug in the microwave to heat.

"I'm still trying to wrap my head around you and what you claim, Maris." Dan crossed his arms over his chest, squinting across the room to make certain the door was, indeed, bolted. "How are you not scared by this life you lead?"

"What happened tonight isn't part of my life. I don't know what the hell it was."

"That's not reassuring at all."

The bell dinged on the oven. Maris removed the steaming potatoes and eased down on the bed's edge, leaving plenty of room between them. Maybe she wasn't as comfortable about the two of them together as she pretended to be.

"So," she said around a mouthful, "you accepted tonight's occurrence, and yet you're hesitant to believe what I've told you about me. I'm not sure most people would have been aware of what took place. There's something in your past that opened you up, whether you are willing to admit it or not."

He muted the volume on the television. "You're right." He dropped the remote onto the bedspread. "You're absolutely right. Two years—no, three years ago now, I was involved in an investigation which brought me in contact with something I hadn't encountered before. I ended up in the ER, thought I was having a heart attack after. I never spoke of it with anyone except the woman directly involved because she had experienced it, too."

Maris scraped the inside of the ceramic to scoop out the last of the potatoes, sucked them off the fork tines, and set the mug aside on the nightstand. She brought her legs up onto the bed, laced-up boots and all, and clenched her hands together in the folds of her skirt. Dan studied the shape of her wrists, narrow-boned, blue-veined, and waited.

"Thank you."

Dan stirred, shifting around on the bed to face her. "For what?"

"Being honest. Most people want to hide that type of experience, for many reasons. Denial, avoidance of ridicule, fear. I'm not going to ask you the details. I don't need to know them, but I want you to understand you can talk to me, okay? It's no fun being alone with this."

He pictured what that would be like, sharing things that frightened him with a woman. The things that didn't. The things that mattered.

Beside him, she bit her lip, loosened her hands, reached for the remote. He stopped her, closing his fingers over her own. "Do you read my mind?"

She didn't remove her hand from his grasp, but her entire body went still, like a hunted animal avoiding the notice of the hunter. He flinched, pulled his fingers back, and settled them on his thigh.

"I don't read minds. That *is* a parlor trick. But what I do receive sometimes is the essence of someone's thoughts, or occasionally an actual image. It doesn't happen all the time, and I don't control it."

"But you have known what's been going on in my head at least a few times since we've met."

She cleared her throat delicately. "Yes."

"This could be troublesome."

Maris giggled, the earthy, liquid sound he found so charming. "Or entertaining," she whispered.

"God, no."

"Certain thoughts are subconscious, not the type you'd say to someone's face sort of thoughts. Some are very dark—not yours," she hastened to add. "Evident of places I don't ever want to be."

"And do you...do you ever speak with the dead? See them?" Dan stared at the socks on his feet, the gray toes on white. The same style his dad used to wear. With sandals even, in the summers before he passed.

"Not in the way you're thinking."

"So you know what I'm thinking right now."

"No, Dan, I do not. I'm talking theoretically, what I believe you meant when you asked that question. Good Lord, let's just watch some TV."

Maris turned the volume on, settling down into the pillows at her back and crossing her arms over her breast. Dan slid down beside her, his arms also crossed, keeping the space of convention between them. Okay, so he didn't quite understand what all of this meant, but he was beginning to give more credence to Maris's world. With his personal experience, there was no reason to fight acceptance so much. What had Maris said about a card on her aunt's table?

Suspending disbelief. Right. A lucky guess on her part, that one. He couldn't give her all the credit, after all. But she'd mentioned the Priestess card still lying on his desk, her voice marked by a strange authority as she spoke of changes in the world.

He tightened his arms across his chest. It was too late to return the card now.

Trying to suppress any guilty vibes that might be headed Maris's way, Dan focused on the commercial playing across the television screen.

* * * *

He looked a different man in sleep. Everything gentled, his lashes lying dark against his lower lids, his mouth relaxed, the stern set of his jaw slackened. He must have looked so as a boy. Maris wondered about his parents, his father in particular. She'd gotten that loud and clear. The socks and sandals. Why did some older people wear them paired that way? Were their feet always cold or did the socks cushion thinning skin from the rubbing of leather?

She would have asked Dan about his dad, but she didn't want him freaking out. He'd had enough to deal with tonight.

Easing from the bed, Maris sought the floor with her bare toes and stood. Dan slept on undisturbed, the television playing on low volume, words indistinct. A background sound she chose not to eliminate because the sudden absence of flickering light against his lids, the vanished murmur of voices, might wake him up. She didn't want him to wake up. His presence comforted her.

She went and peed in the dark to avoid the clacking whir of the fan, then brushed the stale beer taste from her mouth. Creeping back into the room, she stopped in the middle of the floor. The bed was empty.

"Dan?"

Movement near the door caught her eye. Standing in shadow, Dan struggled to put on his boots.

"You can sit down to do that, you know."

He paused, footgear in hand. "I can't. I don't want to sit on the bed. I won't want to leave it."

Maris took two steps closer, a warm flush racing over her skin. "You don't have to."

His pale gaze burned in the semi-darkness. "I do."

"Work?"

"No."

"Me?"

"Yes."

"I'm sorry." Maris strode to the end of the bed and sat, cross-legged, watching as Dan attempted to balance himself with fingers splayed across the wall while he tugged his boot on with the other hand. "I didn't even think to ask if you had someone in your life. I guess spending the night, however innocently, with a woman in her room could cause issues."

"I have no one. And it's not innocent. Not entirely. I'm surprised you can't read those thoughts."

Maris pulled her legs up, wrapping her arms around her knees. A chill draft of air swept across her toes. "You don't have to go."

"Don't I?"

"No."

He straightened, his unsuccessful attempt to put on his left boot leaving it swinging in his hand. "I'm a police officer…"

"So what are you saying? Police officers aren't allowed to have sex?"

The boot dropped to the floor. "Jesus, Maris."

"Or is that not what you meant?"

"No. It's exactly what I meant."

"Then don't leave."

He stood there as if undecided. She didn't need to know his thoughts to see he'd already made up his mind. "I shouldn't become involved like this."

"It's…our business. Our secret."

"Sounds like the kind of statement someone makes before they sue."

Maris dropped her hands to the mattress on either side of her hips. "Excuse me?"

"Not you. But I've heard of it happening. A man in a police officer's position, a woman who—"

"—is suspected of something? I thought you said I wasn't. That everything was routine. It's not like I was pulled over under the influence and offered you a—"

"Maris! Stop. Please. I beg you, stop."

"Okay." She stood and closed the gap between them. "Okay." She took his empty hand, tucking two fingers into the curve of his fist, rubbing her thumb across his knuckles. "Thank you for believing me."

He smiled. Not the winning smile he'd given the waitress, but one that seemed meant for Maris alone. "Don't put words in my mouth, Maris."

"I could offer you something more palatable."

He groaned, tightening his fist around her fingers.

"What?" Maris jerked a thumb in the direction of the refrigerator. "I meant the meatloaf."

"No, you didn't."

"You're right," she said. "I didn't."

He snatched his hand free of hers and shoved both into her hair, wrapping his fingers around the back of her head as he brought his mouth down onto her own, open and questing. Clutching his sleeves, she welcomed him, and allowed him to propel her backward to the bed. Inches shy of the mattress, he lifted her up. She wrapped her legs around his hips and pulled back, letting momentum and gravity take care of the rest.

What came next bore no connection to romantic passion, but was a conflagration designed to drive out memory. Hard and fast in places slick with yearning, the scrape of teeth on tender flesh a shock of pleasure, a game of chance, but there was no cruelty in the lightning-swift play. When she cried out, he pressed his fingers to her lips, followed by his mouth on hers, holding her in place beneath him as he pounded the final strokes of his pleasure deep inside. Afterward, he collapsed onto his side breathless and, she thought, half-ashamed.

Yes, that was what she felt from him. Shame.

"Dan."

The television sent muted light flickering over the ceiling, across his face, along the walls. He lay with his eyes shielded by shadow.

"Dan. Say something."

"Like what?" She barely heard his whisper over the muffled volume of the TV.

"Like you're not ashamed of what we did."

For a long moment, he was silent, and then he threw himself off the mattress with a flurry of motion. Standing beside the bed, he yanked his clothes back into place. Only then did she realize they hadn't even taken the time to remove any of them.

"I can't say that," he said, "because it wouldn't be true."

In less than ten seconds, he was gone, his uncooperative boot hanging by its laces from his hand as he exited the room. He latched the door upon departing, but the deadbolt remained open. She would have to remedy that, but not yet. She sat up and slid her body beneath the rumpled covers, staring at the television screen without seeing it. After a minute or two, she felt around for the remote and found it shoved beneath a pillow. The TV went off with one swift blast of static. From outside the window, the neon motel sign colored the slats of the blinds in the darkened room with a dim hue of rose.

"Fuck."

Chapter 10

"Whoa, Stauffer, what the heck happened to you?"

"Not a damned thing. Anyone process the prints from Mabry's yet?" Dan threw his jacket toward the coat rack in the corner and missed. Tossing his keys onto his desk, he retrieved the garment from the floor and took his time draping it over the curved wood. Something crinkled in the pocket. He yanked out a gas receipt and spotted Maris's number written across the back. With a roll of guilt through his gut, he went and tucked the paper into his top drawer.

"Yep. Eliminated all that were the dead woman's. There were quite a few others, mostly downstairs in the parlor where she conducted business, so that's to be expected, but upstairs, too. I'll get them run through the system today. When's that niece of hers coming in?"

"Today. I'll contact her today." Dan lowered himself into the swivel chair, running a hand through his hair.

"You sure you're okay?"

"I'm fine. Appreciate you asking. Might be coming down with something, I guess." Yeah, like a whopping case of shithead-itis. He knew better. He goddamn knew better than to fall into bed with her. This case had been one screw-up after another, and all his to claim. What if she was guilty of the crime? He'd called the motel and found out she'd only checked in yesterday afternoon, not the night she claimed to have gotten here. Just where the hell had she been?

Realizing the threshold still held the junior detective, Dan chewed on the inside of his cheek. Nearly a half year since they'd each been promoted, and Dan still wasn't sure if Jamie Rogers resented him for his senior position. Sometimes it seemed like he did. But right now, he was acting like the same old Jamie. Dan waved him away. "I'm fine. Seriously. Just go."

With a grunt, Jamie pushed off the doorframe with his shoulder. "Want me to call her for you? What's her name? Maris, right?"

"Maris. And I'll do it."

"Some of the guys are saying she's pretty hot. In a bohemian sort of way."

Dan snorted. "Where'd you pick up a word like 'bohemian'?"

"Dunno. You hear it a lot."

"You might want to look it up in the dictionary."

"Fuck you, Stauffer."

"Yeah, you're not my type." Dan stared at the man until he started to back away. "Pull the door shut while you're at it, will you?"

As soon as the door had closed, Dan spun back and forth a few times in his chair. He needed to contact Maris, have her come in, but what in bloody hell was he going to say to her? He couldn't act as if none of it had happened—not the incident in the stone circle or the confessions in her motel room, not the incendiary sex. They'd both needed the latter, he understood that, but he should have kept it in his pants. And afterward—God, he hated himself for speaking those words despite the truth of them. Even in the dark, he could see the hurt in her eyes, the shock.

Forget the unexplained bond, the flash of hope in which he foolishly thought she might be the perfect partner because she understood where he had been. Forget the comfort, the intrigue, the heated lust. Unless he could prove otherwise, she might end up his prime suspect for the murder of Alva Mabry. He had not only literally slept in her bed, he'd slept with her. Too mild a term for what had passed between them, lightning hot and just as fast, but even if it had been drawn out and taken all night with declarations of adoration and lasting fidelity, would he be any less culpable for his part in it? Of course not.

She had asked him to tell her he wasn't ashamed of what they had done. He could have said no. He should have said no. Why couldn't he lie to her? In many of their conversations, he'd hedged, danced around the truth, but he couldn't lie. Not outright, not even to save her pain. Because she only asked him what she already knew with that damned "sight" of hers. It wasn't exactly fair, now was it?

And it sure as hell wasn't convenient.

Dan lifted the receiver, cradled it under his ear, determined to get this conversation over. He yanked open the drawer for another glance at her phone number and punched the digits on the keypad before whipping the drawer shut. After several rings, her voice mail picked up.

"If this is Dan, go fuck yourself. Anyone else, please leave a message."

Shit! Grateful he hadn't taken Jamie up on his offer to make the call, Dan tried to compose himself enough to leave a message for her. At the sound of the beep, he was forced to rush his message and ended up prefacing the whole thing with the words "I'm sorry" and, following the plummeting realization it was too late to take the sentiment back, added "for inconveniencing you, but I need you to come to the station at"—he glanced at the clock—"eleven this morning for fingerprints and a few questions. Please be prompt. Don't make me come get you."

Oh, for the love of God, why had he said *that*? He slammed the phone down, only to have the receiver bounce across the blotter and drop behind the desk. Cursing, he jumped up and, after several attempts, retrieved it by the cord.

A light tap sounded at the door.

"Come in!"

The door opened wide enough for a face to peer in. "You okay?"

Sally, the newest police clerk. She looked half his age and probably wasn't much older than that. She'd been making eyes at him for the past month. Well, he wasn't interested in any of what she was offering. Or any woman, period. Enough was enough. "I'm fine. Dropped the phone."

"Good. There's someone here to see you."

"I don't want—"

Before he could finish his sentence, the door swung open. Maris walked in, thanked the girl sweetly, and pushed the door shut. She turned to face him, holding up her cell phone. He heard his voice coming through it. After a second, she hit a number to replay the message, and then did it again and yet again, looping "I'm sorry" like an inane apology.

"You are an insane person," he said.

"You don't really believe that." She slipped the phone into her purse.

He sighed. "No, I don't. Sit down."

She sat in the chair where she'd been seated the first time he'd met her. Was that only yesterday in the wee hours of the morning? Yes. Yes it was. Therefore, the little leap of his heart at the sight of her face was inappropriate. Perhaps he was the insane one.

"I need to take your fingerprints."

"So I heard." She nodded in the direction of the cell phone sticking up from the pocket in her purse.

"Where were you when I made that call?"

"In the lobby. You said yesterday that you needed me to come in."

"Yes, I did. I said other things, too, and yet you came anyway."

"Well, you apologized after all." She grinned.

He broke into laughter, but sobered after a moment , experiencing a gut-wrenching urge to apologize for real. Maybe even cry a little. God, what was wrong with him?

"Maris, I don't know what to do."

"About what?"

"About us."

She tipped her head to one side. "Is there an 'us'?"

"It feels like there is." He spun his chair and leaned forward, hands folded between his knees. "Which is absurd. That's not an insult, just reality. It's been twenty-four freaking hours, give or take, and I don't know you—"

"You know me."

He shook his head. "I don't. It feels like I do, but I don't. And I..." He stopped, staring down at his clasped hands at the scar on his thumb from a slippery blade when cleaning fish with his father their last time out on the ocean. He glanced back up. "I have to ask you this question, Maris. I have to."

She nodded encouragement, the expression on her face wary. "Go ahead."

"Did you kill your aunt? Did you poison Alva Mabry?"

A transition took place in her eyes. He couldn't tell if those gray orbs displayed disbelief or guilt or some other reaction he couldn't figure out since her facial expression didn't alter at all. Had she practiced for this moment? He didn't want to believe something so cold about her, but he had to take a step back and view the situation from an investigative standpoint, without prejudice or sentiment.

She shook her head. "Why would I do that?"

"Don't answer a question with a question, Maris. It doesn't bode well for your innocence."

"Ouch. Fine." She shifted in her chair. "Tell me why you think I did. What motive are you trying on for size? The whole estate thing you threw at me yesterday? Do you know for fact there is anything to be gained financially from her demise? And why would I suddenly decide to come back to Alcina Cove and kill my ninety-three-year-old aunt? Time was on my side, and it certainly wouldn't be worth the risk if I wanted to make sure I profited from her death."

He stared at her, mouth dropping open, at a loss for a response.

"Besides," she went on, "I loved my aunt. Not the way I did as a child, but the fondness, the loyalty, the memories I had of her—not all of them perfect, of course—didn't fade completely. I had no reason to harm her. I came here because she needed me. I just didn't know why."

He tightened the twisted grip of his fingers between his legs. "You still haven't answered my question."

Tears glistened abruptly on her lashes. She blinked them away. "I did not."

Dan threw up his hands. "Is that your answer, or are you just agreeing with my statement?"

"You're an ass, Detective Stauffer."

He stood. "And you're infuriating. How can I protect you if you won't be honest with me?"

"Is that what you're trying to do? Protect me?"

Dan pulled the keys from the desktop and shoved them in his pocket. "You wanted me to figure out what happened to your aunt. That's what I'm trying to do. If you're guilty of the crime, I'll deal with that, but if you're not—and I really hope to God you're not—then I need to protect you from the accusations. Now let's go."

She rose, too, standing before him, the top of her head in line with his chin. A light fragrance drifted into his nostrils from her hair. As she moved her head, lifting her gaze to his, he saw she'd changed out the studs in her ears from minuscule gold balls to amethyst stones, but the feather remained, drifting back and forth in a current of air like the hand on an upside down metronome.

"Where are we going?" she asked, tucking her purse under her arm.

"Fingerprints."

Dan yanked open the door. Jamie stood on the other side, hastily lifting his hand as if to knock. Dan shot him a look he couldn't possibly misunderstand, and the man backed away with a less-than-discreet onceover of Maris as she crossed the threshold into the corridor beyond.

"Left," Dan said, following her. "Then second door on the right. I'll need to unlock it."

"No need," said Jamie from behind him. "Already open."

"Yeah, thanks," Dan shot over his shoulder, tone surly. Ahead of him, Maris had her hand on the knob. She turned it and went inside, spine ramrod straight. Dan entered less than two seconds behind and shut the door before Jamie could join them.

"You sound annoyed," Maris commented.

"I am annoyed."

Dan opened the cover to the chemically pre-treated pad while Maris stepped aside in frowning observation. Dan pulled out a ten-print fingerprint card and laid it on the counter.

"That doesn't look like ink."

Dan glanced at her. "It isn't. We use inkless. It's more accurate. Don't want any mistakes."

She held out her left hand. "Does it matter which one is first?"

"Nope."

Dan took her hand in both of his, working his digits along her thumb until he had it turned properly. Her hands were remarkably soft and warm. He'd lost himself inside her the night before and hadn't noticed the texture or temperature of her fingers, hadn't so much as caressed her face, held her hand. He really was a bastard.

One by one, he rolled her fingers over the pad and then onto the fingerprint card, aware of the curves of her body pressed lightly against his side as she leaned in to comply. He could hardly breathe.

"Next."

She obeyed wordlessly, placing her other hand in his. He extended his ring finger toward her wrist, settling it against her veins, to the pulse racing beneath the skin.

"Maris..."

"Don't say anything."

If he walked out of here with a hard-on, he'd be sunk. What the hell was wrong with him? Such a condition wouldn't go unnoticed by a bunch of guys who obviously possessed strong opinions about Maris's appeal.

He turned her pinkie over the card and then pulled it away, releasing her hand. "Okay, finished. You can wipe your fingers with one of those baby-wipes. I have to put the card in the developer chamber."

"How long do they take to develop?" She scrubbed the powder-scented wipe across her fingertips as she tipped her chin up in order to see what he was doing.

"I'll have a perfect, high-contrast print shortly." He glanced at her, telling himself he was gauging her reaction to his words, but was more intent on the swing of her hair across her neck.

She tossed the wipe in the trash can, jerking her chin in his direction. "Where'd that scar on your thumb come from?"

"What scar?"

"That scar right there." She pressed the curve of her nail against the pale cicatrix. Her eyes went momentarily blank. "You were... were you fishing?"

He jerked his hand away. "Come with me. I have a few more questions."

Dan brought Maris into the interview room and indicated she should take a seat. She did, slowly. He felt the weight of her gaze following his movements as he crossed to the other side of the table and sat opposite her.

"Maris, I called the motel and—"

"I was at my aunt's."

He went silent. Was she about to confess?

"After you and I were there, I returned. You'll find my fingerprints upstairs, I'm sure. I used the bathroom and then went into my old room where I slept for a couple of hours. When it got light, I went for a walk. Some of the neighbors probably saw me. Then I came back and waited for you."

"How did you get in?"

"I had an old key in my possession. I wasn't sure it would work, but it did."

"And then you rearranged the cards."

"I did not."

Dan drummed the tabletop in one quick roll, a seething hole opening up in his chest. "So I won't find your fingerprints on those cards? We took them, you know, as evidence. They're being processed. I'd be honest with me right now if I were you. Because you've lied enough."

She closed her eyes. "I know I did. I didn't know if I could trust you."

"And you trust me now that I've found out you've been lying to me? Convenient."

Maris threw her purse up onto the table. Her cell phone popped out along with a tube of lip gloss. She shoved them both back inside. "Dan—"

"Don't call me that."

"Fine. Detective Stauffer, then. We've been lying to each other. Seems that's the way we operate, you and I. A form of protection, of self-preservation, but not the types of lies that hurt people. Merely the type that keep boundaries in place. I did not touch those cards, and unless the prints are twenty years old, you won't find mine on them. I spent the night in Aunt Alva's home to try and get a feel for what had happened. I received no information. I have a key, yes, and told you I didn't. I understand how bad that looks, but would you have let me return to the house if I had told you, even though you insisted my aunt's death was one of natural causes? I don't think so. Because somewhere inside, you thought the possibility existed she hadn't, from the moment I opened my mouth to you about being called here."

He frowned at her, part of him recognizing a kernel of truth in her rant. "Are you finished? Or is there something else you'd like to confess?"

"What, like killing her? No."

Dan opened his fist and smacked his palm on the laminate tabletop. "There you go again, Maris. Don't you hear yourself? You're very keen on words, aren't you? On using them in a way you hope somebody won't catch in order to avoid a straight answer. So let's try this again. Did you kill your aunt?"

She stared him straight in the eye, a woman who had admitted to lying to protect herself, and whispered one syllable. "No."

And he wanted to believe her. God, he wanted to believe her.

"Okay," he said, "let's start from the beginning. And I'm going to take notes so there's no inaccuracy in my memory of this conversation." He slid a pad and a mechanical pencil from the drawer centered beneath the table and laid them on top. Across from him, she pulled out the lip gloss she'd tossed back into her purse a moment before and applied it quickly to her mouth. Setting the cap with a small click, she clutched the tube in her hand.

"Name."

"Maris Granger."

He wrote it down in bold block print. "Address? Again please, yes," he added, forestalling any protest. She gave it to him, and he wrote that down, too. "And you left your house there in the middle of the night because of a dream."

"Yes."

He glanced at her. "And how long did it take you to get here?"

"Three and a half hours. Maybe a little longer."

"Did you stop anywhere? Would someone remember seeing you?"

She rocked on the chair, rearranging her skirt beneath her hips. "I have no idea if someone would remember seeing me, but yes, I did stop. I had to get gas along the way. And use the ladies room, which was fairly disgusting."

Don't make jokes, Maris. "Did you make a complaint of that to someone there?"

"A passing remark maybe when I bought a bottle of water."

"And do you remember the name of the station?"

"I paid cash for the gas. I'll look for the receipt and let you know."

Dan made the notation *gas station* and nodded. "Yes. You will. When you got here, you drove straight to the police department, or so you told me. How did you know where to find the building? And don't say you dreamt—"

"There were signs."

He opened his mouth.

"I mean the kind on metal posts."

"Right." He wrote a word in the margin of the pad but then realized with a start he'd written *Maris*, which he crossed out with such force the lead broke. He pushed out a bit more with a click to the back of the pencil. "But you came looking for me."

"I did."

"Why?" When she didn't answer, he looked up. "Why?"

Her smoke-gray eyes widened. "I saw you. I heard your name. I knew where I should be able to find you."

Dan's breath rushed out his nose. "We'll leave that for now. What time did you arrive here?"

"I don't know exactly. Within a few minutes of when the man at the front desk called you to let you know. You could check with him."

"And at what point did you decide the best course of action would be to lie to me? Right away, or did you size me up and determine I might just be gullible enough for you to pull it off?"

Maris yanked her purse from the table into her lap where it landed with a jangle of coins and keys. She pulled out the latter. He eyed them through narrowed lids. "Going somewhere?"

"Are you arresting me, Dan—Detective?"

He tapped the eraser once on the table, causing the lead to rattle in the pencil casing. "I am not. Not yet."

"Good. I'm leaving." She stood, hooking purse straps over her shoulder. Her shadow flickered up the wall behind her. Dan glanced at the overhead fluorescents in an instinctive search for the cause and found the illumination unwavering.

"I'm sure you'll call me when you have some real news to impart, Detective Stauffer. Some accurate news."

He stood as well, wanting to snatch her into his arms and stop her. Instead, he held the pad close to his chest and watched her go. After the door had closed behind her, he tossed pad and pencil onto the table. The pencil rolled to the edge and caught before toppling over. He looked down at the yellow page on which he'd been scratching his notes. Scrawled across the bottom in a shaky hand so unlike his normal script as to be nearly unrecognizable were the words *listen to her.*

Chapter 11

Maris marched across the graveled lot toward the path leading to the naturalist's residence, arguing in her head against both fear at the escalation of events and her anger at Dan. She knew the statistics. Most murders were not arbitrary occurrence. Most killings took place between people who knew each other one way or another, and the police always looked to the husband, wife, family member first. A homicide involving poison was personal. Random poisoners didn't exist. Since there were no other family members to look at, she was the natural choice. Maris doubted the investigation would ever get as far as a neighbor or a customer because the police viewed her as the most likely suspect, and all efforts would be expended toward proving that. Dan was just doing his job, despite all the misgivings she sensed in him. He was quite good at his work, and the mistakes he'd made did not sit well with him. Like sleeping with her. A big one, that. He'd strive even harder to get at the truth, even if it wasn't the correct truth.

At the door to a one-story addition on the naturalist's home, built to accommodate a small shop, Maris turned the knob and went in. Overhead a small bell jangled, announcing her arrival. A woman in her mid-fifties perched on a stepladder at the far side of the room paused with an armful of books and looked back at her.

Maris stopped dead, a warm thrill running through her at recognition of a kindred spirit. It had been years since she'd experienced such knowledge. "Hi."

The woman stepped down off the ladder and dumped the books onto a nearby counter. She hurried across the floor and took one of Maris's hands in both of hers, squeezing lightly. "Welcome," she said, then caught herself on whatever she'd been about to say next before adding, "to Alcina Cove Nature Preserve."

Still, the woman didn't release her hand. Maris smiled. "Thank you."

The woman searched her eyes. "I'm Felicia. Felicia Woodward. You're not new to the area, but it's been a while, hasn't it?"

"Almost twenty years since I left with my family."

Felicia dropped her hand and strode back toward the counter with a wave of her fingers, indicating Maris should follow. "Welcome home, then."

"That was what you were going to say first, isn't it? Welcome home."

Felicia's laughter rang clearer than the brass bell hanging above the door. "It was."

Maris trailed after her. Felicia stepped behind the counter and pulled out two mugs and a pair of tea bags. A small teapot on a hotplate already sent steam into the air.

"Too early for alcohol and no need for it either, so tea will do," Felicia said as she poured the water. Maris watched in fascination the brisk efficiency of the woman's movements.

"I'm Maris Granger. Alva Mabry's grand-niece."

With a finger pressed to the lid of the upended pot, Felicia gave her a long look. "She's gone, isn't she?"

Maris didn't need to ask her how she knew. "Yes."

"I'm sorry to hear that." Felicia set a sugar bowl on the counter, laying a spoon beside the ceramic container with its depiction of the stone circle. "But at her age, I guess it was expected...or wasn't it?"

Maris pulled one of the mugs close, swinging the dangling tag of the tea bag with her pointer finger. "Apparently she was murdered."

Felicia turned away to place the pot on the burner. "How? Do you know?"

"The medical examiner says poison. Not sure what kind yet. I've heard poison is a very personal method of execution. Dan Stauffer is narrowing down his list of suspects at this time, I expect."

Felicia spun back around, grasping the other mug in both hands, and brought it close to her face, chest expanding as she breathed in the aroma. "So you've met our Detective Stauffer, have you?"

"Oh, yeah." Maris sipped the herbal beverage, letting the hot liquid rest in her mouth a moment before swallowing.

"He's always acted the ladies' man, but I think that persona hides a deeper need. I think he wants someone special, someone different, and someone he can trust."

Maris made no comment, drinking another mouthful.

"I bet he likes you."

A blush heated Maris's cheeks. She kept her eyes downcast, pretending concentration on the tea. "Why would you think that? Am I his type?"

"You're exactly not his type, which makes you what he needs."

Maris cleared her throat, holding her mug in one hand and running the fingers of the other over a series of photographs contained beneath the glass countertop. "I've only been here two days. We don't know each other."

"Uh-huh."

"Besides, liking me would definitely conflict with his job. He fancies me the prime suspect."

Felicia was silent. Maris returned her attention to the woman.

"And are you?" Felicia asked.

"The prime suspect? It would seem so. But did I do anything to hurt my aunt? With the exception of certain things I said to her many years ago, no."

Felicia set her mug down. "He doesn't believe you?"

"He doesn't want to believe me. He's afraid to believe me. He's fearful and ashamed of what he feels."

"For you."

"For me."

"Huh." With a smug expression, Felicia resumed her tea, both elbows on the counter. She stretched out an arm to point at a photo by Maris's hand. "You can see how overgrown and damaged the circle was in this one. I'm surprised anyone recognized it for what it was."

Maris bent to peer closer. "Do you think nature did that, or people?"

"What do you think?"

Maris pressed her fingertip to the glass, causing a halo from her skin's warmth. "Unless there was a massive tremor, those stones wouldn't have gone down. I think they were pulled down out of fear."

"Fear of what?"

Raising her gaze to Felicia's, Maris studied her expression. "Have you seen him, it, whatever guards that place?"

"I have. I'm assuming you have, too. When?"

"Yesterday evening. What is it?"

Felicia shook her head. "I'm not sure. Sometimes I think it's an elemental, other times a Native American spirit. I don't know, though. But I've learned not to be afraid."

"It knew me. It said I knew it, too."

"I think it knows all of us, all who have the gift we do, back through the ages and into the future. I've heard some odd tales about the circle but, as I said, I've learned not to fear it."

Maris shuddered. "It has to make people afraid. People not as understanding as you."

"Is that why you think the circle was torn down?"

Maris straightened. "It would make sense, yet I don't think everyone can actually see it. Dan did, though. Or he sensed it at any rate. I'm sure others have as well."

Felicia's brows shot up. "Really? Dan? That's interesting in many ways."

"You would know the history of this area, though. Did women...like us...meet there?"

Mouth lifting at the corner, Felicia nodded. "Still do on occasion."

Come home, Maris. This is where you belong. "When I stood in the center of the circle, I sensed that gathering going back through hundreds of years. But I sensed a break or an event, too, which caused a change."

Felicia touched Maris's wrist. "How long ago, do you think?"

"Not this century, certainly, nor the one just past. I don't know really."

Poking Maris's mug at her, Felicia stood tall and then stretched. "Drink up. I'm assuming that's why you came here today? To ask about that?"

"Yes."

"And you'll come back and visit me again before you leave?"

"I don't want to leave, Felicia. I want to stay here in Alcina Cove where I was born."

"By the sea."

"Yes."

Felicia reached over the counter and pulled Maris close for a quick, tight hug. "If Dan arrests you, you might have no choice. But if he doesn't, well, you will have a choice. I would think long and hard about leaving, because you belong here."

Hearing that sentiment from a stranger made Maris miss all the more the camaraderie she had once shared with Alva and women of her aunt's acquaintance. Maris hadn't had much experience outside the family with others like herself, but once she and her parents moved away, she'd had none.

"I'll come back in a couple of days. I've been remanded to the area until I'm cleared, so..."

"Dan wants you to stick close."

"He doesn't want to have to track me down with an arrest warrant, I guess."

Felicia laughed. "Everything will work out fine. You'll see." But even as the woman spoke the words, a dark change occurred in her eyes, only to vanish a moment later. She glanced at Maris, her expression a little less certain.

"It's all right," Maris said. "I know. I've seen the aura around him. I don't know what to tell him, or even if I should. He's asked. He's seen the same look in my eyes I've just seen in yours." Maris backed away, heading for the door. "Thanks for the tea. And thanks for being who you are."

Outside, Maris headed for her car, but faltered halfway across the lot, her attention drawn to the path leading to the Circle of Alcina. The temptation to explore it again was strong, especially now that she knew Felicia Woodward lived cheek by jowl with the entity of the stones and held no fear. Curiosity got the better of her, and Maris strolled in that direction. She paused for further reading of the sign's information. After a few minutes, she continued along the path she and Dan had taken by flashlight the night before.

In the sunlight, the stones were more impressive than they had been in the dark. Alone, Maris strode in and out of the circle, weaving a pattern as she traversed the circumference. Birds trilled in the undergrowth, a sign that all was well since they would have fallen silent if frightened. Overhead, a raven winged its way to a stand of wind-bitten pines. Maris returned to the center of the circle and stood with her eyes closed, opening herself again to contact.

Silence. Well, fine. Nothing happened on command. Maybe she would go into town and walk the main street for a while, get some lunch, make a climb around the jetty beyond the sailor's cross, and wait for Dan to contact her with his next move.

She really wished the move would be toward her and not away, but she'd known from the very beginning where this story was headed.

Chapter 12

Dan closed the door to his office with all the control he could muster. The latch barely made a sound. He sat in the swivel chair and leaned back, propping his feet up on the desk. With conscious spacing in between, he counted backward from ten beneath his breath.

A knock sounded on the door at the same time it opened, not giving him a chance to answer. Jamie stuck his head in. "You okay?"

"Yep."

"You seem remarkably calm, considering."

Dan waved a hand in front of his face. "Don't let this demeanor fool you."

"Taken off the case. That sucks."

"Yeah, I don't need a recap. I know how much that sucks."

"But nobody's talking about bringing her in yet, so that's cool."

Dan grunted. It was only a matter of time.

"What made you let her in the house?"

"I took her when there was no clue this was anything other than a natural death." The same words he'd used five minutes ago with the Chief, to no avail. "She went in later by herself and, unless she really is the killer, she had no idea there was anything amiss then either."

"But you—"

"Had sex with her. I know. Fuck off." Dan had no clue how that had gotten out, but the most likely scenario was being spotted walking across to the motel, and then whoever had it in for him had stuck around long enough to see when he exited—carrying one of his boots in his hand for good measure.

"You dog you, how was it?"

Dan leaned back farther, hooking his hands behind his head. He closed his eyes. "I'm already in deep crap. I really wouldn't want to compound matters by kicking your ass."

The door closed.

He'd had to turn over his case notes, which were few. The fingerprints matched the locations she told him her prints would be found. To him, that indicated innocence. Either that, or someone so conniving she'd deliberately placed them for the sole purpose of appearing innocent when she confessed to her presence in the house…And this was exactly what had prompted his removal from the case. He'd lost his detached perspective. His head was spinning in circles.

He'd always thought himself a good cop. Good enough to be detective, and he'd proved as much. But this?

"Shit."

Opening his eyes, his gaze fell on his cell phone lying in the middle of the blotter. In for a penny in for a pound, the saying went. He snatched up the instrument and dialed. At least she'd changed her voice mail message.

"Maris, it's Dan. I'm heading home. When you have a second, give me a call, will you?"

Hanging up, he dropped his feet to the floor and stood. After shoving his arms into his jacket, he gathered a few things and opened the door. Several officers and Sally scattered like birds away from the front desk. Without a word, Dan left the building.

By the time he reached his townhouse, Maris had not returned his call. He parked the car, collected his mail, and went inside, locking the door behind him. After dropping the junk mail into the bin he kept beside the foyer table, he took the bills upstairs to his room in order to change his clothes. He knew he should eat, but he had no more desire for sustenance than he did for another reaming out. A can of soup in a while would work, then early to bed and, finally, a good night's sleep. He'd been requested to take the next couple of days off. At least he hadn't been put under official suspension. He would have gone to his rep over that one. There would have been no sound cause for that kind of discipline. Well, except having relations with a woman after he discovered she belonged smack dab in the middle of the investigation.

"Damn it, Maris."

Not her fault, though. Not really. It was something they'd done together, and he the only one with something to lose. He went into it anyway, with eyes wide open.

Upstairs, he stripped out of his clothes in preparation for a shower, pausing with his shirt in hand to peer through the slats in the blinds. The blue shadows of evening played across lawns and houses and streets, marking time until nightfall. He glanced down suddenly to make sure the blinds remained secured. All he needed was a charge of indecency.

When he looked again toward the street, he spied a figure standing on the opposite curb. Tall and willowy, the partial silhouette held a familiar, narrow, feminine shape. As did his sighting of the streetlight post through her.

Cursing, he shimmied back into his pants and pulled the shirt over his head as he raced back down the steps. He threw open the door. Except for a little girl skipping beside her mother, the sidewalk was empty. Dan went back inside and up the stairs again, wanting more than ever to talk to Maris about his experience. Even if she didn't understand, she wouldn't look at him as if he'd lost his mind.

He stopped dead in the middle of the room. Lying in a central position on his neatly made bed, the Priestess card reflected the last shreds of daylight. His first mistake. Well, he wasn't running back to the station with that card now, but it looked to have been his idea this morning if it had fallen from his pocket onto the bed. If? Of course he meant when. The damned thing couldn't move from his desk under its own volition, and no one had been in the house. After his unsettling dream—when was that? Yesterday morning?—he'd remembered to turn on the alarm.

Grabbing the card by the corner, he tossed it into his desk and slammed the drawer shut. Shower, soup, bed. That was the night's itinerary. Heading into the bathroom, he was stopped by his ringing phone.

"Dan, hi. It's Maris."

He sat on the edge of his bed with a sudden raging hard-on from the sound of her voice. Damn it, she wasn't *that* hot. Maybe what had him vacillating between running away and sprinting straight toward her was the fact she didn't need to be crazy hot for him to want her. She only needed to be Maris. "Thanks for calling me back."

"Why would I not? You asked me to. Today at the station you were doing your job. I get that."

"Not my job anymore."

"What do you mean?"

"I got pulled from the case. Made a couple of rookie-type mistakes and then, worst of all, I ended up in your bed." Waiting for her response, he listened to the sound of the ticking clock on the chest of drawers.

"Who—how did they find out?"

"My theory? Someone saw me go in and stuck around long enough to see me come out. It only takes a hint of that type of impropriety to cause a problem."

"I'm sorry."

He threw himself back onto the bed, one arm flung above his head, the phone pressed to his ear, and his dick standing at attention away from his belly. He touched himself and then immediately let go, glancing at his strewn clothes awaiting the hamper. "Care for a real dinner?"

"Didn't you just say—"

"Yes, and I also say screw it. Unless you prove to be a cold-blooded killer—in which case I'm better off sticking to you like glue—then I'm on a short-term unofficial leave of absence slash vacation, and I say we have dinner. I'm not investigating Alva Mabry's murder anymore."

Silence again. What was the matter now? His erection started to wilt.

"But I wanted…I need you on the case, no matter where it leads you."

He sat up, his jets effectively cooled. "Why?"

"Don't ask me that, Dan. You don't really want to know the answer."

"I do want to know the answer. You can give it to me over dinner. I'd like to shower first. Let's say I pick you up in forty-five minutes?"

"Forty-five? Sure. And this time bring a condom."

She hung up. His penis was at full alert again.

* * * *

Maris paced back and forth in her motel room. Dan's dismissal from the case was a totally unexpected turn of events. His eyes, his name, had been revealed to her for a reason. He needed to investigate even if he drew the wrong conclusions, because the ultimate answers wouldn't be uncovered without him. This much she had known somehow. Now, she had lost her way.

She paused in front of the mirror, studying her reflection. Her fashion sense had always been a product of whim, following her mood more than trend or a desire to please someone else. Yet tonight she had dressed for Dan Stauffer with a deliberate thought to seduction. A brand-new blouse purchased today, soft and loose, because tactile sensation could be a turn-on, the white fabric swirling with her movements like mist on the wind. On her lower half she'd pulled on a pair of tight jeans and boots laced up to her knee. Nothing flashy, but all designed to hint at what lay beneath.

She didn't expect to bed him and then convince him to pursue the case. He was out. Nothing she could do about it, as disturbing as those facts were. She only wanted closeness and hoped to persuade him to the same. Not a wham-bam-thank-you kind of encounter, but something warm and lingering. Despite her meeting with Felicia Woodward earlier in the day and the positive impressions, she felt remarkably alone.

Leaning forward, she stretched her lips back from her teeth, checking the thoroughness of her recent flossing. To be on the safe side, she returned to the bathroom to gargle with mouthwash and applied a fresh coat of lip gloss. In front of that mirror, she adjusted her small breasts in the new lacy bra beneath her blouse, then spent a long time gazing into her own eyes, seeking a deeper motivation to her actions. Finding nothing but a fundamental desire, she returned to the room and put on her coat, flipping the blunt ends of her short hair away from the collar. She ran a finger down the feather in her ear. Peace, yes. She would find that after, her body replete with endorphins. She hoped Dan would receive the same respite from the world. Even more than she, he needed serenity.

At a dull rap of knuckles on wood, Maris snatched her purse from the chair, slid the security chain from its housing, and pulled open the door. "Dan—"

Not Dan. A tall man in a dark, sleeveless shirt that exposed two arms covered in tattoos stood on the narrow sidewalk that ran the length of the building. Recovering from her surprise, Maris gave the man a curt nod. "I think you have the wrong room. I'm expecting—oh, there he is." Maris lifted her arm in greeting at the incoming car. It looked like Dan's vehicle, but even if the car belonged to a perfect stranger, Maris would act welcoming because the man standing before her made the hair stand up on her arms. The stranger turned his head to follow her gaze. With a monosyllabic reaction to her statement, he pivoted on his heel and strode away. The car whipped into the space beside hers, door swinging open.

"Who was that?" Dan slammed his door and joined her on the sidewalk in two strides. "What did he want?"

Maris shook her head. "I don't know. I think he had the wrong room."

"Wait here."

Dan took off down the sidewalk. He returned a few minutes later pushing his fingers through his sandy hair. "Didn't see him. What did he say?"

"Nothing. He grunted and left when I waved at you."

Dan slipped his hands into his jacket pockets as he frowned in both directions along the sidewalk and then over the parking lot. "This place has never had the best reputation."

"Okay," Maris responded, wondering where he was headed.

"I've made a few drug busts here, arrested a couple of parolees who'd violated their conditions, one reported rape, and rooms have been broken into more than once."

"If you're trying to unnerve me, you're almost there." Maris clung more tightly to her purse, shooting a glance in the direction the tattooed man had gone.

"You might consider relocating to another motel for the time you're here." He looked at her as if expecting an argument.

Maris went back into her room through the open door. Dan followed a moment later. He stood a few feet away as she pulled out her bag and began to repack it.

"What are you doing?"

Maris lifted a brow. "Taking your advice. I didn't like the looks of that guy or the vibe he was giving off. I'll turn in my key and follow you to wherever we're going for dinner, then I'll find someplace else to stay." Maris set her laptop on the bed beside her packed bag and took a turn around the room, including popping into the bathroom to make sure she hadn't forgotten anything. When she came out, Dan had a grip on her suitcase and the strap from her laptop case hung over his shoulder.

"My friends at the Timeless recently put on an addition, opening it up to the general public for dining. Good move on their part because it's increased their business income considerably. We're going there to eat. You can ask them if they have any open rooms. If not, there's one of the big chains outside of town a few miles."

Maris retrieved her purse again. "I thought you told me I couldn't leave town."

"That's not really leaving town. What I meant was that you couldn't go home."

But I am *home.*

As she loaded her belongings into her trunk, she realized she both was and wasn't home, like standing on a line of physical demarcation, one foot in a certain county, one foot in another, and not belonging in either. Not anymore. Returning to Alcina Cove had altered her mindset, made her yearn for the place, as did her rather iffy relationship with Dan, but did she really belong? Felicia said she did, but nothing else here had.

Dan stood with one leg inside his car, fingers folded over the open door. "Do you remember the way, or do you want to follow me?"

Maris leaned her chin on her hand on the roof of her vehicle, smiling at him across the open space. "You're cute when you're not all angry and blustery."

He sighed. "As usual, simple question, no answer."

"I'll follow you." Maris dropped down into her seat. *Wherever you go.*

Chapter 13

The addition had been placed where Maris's former home had possessed a screened porch. What had been a backyard with a swing set and a garden shed for the mower had been landscaped to further resemble the English-style garden at the front of the Timeless Inn. Five-foot-tall windows on three sides of the room looked out over potted mums, leaves turning gold on the nearby bushes, and a garden marked by shadow beyond the series of small lampposts lighting the pathways. Maris disentangled a pale green tablecloth from around her knees. "It's charming. Too bad there's no room left at the Timeless. Being here makes me wish I had more talent, though. What an amazing job they've made of it."

She'd been introduced upon arrival to Pete and Constance—or Connie, as both Dan and her husband referred to her, although the woman had used her full name in introduction. Constance was heavily pregnant, gravid with life and glowing. When asked if they knew the sex of the child, Pete had piped up with, "Nope, but if it's a boy, we're going to call him Re-Pete." Constance had rolled her eyes and punched him in the arm. Dan appeared relaxed and contented in their company, and perhaps a little envious. Maris watched him now across the table with a single candle burning behind glass between them and wondered what he wanted from life and why he hadn't gotten it.

"They left the force to start this place. It's nice."

Nice. Seemed to Maris he avoided the enthusiasm he would have revealed if he had the inclination to open up. Played it close to his chest, her detective did. Her detective? Good God. She hadn't meant that. She grabbed her menu and studied it. "Different atmosphere from last night's dinner. I know you said you like that place, but this is…I don't know. Special."

"Yep."

She glanced from the menu to his face. The expression in his eyes warmed her cheeks. She went back to reading. "What do you suggest?"

"The filet mignon. The pasta primavera. The salmon. They're all good. Whatever you want. I asked you, so my treat."

Maris nodded, considering. "Aren't you worried about being seen with me here?"

"I don't give a flying fuck."

"Wow. Those're sum purty strong fightin' werds."

His mouth twisted into a half-hearted grin.

"Don't risk your job for me."

"Let me worry about that." He picked up his own menu, his eyes moving back and forth as he perused selections he appeared to already know by heart.

"I'm serious, Dan."

"So am I."

Maris experienced a little leap in the physical vicinity of her heart. Gratitude, she supposed. Nothing more. But when she felt the hook of his foot behind her boot, pulling her leg closer to his beneath the table, a reaction she both recognized and expected seared through her like a flame.

* * * *

"What kind of convention fills up an entire hotel?"

Dan dropped Maris's zippered case on the sofa and set her laptop beside it on the floor, leaning it back against the cushioned edge. "A handmade soap maker's convention, apparently."

"I was being facetious. I heard the desk clerk as clearly as you did. I make my own soap. How come I never heard of this organization?"

"You make soap?" he said, eyeing her as she moved about the room like a cat scoping out the escape route. "Of course you do."

"I have several bars in my bag. You'd probably like the lemongrass lavender, even if you are a man."

"If?"

"Sorry. Though. Even though you are a man."

"Thanks for the clarification."

"No problem."

She stopped at the island counter, picking up a law enforcement magazine and laying it down again before moving on.

"Maris, calm down."

She glanced back at him. "Now who's reading minds?"

"Reading body language. Just like you."

"Hmm." She went into the kitchen, moving alongside the counters, fingers trailing over the polished stone surface. She paused and picked up a prescription bottle. "What's this for?"

"Boundaries, my dear."

She put the bottle back down.

"Antibiotics for a sinus infection about a year ago. I didn't quite finish them off."

"Bad boy. You know better than that." She turned to face him, arms bent, palms cupped around the bull-nose edge of the counter. "I have a prescription for sleeping pills. I haven't taken any since I've been in Alcina Cove."

He wanted to ask her what necessitated the prescription but he had a feeling she wouldn't say, that she was merely talking for the sake of conversation because she really didn't want to talk at all. Neither did he. "The bed in the guestroom is comfortable I've been told. You might take one of those pills tonight if you need it. I think you haven't been sleeping much since you've been here. I know I haven't."

"I take them when I need to keep the dreams at bay. Sounds ominous, doesn't it? But I don't think I need the pills right now. I want the dreams."

He watched her breathe, the silky white shirt lifting and falling over her torso. Her jeans defined the curve of her hips, the length of her legs. She'd dressed differently tonight, in a casually sexy and provocative manner. He would have liked to take those clothes off her, but they were still dancing their dance.

"Are you really relegating me to the guestroom?"

Or maybe the dance had ended, and they were about to proceed into a long and glorious fall from grace. "I don't want to."

"Then don't. At least not this night."

He went to her, took her hand, turned, and led her back across the floor. Her first step had held a little hitch, as if she was having second thoughts, and then she fell in beside him. She leaned her head sideways against his upper arm.

"Last night," she said, "you fell asleep in the bed beside me. If you really believed I could poison someone, would you have done that?"

He considered a moment, contemplating his inability to tell her an outright lie, despite what she'd said to him earlier today. But he hadn't been asleep. He'd figured by the way she'd crept from the bed that she had thought he was. "You're right. I wouldn't have fallen asleep beside you if I believed you could poison someone."

She said nothing. He knew she hadn't been fooled, but she didn't seem to care. She continued to walk beside him, her sweet-smelling hair falling across his bicep, her fingers caressing the palm of his hand. At the base of the stairs she turned to face him, grasping his belt buckle and working it loose. She slipped her hand inside his jeans.

He sucked in his breath and let it out slowly. "No romance?"

"No time for romance."

He could still differentiate between verbal foreplay and a statement reverberating with foresight despite her fingers closed around him. "What does that mean?" he whispered.

"I can sense the world closing in like night's darkness without moonlight, without stars. I don't want to know it, I don't want to feel it, but it pulses against the back of my thoughts with the insistence of someone hammering on the door. I'm sorry, Dan."

Holy crap. "For what?"

"The lack of time for us."

She was leaving something major out, something he knew would scare the hell out of him. Two days ago, it would have been easy to dismiss her words as nonsense, a flagrant display to make herself important, but he knew better now. A chill worked its way up his spine to the base of his skull. Suddenly he remembered again what she had said about the cards rearranged across her aunt's table. The suspension of disbelief. Becoming a new person. Truce. Despair.

And the Priestess card, lying hidden in the dark drawer of his desk. Secrets and choices made.

He unzipped his jeans and removed her hand, then bent forward and scooped her up into his arms. She wrapped her own around his shoulders, burying her face against his neck, her breath warm and moist on the flesh where his pulse beat heavily. He climbed the stairs with his cheek pressed close to her ear, whispering endearments he hadn't used in years.

By the time they reached the door to his room, he was throbbing with need far beyond the engorging rush of blood to a place that required little encouragement. With a word from him, Maris stretched one arm behind and turned the knob, giving the door a shove with her fist. He stumbled inside and kicked the door shut. Maris wriggled out of his arms.

Striped by the cool glow of the streetlamp through the blinds, she took off her clothes. No preamble, no coyness. Her skin glowed, pale and blue-white as if it had never seen the sun. Prevalent pelvic bones cast a deep shadow that nearly masked the curling, dark triangle of hair. He ran his fingers across her abdomen and down between her legs. He stroked her sodden folds, curled his finger in lazy circles around the nub of swollen flesh until she moaned.

"Take off your clothes, Dan. Now."

He stripped, staring a moment at the shape their clothes made on the floor. She touched his jaw, turned his face away.

"Look at me. Just me." With a sweep of her leg, she kicked their discarded garments across the rug.

"But—"

"Only me."

She urged him across the floor with his face in her hands, her eyes steady and luminous, the hard-on he'd almost forgotten for a second still powerful and throbbing. When they reached the bed she climbed backward onto it, first one foot, then the other, until she stood balanced as if on the prow of a ship. The mattress dipped beneath the weight of his knee. He stroked her again, with the ball of his thumb this time, slow circular motions before he darted in with his tongue to taste her. Last night had been brimstone. Tonight was the sweet, slow drip of honey.

She came without noise, which surprised him. He felt it, though, in the warm contraction around his fingers. "I'm sorry," she whispered, a sound like velvet on sand. "I don't know if I could have stopped it."

"I wouldn't want you to. We still have time to make that happen again."

Maris dropped to her buttocks on the rumpled bedclothes, scooting toward the head of the bed. She clasped the metal frame with both hands, knees drawn up and spread for him in invitation. He didn't hesitate. The noise she made in her throat was the kind of thrum that visited the edge of hearing, sounding deep in the bone and rising until she cried out loud. Unable to hold back any longer, he pulled her down beneath him and drove hard inside until the sound of his pending release joined hers. She silenced him with her mouth on his, pulling him down into that small death no man could live without.

* * * *

Maris rose up onto her elbow, peering down into Dan's face. Yes, asleep this time. She'd thought he'd been sleeping last night as well, but she'd been wrong. His stumble earlier, a bad attempt to deflect her question, had told her that. Tonight he slept well, his mouth open and the smallest sound of untroubled respiration coming from it. When he awoke, would he remember what he'd said to her on the stairs? She hoped not. They'd been intimate words she wasn't ready to hear from him and he sure as hell wasn't ready to say.

She climbed carefully from the bed and searched the floor for his shirt. She would wear that since it would cover more of her bare ass than her own would. After slipping the garment over her head, Maris held the fabric to her face for a brief inhalation of Dan's scent prior to pulling it down over her body. Before heading to the bathroom, she stared at the pile of clothing.

Dan had noticed something there earlier. Although she didn't believe he recognized what had drawn his attention, she had witnessed the change in his face before she kicked their clothing away. An ill-omened trick of light and shadow, as serpentine sleeves and humped denim created the spectral inference of a lighthouse lying along the rug. Not alarming in itself. People saw shapes in clouds all the time—made a game of naming them—and in photographs as well, claiming to have captured the spirit world on film. But this particular form harked back to the dream of Great-Aunt Alva that had returned Maris to Alcina Cove. Dan and death were connected as one in the vision of that lighthouse, a landmark structure only a short distance up the coastline that sent its beam across the ocean tides nightly. She could try to keep Dan away from the sea, but it was far more likely the correlation was abstract rather than direct. In fact, it wasn't until she'd met Dan, witnessed the darkness dogging him like a second skin, that she had recalled that part of her dream. Assumptions could be dangerous, blinding one to the heart of the matter.

Maris tucked Dan's shirt along her thighs and climbed up to sit cross-legged on the cleared end of his desk. She pulled down on one of the slats in order to peer out to the street below. Behind her, the bedsprings creaked, followed by the soft tread of bare feet across the carpet.

Dan's arm slipped around her from behind, forearm resting against her collarbones, fingers wrapped around her upper arm. "What's up?"

Maris grabbed the pull cord for the blinds and raised them about eighteen inches from the sill. Over her head, Dan's breath rasped into his lungs.

"I've seen that twice now. The night Alva Mabry died, and last night as well. Is it…is it her, do you think?"

"My, how far you have come in two days' time, Dan Stauffer." Maris leaned forward, fingers splayed across the glass. Dan followed her movements, his chest warm against her back.

"Is it?"

"It could be, Dan. It upsets me to admit it, but Aunt Alva could be that determined."

"You mean you don't know for sure?"

Maris shook her head. "Many spirits take the form of the crone, but my gut feeling is that it is Alva. Yet she's not speaking to me. I'm looking right at her, and there's not a single word." As she spoke, the translucent silhouette vanished with an upward curl like smoke. Maris lowered the blinds to their former position. "What time is it?"

"Two? Two-thirty?"

She skated her fingers between his, fitting them together. Lifting his hand, she pressed her lips against his knuckles and slid her tongue into the place where his fingers met hers. "One more time into the fray?"

He didn't say no.

Chapter 14

When Maris awoke in the morning, she discovered Dan energized, dressed, and tying a pair of running shoes on his feet, declaring his intention of taking the first run he had in weeks. She waved him on his way with a flutter of her fingers before rolling over to bury her head beneath the pillow. "You have fun with that."

As soon as she heard the front door shut, she sat up. What was she doing here? They were suddenly like a couple, the little woman staying in bed to rest up after a hard night while the man took off on his jock pursuits, showered and shaved and revitalized. Maris swung her legs over the edge of the bed. She needed her own shower. Desperately. And a plan. Some kind of plan. She couldn't have Dan risking his livelihood, his safety to save her. Because he would. He would do all of that without understanding why. He certainly wasn't in love with her, but a link existed between them that couldn't be explained away. Sex, sure, that had been a blast. Fulfilling and hot enough to burn away some of the blackness adhering to them both. If she stayed by his side, though, the doom she sensed waiting would claim him, and somehow her hand would be in that dark destiny.

"Aunt Alva, I need you. I need you to explain this to me."

The distance between them had been too great for too long, and now... well, if Alva Mabry chose not to speak to her, nothing on this earth could change that.

Maris showered, using Dan's shampoo and Dan's soap, realizing she would smell like him for the rest of the day. His scent would be in her hair, on her skin. As unsettling as that was, the recognition would comfort her. She considered dumping a bit of his shampoo into a plastic bag, enough to open and breathe in as necessary in a kind of stalker-ish aromatherapy.

She had nearly finished dressing and was putting her earrings back in when she heard the front door open. Walking barefoot down the stairs, she called Dan's name. A male voice answered her that wasn't his.

"Hello? Who's that?"

Maris stopped, fingers tight around the handrail. If the person was someone Dan worked with, she couldn't let him know her identity. Things would only go from bad to worse. As she was deciding what to do, a man walked from the living room back into the foyer. She recognized him. He'd been the other detective following them down the hall toward the room where Dan had fingerprinted her. Dan had practically shut the door in his face.

"Ah, shit," the man said upon sight of her. "That guy has fucked himself good this time. Where is he?"

Maris sat on the step, tucking her hands into the folds of her skirt. "He...he went for a run."

"A run? Feeling proud of himself, is he?"

Maris frowned at the man. "Jamie, isn't it?"

"Yeah."

"Don't be like that. He's a good man. And a good cop, I'm sure."

Jamie sat down on the step below her, leaning his back against the wall. "You don't even know the guy."

"Maybe not. At least not the way you know him. Obviously, you're shocked because his behavior is uncharacteristic. That should tell you something."

"Then he better start acting like the guy I know. I mean, how long have you been in town? Two days? A perfect stranger, and possibly the only one who might have had reason to off old lady Mabry—sorry. But you know what I'm saying is true. He's walking a dangerous path. What did you do to him? I can't see him taking a risk like this if he was thinking with his brains and not another part of his anatomy."

Maris crushed fabric between her fingers and slowly let it go. "I did nothing *to* him. And I didn't kill my aunt. You're a rude man, considering you don't know me either."

Jamie puffed a breath out through his nose. He reached up and scratched his scalp through short, auburn hair. "I'm sorry. It's just—I'm worried, you know?"

As am I, she wanted to say. *For so many reasons.*

He dropped both forearms onto his thighs, clasping his hands together between his knees. "How long has he been gone?"

"Half an hour or so. I'm sure he'll be back soon. You should wait for him." A thought occurred to her. "Did you find out something new?"

"I'm not discussing the case with you. I...I can't."

"Since you haven't yet broken out the handcuffs, I can only assume it doesn't point a finger definitively at me."

He frowned. "You could be in real trouble, very soon. Are you always so flippant?"

"Don't confuse straightforward with dismissive. And learn to listen." Maris rose and turned, heading back up the stairs.

"Where are you going?"

She paused, looking back down at him. "To finish getting dressed. I don't want to see Dan in trouble any more than you do. I hadn't intended to stay here last night. I only hope that damned soap convention has ended and will empty out the hotel outside of town."

"Right. Look, you seem nice enough, but that doesn't mean anything. Take Ted Bundy, for instance—"

"Once again, you're confusing two totally separate things. You've mistaken charm and looks for character. He was able to fool people into trusting him, mostly because of the way he looked. And Bundy was a serial killer. Unless someone else shows up with a needle full of poison in their neck—"

"What did you say?" Jamie rose, his whole demeanor altering.

Oh God, oh God, that came from him, from his mind. Jamie would never believe she was anything but guilty now. Why had she spoken his thoughts aloud?

Jamie repeated his question, face hard.

Maris rubbed her eyes with the back of her hand. "I know I shouldn't be listening, but I can't help it."

"What do you mean? Did Dan get a call from someone this morning?"

"Yes," she lied, glibly, compounding her own damnation. "I don't know who it was, but I overheard part of the conversation." Hopefully that would keep the detective satisfied, or at least in doubt, until she had an opportunity to speak to Dan. Chances were that Dan would side with Jamie anyway on this. Dan struggled every moment with what made sense in his logical mind and what he knew in a place that operated on elemental understanding. A statement like the one she'd made could tip the scale in the wrong direction.

"Is that how Aunt Alva was killed?" She had to ask, not to throw Jamie off, but because she wanted the information.

"I'm not saying that. In fact, in case you didn't get it, I'm not saying anything to you about the investigation. Fuck."

Maris hurried upstairs to Dan's bedroom and shut the door, resisting the urge to lock it. If either officer was determined enough, a door wouldn't keep them out. She paced back and forth across the room, toes digging into the thick carpet. Frightened, she considered fleeing, but dismissed flight as a foolish response. Wasn't that what guilty people did? Run? Lying and running. The occupation of the morally challenged.

Maris grabbed her zippered case and threw all her belongings back inside with the exception of a pair of tights, which she slipped on under her skirt. After, she fit the diary between the folded legs of her jeans and zipped the bag shut, because despite her self-scolding not to run, the urge to do so was nearly overwhelming. She couldn't climb out a window, which meant she'd have to walk down the stairs again. Well, her laptop remained on the floor in front of the sofa. She'd have to grab that anyway. If Jamie even let her past him.

How could she have blurted out a statement that made her appear guilty as hell? Would she even believe herself after these last two days? What was she going to do?

Maris slammed her hand on the desk top. The impact caused the top drawer to slide open a few inches, revealing the edge of a thick, illustrated card. Pulling the drawer out farther, she gazed down at a Tarot card inside. Her heart began a rapid fluttering as she recognized what could only be one of Alva's. How had Dan come into possession of the High Priestess card? Maris's mind rushed to an ill-borne conclusion involving guilt as ridiculous as her own. Dan wouldn't have hurt Alva. He didn't even know her. Did he? But if he didn't, what was the card doing hidden away in his desk?

Closing the drawer, Maris sat in the chair, spinning a little on the swivel mount until her knee came to rest against the desk itself. Morning light shone through the slats of the blinds, illuminating the wood with diffuse geometric shapes. No running. There was a saying: The Truth Will Out. The police department would require hard evidence to charge her. With the exception of her fingerprints, explained to Dan and which she would reiterate to anyone else who asked, there was none to point conclusively in her direction. Her recent utterance followed by the poorly executed falsehood wouldn't help her, but it couldn't convict her either.

Aunt Alva, who would do this to you? Can't you help me find out?

No answers came, but she hadn't expected them to. Except for the undeniable call for her return to Alcina Cove, Maris had received no further information since her arrival. Not about Alva. Plenty about Dan Stauffer, though. What did that mean?

Voices came to her, muffled by the wooden door. Dan had returned.

* * * *

Dan slowly climbed the stairs. Sweat glued the T-shirt to his back. He stood listening outside his closed bedroom door. After a moment, he heard the squeak of the desk chair. He pushed the door open.

Maris sat facing the window, staring out through the raised blinds. She had a look about her, in her eyes, her position, as if yearning for wings so she could fly. At her back on his bed, her bag lay on its side, packed. Dan crossed the room and sat beside it, He leaned forward with his elbows planted on his sweaty thighs. "Are you leaving?"

"I thought I should see if any rooms have opened up at the hotel."

"That inquiry could be accomplished with a phone call, couldn't it?"

Maris drew a steadying breath. "It's better if I leave—"

"Not for me, it isn't."

"I think Jamie's going to arrest me."

"No. He's not."

"I told a lie. I told him I overheard a conversation you had on the phone, but it was what I heard in his thoughts."

"Will you look at me?"

"I can't."

Dropping his head forward, Dan pushed his fingers through his hair. "I wasted a shower. I freaking stink."

He thought she laughed, but when he looked up again, she was crying. "What is it? Sweetheart, tell me." At the endearment, she cried harder. He started to get up.

"No. Stay there," she whispered hoarsely. "If you touch me, I'll turn into a crazy person. I swear I will."

"Turn into one? What the heck are you now?"

She shrugged, wiping at her face with the heel of her palm. "Dan, have you ever heard people talk about past lives?"

"Yeah," he said slowly.

"Do you think there is such a thing?"

"I don't know."

She slid down on the seat, crossing her legs over the edge of the desk and leaning her head against the cushioned chair back. "There has to be because I barely know you, and yet the idea I could let you down is breaking my heart."

The muscles in Dan's abdominal wall tightened. He felt momentarily dizzy and realized he hadn't eaten. Stretching out his left arm until it bridged the gap between them, Dan closed his fingers around Maris's hand. He gave her arm a tug. "Come over here and sit next to me."

She dropped her feet to the floor and stood. Her head turned abruptly toward the door. "Is Jamie waiting in the hallway? Handcuffs at the ready, I suppose."

Dan followed her gaze, spotting the shadowed movement visible under the barrier of wood. Releasing her arm, he hurried to the door and yanked it open. He stepped into the hall, glancing the short distance to either side. "Rogers! Where are you?"

The sound of footsteps on carpet preceded Jamie Rogers's appearance on the upper half of the stairs. "Where I have been. Sitting on the step. You told me to wait."

"No one went past you?"

Jamie's brows lowered. "Are you joking around? No one's come in. They would have had to step on me. I haven't moved."

"Shit." Dan ran to the bathroom and checked inside, then onto the small guestroom, also empty. When he came out, he found Jamie and Maris standing side by side. Jamie's realization of his vicinity to Maris's person spread across his face. He sidled a couple of feet away.

Maris took a step forward. "I saw someone—"

"So did I. But there's no one up here. And your friend there was on the steps, so no one passed him."

Maris eyed Jamie up and down. "*My* friend?"

Jamie shot her the same sort of look, but with the whites of his eyes showing all around. *Oh, yeah*, thought Dan. *The guy is spooked.*

"So you both saw someone," Jamie said, "but there's no one up here except you two. Is that what I'm supposed to get out of this conversation?"

"That's exactly what you're supposed to get out of this conversation," Dan said.

"I don't—" Jamie subsided, staring down at his feet.

"It's all right," Maris whispered.

He glared at her, then turned away and stomped down the stairs.

"We'll be right there," Dan called after him. "Park it on the couch for a sec." Cupping the back of Maris's skull in his palm, he tipped her head closer and pressed his lips to her warm, fragrant hair. She smelled like... his shampoo. Right. He laughed.

She pulled away and looked up at him. "What's going on?"

He jerked his head in the direction of the stairs Jamie had descended. "You, me, the upstart down there—we need to have a conversation. Are you ready for that?"

Maris's brows dropped to form a straight line, giving her the expression of a worried cat. "Depends on the topic."

"The topic is you."

Before she could protest, he pulled her to the stairs and down. Jamie waited for them in the living room seated on the edge of a cushion, arms folded over his abdomen. Dan led Maris to the stuffed chair on the opposite side of the coffee table. He perched on the chair arm beside her, conscious of the sweat drying between his shoulder blades.

"I'm going to start."

Both Jamie and Maris looked at him, relief clear on their faces. Obviously, neither of them was ready to say a word.

"A few years back, I had a run-in with something impossible. It still gives me nightmares, and it's not something I've discussed freely with anyone. In fact, I've developed a pretty cocky-assed attitude about things that don't fit into a neat little box labeled *reality* because I figured there could be only one reality—the one that comes under the classification of general acceptance. Because even though I'd experienced something that didn't fit into that box, I wanted to pretend it didn't happen. I never would have admitted to any of it out loud, and I compartmentalized the memory. Still, it was like a door that kept opening I needed to slam shut. Every time I encountered something else, my solution was to turn away in denial." Jamie folded his hands. He ran his thumb over the ridges of his knuckles. Maris slipped her fingers into Dan's.

"Which brings us to what happened in this house. Not upstairs, but the conversation between the two of you." He waited. Outside, children laughed in the yard across the street. The sound seemed oddly muffled.

Finally, Jamie looked up from the study of his interlaced appendages. He turned to Maris. "You scare the hell out of me, lady, plain and simple."

"I've spent my life doing that to people. I don't mean to. I'm sorry."

Dan stirred, squeezing her hand. "Don't apologize." Her lips twisted in something less than a smile.

Jamie cleared his throat. "I think the whole psychic thing is bullshit. No offense meant, but I do. But you were dead on with the needle in the neck remark. Dead on."

Maris tugged her lower lip with her top teeth and released it. "I have to tell you...I heard that thought from you."

"I know you did. If that was the news I'd come to share with Dan, yeah, I would have followed you up those stairs and hauled you back down and to the station. But it's not. It was just a thought in my head, totally random because of what we were saying about Ted Bundy. I don't even know where it came from. But you lied to cover up for what you had said, which troubles me. I pounced on Dan about it the second he walked in. Caught him off guard. I could see he wanted to lie, too, to protect you. Now why, I ask myself, would he want to do that?"

"Don't blame him for anything—"

Dan shook her hand. "Let him talk."

"I'm not blaming him. Not right now, anyway. However, there's been some talk around the station about the crap at the scene yesterday when you were talking about the cards on the table. You were saying things as if it all meant something." He made a gesture with his hands. "But when you spoke those words on these steps a few minutes ago, it was as if they'd come right out of my head and into your mouth."

"That's…that's not how my aunt died?"

"No."

Maris nodded. "Does that mean you no longer suspect me of killing her?"

He snorted. "Hell no. Despite having my sense of logic shaken, I do believe in evidence. And once—until—we have evidence pointing to you without any chance of having the case thrown out of court, I'll keep looking in whatever direction I am taken. As Dan would, if he was still on the case and if he could manage to pull his head out of his ass."

"I'm sitting right here," Dan said. "And as you can see, my head is firmly perched on my shoulders."

"So," said Maris, "what about in the meantime?"

"In the meantime—" Jamie shot another look at Dan.

Dan narrowed his eyes at him. He'd told Jamie to mind his own business, but Dan had known Jamie would ignore that command.

"In the meantime," Jamie went on, "I wish you'd stay the hell away from Dan."

Leaning forward, Maris let go of Dan's hand, her expression earnest. Dan placed his fingers on her back in defiance of whatever she or Jamie would say next.

"I know what I'm doing to him, Jamie. I worry about him. I see the effect I have on him. But he has one on me, too. Things are not simple. In fact, they're complicated in the extreme. We are…bound together. I'm not quite sure why."

"Bound together. Quaint name for fucking his brains ou—"

"Shut up, Rogers." Dan stood. "Not another word."

Jamie rose from the couch, facing him. "I'm sorry. I know I'm out of line. It's just that I feel…"

"Frightened?" Maris supplied.

"Yeah, I suppose I am. And confused. And angry."

"Understood," Dan said. "I've been feeling that way for the past three years, I think. And as to the rest of what we discussed, you'll keep me posted? I know you shouldn't, but I appreciate being kept in the loop." From the corner of his eye, he saw Maris's eyes widen at him. "I can't talk about it with you, Maris."

She nodded and sat back.

"Actually," Jamie said, "there's more. Can we talk in private? Assuming, of course, that would keep things secret."

Maris struggled out of the deep cushion of the chair. Dan grabbed her elbow and assisted. "I don't 'hear' everything," she said. "It doesn't work that way. I would lose my mind if it did. Let me just get my boots on, and I'll go for a walk. When I come back, though, you and I"—she directed to Dan—"need to discuss what I'm going to do. Staying here with you shouldn't be an option. It weighs against your integrity as an officer of the law."

He didn't argue with her. He couldn't, because she was right. But he wished with every speck of the man he used to be and wanted to be again that she wasn't.

* * * *

The day was spot-on lovely, considering how chilly it had been of late. A bit of Indian Summer, as balmy as the temperature ever got this far north. She blamed the weather for the fact she kept on walking, but of course, the weather had nothing to do with it.

She took a right from Church onto Main, making a mental note of the street names. Twenty years was too long to remember every avenue, every lane, and she didn't want to get lost going back. She had her phone tucked into her pocket, so the fact she could make a call for help was reassuring, but the potential humiliation of that call would be a deterrent and keep her wandering the streets in search of the right one.

Her mom was fond of calling her stubborn. Stubborn and ridiculous often walked hand in hand. So far, her phone conversations with her mother had been brief, of necessity. There wasn't much Maris could tell her that wouldn't be upsetting to her parent, so she stuck with her made-up story of a friend in need and hadn't even mentioned where she'd gone.

If her mother knew she was back in Alcina Cove, she'd have a cow. And, Maris mused, with good reason.

Maris walked into the drugstore and bought herself a bottled soda, in the mood for a beverage with a bit more zing than water. Back outside, she continued her stroll, twisting off the cap and drinking a few mouthfuls as she went. She returned to the sailors' cross where she'd been the day before and spent a few minutes studying the etched names again. So many lives lost at sea. It didn't seem possible anyone could view the vast amount of names and still opt for a life on the water. Except for the tales her father had told her, she knew very little of a fisherman's existence. But at least those stories had been colored with enough descriptive detail to be like memories to her now.

Soda bottle in hand, Maris clambered once more out onto the rocks of the jetty. The spume of crashing waves made rainbows in the air. She sat on a flat slab of dark stone with her back to the sun, the bottle cradled in the sling of her skirt between her thighs. Far away, a freighter moved along the horizon, a black speck on the line of infinity. Nearer, a sport boat cruised past, rods secured and upright. Maris closed her eyes.

Dan Stauffer, who are you to me?

She had a suspicion that even if Jamie Rogers had been determined to arrest her, Dan wouldn't have permitted it, effectively ending his career, maybe even resulting in him being jailed. She couldn't let that happen. She would tell Jamie if it came to it, he was to let her know and she would meet him at the station. Dan couldn't be allowed to receive that information. With Dan and Jamie's friendship and the way Jamie felt about Dan and her, she was pretty sure he'd agree without hesitation. Such a conversation with the younger detective certainly might be construed as one of guilt, but so be it.

Maris opened her eyes to the sight of a man at the far end of the jetty. He raised an arm to cast a line out into the water. A familiarity in his stance, the man's posture, his carriage, made her think of her father. A sad smile stole to her lips. Even after all these years, she missed him.

Dan liked to fish. Or at least he had enjoyed going out on the water with his socks-and-sandals-wearing father to do so. Such intimate knowledge of a stranger's flashes of memory was improper, premature, and confusing. She had never in her life experienced the depth of connection she did with Dan. She used to pretend she had it with the imaginary friend of her youth. She'd felt a part of something special. Perhaps that emotion explained her willingness to disregard her former caution. But though she had opened up to warmth and light, she had also exposed herself to the darkness embracing him. She feared that darkness because she feared losing him—a man of two days' acquaintance.

Silhouetted against the sky, the fisherman at the end of the jetty turned and waved to her. Maris scrambled upright. She choked in a breath. "Daddy?"

No, not possible. This man was solid and real. Nevertheless, she made her way toward him, stumbling over crevices and protrusions of stone. A part of her brain dwelled on the terms of sanity, but the other portion had to *know*. When she reached him, his back was to her. She touched his arm. He glanced at her over his shoulder through eyes shielded by a pair of dark sunglasses. His facial features were those of a stranger, though.

Maris backed away with a hasty apology. "I thought you were someone else. Sorry."

As she reached the street, she noticed a woman and young boy standing there. Probably that guy's family, and the wave a signal to them that he would be done soon. She shouldn't have come back to Alcina Cove, no matter how much the dream, Aunt Alva, had called out to her. Since her return, she'd displayed the behavior of a woman she didn't recognize.

Maris marched back in the direction she'd come. She lifted her arm to search for the hotel business card in the zippered wallet hanging from a strap on her wrist. Finding it, she made a call to check for open rooms. Still booked. Crap. There had to be someplace else. As she hung up, the phone rang.

She answered without looking. "Hello?"

"What are you doing?"

"Who is this?" Maris pulled the phone from her ear, checking the number. Blocked, it read anonymous. For some reason, she looked back toward the man on the jetty. Although he was too far away to see clearly, she could tell he continued to fish, casting out his line with a sweep of his arm. He certainly wasn't on the phone. And why would he be?

Maris, get a grip.

"Who is this?" she asked again.

"You've won a free trip to—"

Depressing the button on the phone's face, she ended the call. "Jerk telemarketer."

She needed a good night's sleep and a place to lay her head. She didn't have the number for the Timeless Inn, but she'd ask Dan for it and give them a call. Unfortunately, if she took a sleeping pill, waking up from a deep sleep in a strange place could be unnerving. She'd have to tough out that effect, though, because she hadn't any choice.

In town, she walked until she saw the sign for Church Street again and made a left at the corner. Halfway down the block, she crossed to a perpendicular street on the other side. Head bent to her phone in order to find Dan's number, she didn't see the car until it was too late.

Chapter 15

"I don't think I can recall hearing such a creatively verbalized string of invectives before."

Maris heard the statement as she was being wheeled around the corner to the emergency room cubicle where she'd started out before being sent for x-rays. She didn't recognize the voice, but she enjoyed the woman's turn of phrase.

"Ah, here's the queen of potty mouth now."

"What? You meant me?"

The nurse nodded with a Cheshire cat grin. "I'm sure you don't remember. You weren't fully with us in this world." Dan stood behind the ER nurse, his face ashen.

"How'd you get here?" Maris asked him.

"I drove."

"I mean, how did you find out?" Maris winced as the portable bed bumped the wall, jostling her. "Who called you? Oh, wait, you heard on the police scanner?"

Dan said nothing, waiting until the nurse had finished hooking all the wires back up to the nearby machines. Maris tipped her head to look at the nurse beyond the fall of the woman's curly hair.

"Can I leave soon?"

The nurse laughed. "No."

As soon as she'd gone, Dan yanked a chair up to the side of the bed. He grabbed her hand. "I didn't hear on the police scanner. I heard the whole thing live. Seems you were in the process of calling me when you got hit. The bastard didn't stop. Hit and run. Witnesses are being questioned."

Maris studied the moisture glistening in his eyes. Not crocodile tears. The real thing. For her. Her throat closed. She cleared it with a small cough. "Are you all right?"

"Me?" he yelled, then lowered his voice. "You're asking how I'm doing? Don't. Don't even worry about me."

"That had to be terrible, hearing something like that…"

"Oh, for the love of God. Not as terrible as following the sound of sirens until I found you. I didn't stop to call the station. I had Jamie do that. I just held the phone to my ear, listening to make sure…to make sure—"

"I was alive?"

"Yes."

Several tears skimmed down Maris's cheeks as she considered how that must have been for him. She looked down at her body loosely wrapped in a hospital gown, name tag on her wrist, pressure cuff on one arm, intravenous tube in the other. A warmed blanket had been flipped over her by the nurse before she departed. Maris would really like one of those cabinets for home. Nothing like a heated blanket.

"Dan…" She felt slightly disassociated from her surroundings and wondered if the hospital personnel had given her something for pain.

"Yes?"

"You really do care, don't you?"

"Fuck. Of course I do."

She pulled her hand free of his grasp and cupped the side of his jaw. He kissed her palm. His skin felt damp.

"You've been crying, haven't you?"

"Maris, would you just shut up?"

"Sure."

"I don't mean that."

"Yes, you do. I'm an idiot and you're…you're a nice man."

He made a face and rolled his shoulders. "I've been called worse."

"I wasn't even looking…I just stepped out in the street. How bad is the damage? Did somebody tell you, at least? Because they've said nothing to me. Not that I remember, anyway."

Dan removed her hand from his face and held it clasped between both of his. "Somehow I always end up in this hospital."

"What?"

"Never mind. No one said anything about broken bones after the x-rays?"

Maris shook her head.

"It takes a while, I suppose. You are splinted up on your leg, but that might be precaution. Does it hurt?"

"At this point, everything hurts."

"Anyway, I think they wouldn't be quite so blasé if there was a possibility of internal bleeding. I did hear a doctor in the hall mention concussion,

though. If that's all you've come out of this with, you're damned lucky."
He turned her hand in his, pressing his thumb into her palm. "One of the
witnesses said the driver pulled out of a parking space without noticing
you were there. Luckily the car hadn't picked up speed yet. Whoever was
behind the wheel stopped momentarily and then sped off."

"Anybody get a tag?"

Dan shook his head. "No. But we've got a pretty good description
of the vehicle."

"We? I thought you were…I don't know. Not suspended, but…" Her
head hurt, making thinking difficult.

"I was only taken off your aunt's case and told to take a couple of days'
vacation. I'm not suspended. I've still got a job. It's still 'we' unless they
actually fire me."

Dan put his head down on the back of her hand. He appeared inclined
to stop speaking for a while so Maris let him because an urge to seek
stillness had come over her, too. She would have closed her eyes, but
if she did have a concussion, she thought she might not be allowed to
sleep. Having never had a head injury, she wasn't sure, so she stared at
a bright orange sign on the wall regarding biohazard and listened to the
silence creeping in. Sound fell away, first voices, then machinery, down
to the ticking clock on the wall, a noise she hadn't previously noticed. A
sudden fear possessed her that despite Dan's non-medical assurances to
the contrary, death had come to claim her.

A mist materialized in the corner of the room, taking undefined shape
as it struggled to manifest. Maris tried to jiggle her hand, to shake Dan to
attention, but found she couldn't move.

Don't give in.

"What?" Had she said that word aloud? Her lips felt stiff and lifeless.

Hold on, child.

"Aunt Alva?"

The machine to her right burst through the bubble of silence with an
ear-piercing clamor.

* * * *

Dan pulled into the hospital parking lot and found a spot a good
distance from the main entrance. Naturally everyone wanted the closest
spaces in the pouring rain. He hadn't brought an umbrella. Who was he
kidding? He never carried an umbrella. Anywhere. Not the manly thing
to do. Getting out of the car, he turned his collar up against the onslaught
and ran across the puddled blacktop. The automatic doors opened for
him, but not quickly enough. He hit the right one with his elbow and

swore. Mouthing an apology at an old lady waiting in a chair at outpatient admissions, he headed for the elevator.

The nurses on the second floor knew him by sight at this point, and he nodded greetings as he passed. At the last room on the left, he paused. He heard voices inside. No, not voices, plural. Only one. Maris was on the phone.

Unabashedly, he listened for a few seconds before entering. Maris's mom had to be on the other end. Maris didn't talk to anyone else in that manner, with a note of impatience mixed with devotion. Maris had told her mother a couple of days ago about Alva's passing, believing her mother wouldn't really care. But she had.

"Yes, the body's been released. I thought I told you that yesterday. There was no one but me to make the decisions, Mom. Give it a little time, and I'll arrange a service. I…I can't right now. There are complications."

Yes, like Alva's murder, the fact Maris had been in the hospital after being struck by a car, and the dead-end of a lead in Alva's case that had pointed to one of the neighbors with a criminal record, leaving only Maris once again. Nothing had yet come of the vehicle that had run Maris down. And Maris didn't mention any of this to her mother.

As soon as she was up to it, Maris had placed a small obituary for Alva. Dan had encouraged her, hoping the announcement might bring a call from an attorney somewhere who'd prepared Alva's Will. A double-edged sword if it proved Maris benefited in any way. Dan hoped it would reveal another beneficiary. Someone hard and cold and not at all like Maris.

Dan moved to stand on the threshold. Maris, dressed and ready to go, waved him inside from her perch on the edge of the hospital bed.

"Mom, I've got to run. I'll call soon. Yes, I promise. Work is okay with my being out. Nothing I can do about it, right? Yeah. Okay. Love you."

Dan eyed the white gauze wrapped around her head and the fuzz of shaved hair showing on the right side. "I thought that was coming off?"

"It is. Do you have time to wait a few minutes? Someone's coming to remove this and give me my release instructions."

He walked up to her and pulled a box from his pocket. "I've been holding onto this for you. I found it on the ground the day of your accident." He pulled off the lid.

She threw her hands over her mouth and gasped in the hollow they made. Then she reached out and snatched her feather earring from the cotton inside. "Oh, Dan, thank you, thank you so, so much. Can you help me put it in?"

He did, fingers lingering against the side of her throat. Her pulse beat steady and strong. When he ran a fingertip over the line of tendon, her skin warmed, but she eased his hand away and made another adjustment to the position of the earring.

She dropped her hands into her lap. "I called that hotel outside of town. Now the damned convention is over, they had plenty of empty rooms, so I—"

"I told you I would take you home with me."

Maris avoided his eye, stroking the feather. "Things haven't changed. With us, perhaps, they have. But not out there in the world where you perform a lawman's job."

Dan threw himself down in the nearest chair, continuing to clutch the empty box in his hand. So much for romantic gestures. Not that he expected her to fall into bed with him again. Not yet. She had some healing to do still.

"You make me sound like a freaking sheriff out of the Old West, Maris. You need someone to look after you. You're not allowed to drive yet, you can't return to work, and it is the preference of the Alcina Cove PD that, if you don't have to leave the area, you don't. If you're going to be that goddamned stubborn, you can have the guestroom."

"And if you're going to be that goddamned stubborn, I'll take it." Maris caressed the feather one more time, lifting her gaze to the doorway.

Two people entered, a floor nurse and the other presumably Maris's doctor. Dan stood. "I'll step out." Before anyone could protest, he darted into the corridor. He strode to the window overlooking the hospital grounds and shoved his hands into his pockets. Rainwater dripped off his hair and down his back beneath his jacket. He shivered. Outside, the day was gray, wet, and miserable. Plumes of water arced behind the tires of a vehicle departing the lot. As he would be required to pull the car to the entrance for pickup, he had no worries about Maris getting wet, though.

His gaze shifted to the wide, brightly lit corridor reflected behind him, U-shaped stations running down the center all the way to the far end. Hospital personnel and visitors moved in and out of rooms with a drone of quiet conversation. From Maris's door, the doctor raised a hand to get his attention. Dan started to make his way back, halting at the sight of a figure standing beneath the exit sign halfway down the lengthy hall. Dan narrowed his eyes, bringing the man into sharper focus. Dan had seen him somewhere before. Of course, he came into contact with hundreds of people every year. The guy carried a bouquet of flowers wrapped in cellophane. After reading the sign directing visitors to certain room numbers, he started making his way in Dan's direction, pausing outside each door to check the numbered plaque.

Dan turned away. Where he'd seen the guy would come to him, probably in the middle of the night. Right now he didn't want to get into any conversations. After nearly a week in the hospital, Maris was ready to leave. The first two or three days he'd been mired in worry and senseless guilt, but after that…

After that, he'd been filled with a sense of liberation like the shift of the atmosphere after a long, hot summer. He felt lighter, somehow. Physically lighter. Made no sense, but he found himself sloughing off long-term anxiety like dead skin.

Entering the hospital room, he studied the un-bandaged right side of Maris's head. A growth resembling a week's worth of soft beard shadowed her scalp around the edges of an oversized band-aid. Beneath it, so he had been told, the scar of a very precise incision would one day shine like a thin silver line. Right now, he suspected it resembled nothing quite so picturesque. A hand span below the new bandage, the plume of Maris's feather swung in a draft of air.

"Your girl's ready to go, Detective."

Maris's gaze jerked toward the doctor at his words. Her shoulders shifted in a dismissive shrug. She rose from the bed, gathering her plastic hospital bag from the mattress. The cream-colored teddy bear Felicia Woodward had given her peered out the top.

"I'll go bring the car up. See you in a few minutes, Maris."

"I—can't I walk with you?"

"No," said the doctor. "Definitely not. Hospital policy. Sit tight and wait for the wheelchair."

Dan left the room, walking quickly in case Maris took it into her head to disobey the doctor's orders. Glancing aside into one of the rooms, he spotted the fellow with the flowers. The man turned and looked at him with no sign of recognition at all. Dan continued down the hall, figuring he had to be wrong. Still, something seemed familiar. Had he become like Maris, seeking relevance in everything? Oddly, though, she'd said very little along those lines this past week. She had been quite pensive instead. He supposed he would be, too, after a brush with death. But the head injury…could it have altered her perception of things? Life would be a hell of a lot easier if she were normal. That was unfair, though, to judge her on the basis of his own existence. Did he expect her to live without her gift because he'd be more comfortable? Besides, she wouldn't be Maris then, would she?

That gave him pause. What if Maris was different now?

Five minutes later, Dan pulled his car into a space in front of the older entrance, the one where aids brought patients to be released to whoever would be driving them home. The rain had gotten chilly, so he kept the car running, heater on high. After a moment, he snatched a towel from the back seat to dry his hair, glancing in the mirror every few seconds for Maris's arrival. When she finally wheeled up with an aid at her back, she looked pale and shaken. The aid pulled the chair off the curb and closer to the car. Dan hopped out.

"Are you all right? Not dizzy or anything?"

Maris handed him her belongings and pushed up out of the chair. "I'm fine."

As he helped Maris into the front passenger seat, Dan glanced back at the aid holding the chair handles.

"A man got in the elevator with us," the woman said. "Made small talk, mostly about the weather. And then he asked your wife—"

"Not his wife," Maris said, buckling her seat belt.

"He asked her if he knew her. She said no, but he persisted. That was a little annoying, yes, but something about the exchange"—the aid tipped her head in Maris's direction—"upset her."

"I'm fine," Maris repeated.

Dan thanked the woman and helped her lift the empty wheelchair up onto the sidewalk. After, he got in the car and swiveled to face Maris. "Warm enough?"

"Getting there."

"Is there a possibility this guy recognized you from before?"

"I was twelve when I left, Dan. I had buck teeth and braids and was a good five inches shorter than I am now. I was a late bloomer, one of those girls who doesn't reach full height until her mid-teens."

"What about him upset you, then?" Dan put the car in gear and rolled away from the curb.

"I…I sensed something about him. Something not good."

Ah. Maris had returned. "Like what?"

"I don't know. Apprehension. Regret, possibly. Anger. A lot of mixed-up crap going on in that guy's head. With the exception of you, I don't usually get that clear a message. And those freaking flowers in his hand. He kept waving them around like he was trying to punctuate his words in the air. He threw them away when he got off the elevator a floor before we did."

Dan inhaled, willing himself calm. "Flowers? What kind of flowers?"

"A variety of daisies, shastas and gerbers, and something purple in there, too, all wrapped up in cellophane with a green ribbon. Does it matter?"

Yes, he thought. It very well might if it was the same guy he'd noticed. "Think hard. Are you sure you haven't seen him somewhere?"

She shook her head.

"Perhaps behind the wheel of the car that hit you?"

"What?"

Dan tightened his grip on the steering wheel. "The accident was in the paper, including your name. Anyone would have figured you'd been brought to this hospital. He might have been driven by guilt to seek you out. That would explain him asking if you knew him, if you recognized him. I should have paid closer attention."

"To what?"

"To that guy. I'm pretty sure I saw him on your floor. He'd gone into a room a few doors down from yours, but now that I think about it, the bed in that room was empty. I think the patient might have been out walking, and he ducked in there when he saw you weren't alone."

Maris's fingers tightened on the side of her seat. "You don't think those flowers were for me, do you? That's creepy as hell."

"I don't know. He could be feeling really bad about what happened. That doesn't mean he isn't going to be charged, though. The sketch artist we sometimes work with is a friend of mine. I'd like to ask her to come in while the guy's face is still fresh in my head. But I'll see you settled in first."

"What would be the purpose of having a sketch? You don't know it was the driver. I really don't recall much of that day."

"I don't need to. We can put the likeness in the paper as a person of interest. We don't need to specify suspect. He could be a witness for all anyone might know. But the sketch could turn up a name."

"Okay." Maris hadn't quite settled down.

Dan wondered what she might be hiding from him. He didn't need to be protected. He needed to be informed. "Maris, remember what you said about the two of us lying to protect others and for self-preservation? Do you remember that?"

She nodded again.

"We've been through a lot together this past week. Prematurely, yes, but true. I think we need to start being honest, all the time, no matter what."

Her head bobbed one more time, a small movement hardly noticeable in the gloom of rain. "Okay."

"Okay" was not an agreement. It was not even an answer. Well, it was a Maris-type answer, open-ended and vague. In her head, she probably understood what she meant, but there was no point in seeking clarification. Not right now. When he needed a more definitive answer, he would bring it up again.

As he'd been doing every day, Dan drove down the street where Maris had been hit. Did he hope to find a blue Chevy with front-end damage and a shattered windshield parked as bold as brass at the curb? Stupid, this daily ritual, and obsessive. He thought about the guy in the hospital, a man familiar to him and not to Maris, but as the hit-and-run had taken place fairly close to Dan's house, it might be a friend of a neighbor he had seen on occasion. The picture in the paper ought to help. He kept an eye on Maris as he drove along the road in case she got upset, but she didn't appear to recognize the location when they passed it, staring out the window with a tired, disinterested expression. When he got her back to his place, he'd make sure she was tucked in and comfortable before heading to the station.

No one but Jamie knew she'd be staying with him, and that was the way he planned on keeping it. Jamie thought he'd gone off the deep end with a decision like that. How much crazier would Jamie view him if he found out Dan had fallen for her? Because despite the certainty of heartache Dan saw in his future—as clearly as Maris picked up on people's thoughts circling in the air—he couldn't help himself. His race along the sidewalks, listening to the commotion of the accident through his phone, had pretty much clinched it for him. Sitting at her side during her days of recovery from a hemorrhage in the vessels around her brain had sealed the deal, tied up as neatly as the laces on his boots.

And if she was guilty of murder, what then? Would his emotions just stop? He doubted it, but he wouldn't stand in the way of justice. He couldn't, no matter how slow and painful the death inside of him would be.

Chapter 16

Dan tucked the blankets around her shoulders as if she were a child. Maris shook her head at him. "Do you have children?"

"No. My ex-wife and I…we didn't want to have any for a while and then, well, we didn't. I guess that's a good thing."

Maris wriggled her arm free. She reached for the magazine he'd placed on the nightstand. "I'm not really tired."

"I don't care. Last thing I need is you stumbling down the stairs or something while I'm gone. I'd appreciate it if you'd stay put." He removed the magazine from her hand. "Even though I gave you that, you shouldn't be reading it. I think the term is 'brain rest.' Close your eyes."

She snorted. "Yes, sir." A second later, she cracked one lid apart and discovered he hadn't moved. *Dan, don't look at me like that.* "What's wrong?"

"Nothing's wrong. I'll be back in an hour or so. I'll bring some soup."

"I don't have a cold."

"Will you just let me be kind in my own way? Please? Besides, there are no groceries in the house."

She grabbed his hand and folded her fingers over digits still chilled from the cold rain. "Thank you. I appreciate that you came to the hospital and sat with me every day, too. The nurses told me," she added, before he assumed otherwise. She'd lost her psychic connection with him until the fourth day of her hospital stay when she'd opened her eyes and heard footsteps in the hallway, followed by his voice in her head. *You'll be awake today, Maris Granger. Today is the day.* She'd been moved from ICU that afternoon to a regular room.

Dan pulled his hand back. "I've got to go."

He shut the guestroom door as he departed, and several minutes later she heard the front door close. The rain pounded harder on the roof.

He'd been puzzled by her insistence of taking the spare room but hadn't argued. She didn't belong in his bed. Not in that way. Theirs was a relationship rushing backward. She visualized it as a time-lapse video in reverse, the flower starting in full bloom and minimizing in growth until the green sprout disappeared into the earth, a seed closed and awaiting sunlight and warmth that would never come.

There was no hope for them. The aura like a dark second skin, flaring and shrinking around Dan's body, was still there, and she had no idea what to do about it.

* * * *

Dan handed Jamie Rogers the sketch. "So, you think you could get that in the paper?"

"What really makes you think this might be the guy?"

"Nothing stronger than a hunch." Dan ground a knuckle into the base of his skull. "Got any aspirin?"

"A hunch, huh?" Jamie pulled a bottle out of his drawer and tossed it in Dan's direction.

Dan popped the cap and took one without water, grimacing at the taste, but the pill went down. "One of my own. Not hers."

"How's Maris doing?"

"Good." Dan recapped the aspirin and handed the bottle back.

"You don't sound so sure."

"I'm not. I don't mean health-wise. The doctor said she's recovered, rather amazingly, but she can't, you know, drive or anything."

Jamie arched a brow at him. "Anything?"

"Shut it, Rogers. I'm not an animal. That's fine."

"Then what's up?"

"She…she's different somehow. I can't quite explain, but she doesn't seem herself."

Jamie opened the drawer and returned the pain reliever to its place. He slipped the sketch into a folder. "No offense, but how well do you know her that you can tell she's changed at all?"

Dan said nothing.

"Plus she's been through some nastiness. Give her time."

With a snort, Dan crossed his arms over his chest. "Listen to you. I thought you condemned my thing with Maris."

"What makes you think I still don't? But it's your life, and you and I have been friends for a long time. I'm just trying to be there for you, buddy."

"Don't call me buddy."

"It's better than what I'd like to call you for the risks you're taking. What am I supposed to do with this sketch, anyway, since it's only a hunch?"

"Person of interest. Word it so it looks like we think he's a witness. People might be more inclined to come forward with information about him then."

Jamie stared for a few seconds before nodding. He stood. "I'll contact the paper tomorrow. Want to go for a beer or something?"

Dan rose, too. He put the chair back where it belonged. He thought about Maris, hoping she'd fallen asleep. "Sure. Only one and a bite to eat. Somewhere they have soup because I told Maris I'd bring some back for her."

"Listen to you, all domesticated and shit. Don't you have a can in the closet somewhere?"

He glared at Jamie, who burst out laughing.

"Kidding, Stauffer. Just kidding. Follow me to the Sickle. They always have great soup. And it's quiet there." Jamie lowered his voice. "I have a few things to tell you."

Twenty minutes after consumption of their meal and a second beer for both of them, Rogers still hadn't opened up. Dan signaled the waitress and asked her for an order of the minestrone to go.

"What's your hurry?" Jamie said. "Afraid your girlfriend won't be there when you get home?"

Dan lowered his glass to the table. "What's your fucking problem all of a sudden?"

"Sorry. Nothing. Well, that's not true. You…you always were, I don't know, confident? Secure? You've been antsy this whole meal, like you can't wait to get out of here."

Spinning his glass in the ring of condensation, Dan considered his reply before opening his mouth. "I'm not any less confident or secure than I was. What you mean is that I used to treat the women in my life without any real concern. But now, there's someone I worry about. What the hell is wrong with that? You and Roxie have been together how long? Five years? Are you telling me you don't give her any consideration?"

"Of course not, but that's different."

"How?"

Jamie remained silent, his glass wrapped in his fist. His gaze shifted to the remnants on his plate and stayed there.

Dan pulled out his wallet and placed a twenty dollar bill on the table. "I'll leave that with you. I'm assuming you're not ready to leave?"

Jamie lifted his head. "Do you want the latest or not?"

"On what?"

"The Mabry case."

"Yes, but if you're in the mood for being a jackass, I can wait another day."

"I'm…I'm good. Sit down, wouldya?"

Dan hadn't realized he'd gotten up. He eased back into his seat.

"Want another one?" Jamie nodded at Dan's empty glass.

Dan shook his head.

"Suit yourself. Yesterday we pulled a lot of boxes out of the old lady's attic." Jamie rushed right in without preface. "Photo albums and paperwork, in case there's more family than Maris is letting on, or perhaps even knows about. Families get estranged. There's always a possibility of someone else. So far, nothing, since we can't tell who's who in the pictures. There're no names in the albums. No one else knows Maris is out of the hospital. I haven't said anything because the Chief is pushing to get her in to go through them. If we have more names, we can start trying to track people down."

Dan sighed. "Unfortunately, family makes the most sense. But only if one of them had a real vendetta or stood to gain something. I can't see that old woman pissing somebody off at this late stage in her life, can you? What about a Will?"

Jamie's next beer arrived. He took a sip before answering. "Well, that's the kicker, Stauffer. There was a Will, leaving everything to the surviving blood relations in a direct line from the two sisters. With Maris's grandmother's children all dead, I guess that reads any grandchildren now. Alva had an estate worth three million dollars. Who would have thought, huh? According to her solicitor, Alva had been getting ready to change the Will, but she didn't come in to do it. At the time the Will was drafted, the attorney is pretty sure there were several living family members, but the document was signed years ago. He has no idea who has survived. I know Maris insists she's the last in the line, so if we can't locate somebody else in her family, it's going to be down to just her. Any alibi she has better be rock solid at that point."

"Jesus Christ." Was that a prayer? He thought it might be. He'd uttered quite a few of them over the past several days, poorly worded with basic intent. Dan stood again, accepting the bag with the container of soup from the server. Jamie reached out for the check. "Try and get me a couple of days, Jamie, if you can. She's not in good shape. A bit more rest would help so her head is clear. She's concussed and isn't supposed to be engaging in any strenuous brain activity. She can't even read or watch TV. Looking through those photo albums isn't going to help. Or the stress.

She has the instructions she left the hospital with if you need them. They spell her limitations out pretty clearly."

"Okay. As soon as the request is official, I'll let you know. I'll take a copy then."

Dan extended his hand toward Jamie, who took it after a brief hesitation. "Thanks," Dan said. "Sorry for being sensitive. I understand your concerns."

Jamie released the handshake grip and waved in dismissal. "If we don't find any blood relations alive, she's going to need a lawyer. You know that, don't you? A lawyer to present her alibi in concise terms with every ounce of proof available."

His gut in knots, Dan nodded and exited the restaurant.

* * * *

With a finger in each dangling handle, Maris slowly pulled Dan's desk drawer open. She gazed down at the Priestess card, an image that had come to her in a convoluted dream. So much of the dream made no sense, but she remembered the card had a main part. That and the words *don't touch it*. Naturally, she awoke with an intense yearning to disobey and do that very thing.

After a moment, she shut the drawer. Her fingers tingled with the desire to snatch the card out of the darkness within. But the atmosphere of danger pervading the dream was strong enough to deter her foolishness. Turning on her bare heel, she gazed at Dan's neatly made bed. Warmth danced over her skin in memory. Why couldn't she love a man like that?

Because, when he was gone, she'd be a hollow husk. Nothing of herself would remain.

Maris shut off the light and returned to the guestroom. She climbed back beneath the covers. She wanted to write the elements of her dream into her diary, describe the impact of the card, but the journal was tucked away in her canvas bag on the other side of the room. Energy flagging from her stroll in Dan's room, she decided not to get up. Her stomach growled. Where were Dan and the promised soup?

Reaching up to finger the edges of the bandage, Maris listened to the sounds of the house around her. The rain had stopped, but the intermittent drip of water in the downspouts continued. Wind rattled a window frame somewhere, and the compressor behind the refrigerator hummed into life like the distant rumble of a passing car. Too noisy. Possibly needed a cleaning.

Maris snuggled down under the soft sheets and blanket and closed her eyes. She'd hear the front door when he returned and wake up again…

She opened her eyes to a darkened room and a silhouette standing over her. She let out a shriek that would have shamed her if she gave a damn. She flailed out, striking someone squarely in the stomach.

"Maris! It's me!"

Maris heard a scramble in the vicinity of the nightstand. The lamp flared into life. Maris snatched up her pillow and tossed it at Dan. "You scared the living crap out of me!"

"Sorry. I came in, and you were asleep, so I turned off the light."

"Why were you standing over me like that?"

He shifted his weight from one foot to the other, clutching the folded top of a brown bag in one hand. "I…I was listening to make sure you were breathing. I started to worry that maybe…maybe you weren't."

"I'm breathing. I'm fine. I'm only tired. And really, really hungry. Is that soup?"

He held out the bag. "Minestrone."

"Is there a spoon in there?"

"Yep."

"Thank you."

She took the bag from Dan and slid over automatically to make room for him. "Oh. Sorry. You don't have to. I'm sure you have things to do."

He sat, propping several pillows against the headboard for both of them.

Maris pulled the container out of the bag and opened it. Steam rose from the contents. "Want some?"

He shook his head.

"Is it okay to eat in bed? Don't know what your house rules are."

"They're all annulled for an invalid houseguest. Eat up."

She did, with relish. In the hospital she hadn't had much appetite. Gratitude for her release—for her life—probably explained the return of it. He spoke as she ate, his arm draped lightly across her back, his hand at her nape.

"Not now, but soon you will have to go to the station to look through photos. Jamie ordered albums and paperwork removed from your aunt's attic. They're looking for identification of family members to determine if any of them might still be alive."

"I told you—"

"That you're the last one. I know. But are you certain? I have cousins I've never met. You could, too, you know."

Maris dropped the spoon into the container. She looked at him over her shoulder. "My father had two brothers. One died at sea before he'd ever married. The other one was killed in an auto accident quite a long time ago. His wife remarried, but I have no idea where she is. She and my uncle didn't have children."

"Who told you all of this?"

"My mother. After my father passed away. I was curious why only friends came to his funeral and no family." Dan's fingers moved on her neck, soothing a knot away. She closed her eyes, enjoying the sensation. "Is there something you're not telling me?"

Rub, rub, rub. "No."

Liar.

Easing away from his ministrations, she held up the soup container. "Sure you don't want any?"

"Positive." His hand dropped to his lap.

Maris surprised herself by finishing it off. Once again, she dropped the plastic spoon into the bottom of the container and slipped the lid back on. Dan took it from her and set it on the nightstand on the folded bag.

"Thank you."

"You're welcome."

A minute passed. She wished there was a television in the room. She would have turned it on, if only to listen to with her eyes shut. "Is this supposed to be so awkward?"

"I think it's because we are…undefined? And because you insisted on sleeping in the damned guestroom."

Maris giggled. She turned and settled herself on his chest, her arm around his waist. He slid downward until they were both nearly reclining on the mattress, then circled both arms around her. She whipped the blanket up and around until it covered his legs.

"Now isn't this cozy?" he whispered against her crown. His left arm lifted for a moment. The light went out.

After several more minutes of silence, Maris made a decision. "Dan, I'd like you to tell me a story."

He grunted. "What, like a fairy tale?"

"No. Not a fairy tale. I'd like you to tell me the story of how the Priestess card came to be in your desk drawer."

His respiration stilled beneath her ear.

"I wasn't being nosy. The day Jamie was here I bumped the desk and the drawer opened. Tell me that story, Dan, please, because I can't figure it out."

He slid down farther, stroking back her hair until he contacted the bandage and the fuzz beneath. He rested his fingers against the side of her neck. For a few minutes, he remained silent, but then she heard the first rumblings of his voice in his chest as he began to speak into the darkness above her head.

"Once upon a time—that's the proper start to a fairy tale, right? Once upon a time, there was a boy who was afraid of the world. To counter his fears, he worked for and took the job of a brave man, a police officer. And he was good at it. One day, though, he met something dark and evil which changed his view of everything, but he did his best to deny it had ever happened."

Maris closed her eyes, moved by the manner in which he'd chosen to reveal his story to her...and the fact he had at all. She curled her fingers around a handful of his shirt.

"He worked harder at being a police officer, and after completing the tasks presented to him by the...king, he was crowned detective along with another man who became his junior. And all was right with the world again. The dark places didn't exist. He decided to live in the light of his new position.

"But one night an old, um, seer passed away, and while he was in the home where she practiced her craft, he forgot his teachings in the blink of an eye and came home to discover he had taken one of her possessions with him."

"Really? That's what you're going with?"

He pressed a finger to her mouth. "Yes. Are you going to let me finish?"

She nodded against his chest.

"He didn't even remember doing it. But before he knew it, it was too late to return the object to the place where it belonged because he feared his folly would condemn him, and he...he was a bit of a coward, I guess."

"Dan..."

"Quiet. Were you this much of a pain in the ass when you were a kid?"

"Sorry."

"Then the detective made a second mistake when he met the Priestess in the flesh and was blinded by so many things that he didn't want to believe about her. He took her to the seer's house in direct opposition to what he knew was right, and to make matters worse, they lay together— isn't that the term used in old books?"

Maris nodded on his chest.

"The detective was transformed and lost and guilt-ridden all at the same time. But the one thing that saved him was the fact he'd found someone he could share the unknown world with and maybe, one day, understand."

"Dan, I—"

"Hush. I'm almost done. If you interrupt me, I don't think I'll be able to finish. This isn't my forte."

"Storytelling?"

"No. Honesty. Not this kind of honesty."

Maris swallowed, hard, but the lump refused to budge.

"An evil, uh…"

"Chariot driver?"

"Sure, that works. An evil chariot driver tried to take the Priestess from him, and in the days of her healing, the detective who had fallen from grace realized he hadn't. Not really. Because deep inside him something had been reborn, something he didn't think to know again. And that's the end of the story. Or maybe the beginning. I guess we'll see where it goes from here."

Maris burrowed her face against his shirt, tears dampening the cloth.

"Are you crying?"

"No. There's no crying in fairy tales."

"Bullshit. I seem to remember plenty of weeping and gnashing of teeth in those stories when I was a kid." He kissed the top of her head. "I'm glad you came into my life, Maris. I just wish I knew what the future would bring. But that's your territory."

"I don't know what the future holds for us either, Dan." She caressed his chest beside her cheek. "I do know this, though. Don't touch that card again."

"Why?"

"I'm not sure, but I think you have to take my word for it."

"I'm taking your word for a lot of things, my dear. I only hope I don't live to regret it."

He lapsed into silence then. After several minutes, his breathing grew deep and even. She smelled the faint, yeasty scent of beer on his breath and an uncertain spice. Far from offensive, the evidence of a taken meal was comforting.

She knew Dan found her care with words a frustration at times, but she wished he had spoken his last sentence differently. He should have left out the words "live to." Fate could so easily turn against his hope as he'd expressed it.

Chapter 17

"Ow."

Dan's arm had fallen asleep, and moving it brought tingling pain to the extremity. He shifted again, trying to ease himself out from beneath Maris's sleeping form. She slipped off his chest. He caught her before her head bounced on the mattress and slid a pillow into place. After pressing his mouth to the side of her head, he left the room and went into his own.

He stripped out of his clothes and into a pair of sleep pants, then went to the bathroom to brush his teeth, lingering before the mirror in a frowning study of his face. Where had that fairy tale come from? It had been easier to confess his story in that way rather than tell her outright. He wondered what she'd meant afterward about not touching the card. He assumed she meant physically, although he couldn't imagine why. Perhaps there was a certain Tarot reader's taboo involved. Either way, he couldn't ignore the fact of his misappropriation of evidence. If not evidence, then a woman's property. Perhaps Maris's property now.

God, he hoped not. He needed to speak with her in more detail about an accounting of her time the night her aunt died, although such questioning might be construed as assisting her to create an alibi. After all, he had no official reason for the discussion. One thing he knew for sure—there was no longer any point in denying his involvement with her. He wouldn't add to her burden with a lie of that magnitude. It certainly wouldn't help either one of them.

Dan went to his desk and opened the drawer. He studied the card that had so fascinated him. He honestly couldn't recall putting the thing in his pocket. Was there some significance to that? Maris would think so. To him, it was a mistake. A stupid mistake that might end up with consequences he hadn't foreseen at the time. Certainly the scale of his error in judgment had been intensified by everything that followed.

The lamp shimmered over the varnished colors of the High Priestess with her jet-black hair and enigmatic expression. The blue of her attire was very like the predominant color in the skirt Maris had been wearing that first night. He remembered thinking she'd known he'd taken the card. Nothing more than a reaction of guilty conscience, that one, as her question tonight indicated she'd had no idea. How many other reactions of his were based on his own suspicions and culpability rather than some special insight of hers?

He slammed the drawer shut. He couldn't begin doubting her again. The vicious circle he would create for himself would suck him down like a whirlpool. He trusted her. He had just proven how much with that silly little tale.

Turning around, he studied his empty bed, neatly made and sterile. Had it ever truly appealed to him, this semi-bachelor existence?

The door squeaked open behind him. "I'm sorry. I should have knocked."

"Did I wake you up?"

"Not deliberately. It was your absence." She stood in the doorway dressed in flannel pajama bottoms and a long-sleeved cotton shirt, holding the soup bag from the nightstand. At least she hadn't suffered any broken bones, but the blue bruising beneath the shaved portion of her head was more evident in the light of the desk lamp than it had been in the hospital. Her gray eyes looked huge.

"You remind me of a picture my grandmother used to have hanging in her hallway," he said. "They were popular back in the nineteen-sixties. Big eyes. Very waif-like."

Her lips curved into a crooked smile. "I'm going to bring this down to the kitchen for the trash and get a glass of water. Do you want anything?"

"I'll do it. I'd rather you stayed away from the stairs for a while."

He grabbed the paper sack from her hand as he passed and trotted down the steps. On sock feet, he skated into the dark kitchen. Although the rain had stopped some time ago, the night remained overcast, confining the light of the streetlamp outside to a small and feeble circle. Fine hairs lifting on his nape, Dan leaned over the sink and looked out, expecting to see again the translucent figure. The sidewalk, the patch of grass, the street were all empty. With a small laugh of relief, he reached for a tumbler from the drain board. A gloved hand slammed down across his wrist.

Adrenaline exploded through Dan's heart. He acted without conscious thought, stepping into the attack and tossing the man to the floor. The intruder rolled upright to his feet before Dan fully regained his.

The intruder lunged at him again in a feint, but turned instead and darted toward the front door. He managed to yank it open and run out into the night before Dan reached him. Dan gave chase but lost him quickly when the man disappeared behind the next row of townhouses. Dan pursued anyway on the chance his attacker hadn't vanished entirely but was lurking beneath a deck or behind a screen of bushes. By the time Dan returned home, socks soaked and limping from a bruised arch, sirens wailed in the near distance.

Charging up the stairs despite his injury, he shouted Maris's name before he burst through the unlocked bedroom door. He circled around the room in a wide arc, trying to rid himself of the picture in his head of Maris and the stranger in confrontation. But except for Maris, the room was empty. No one had doubled back and gone after her. "You're all right?"

She nodded. Only then did he notice what she held in her two hands. Seeing where his gaze had gone, she lowered the glass quart bottle filled with coins to the floor.

"You could have done some damage with that."

"I meant to," she said.

Dan sat abruptly on the bed. He whipped off his sodden socks. Maris took them to the bathroom and returned. "I called the police. Two cars are outside. What do you want me to do? Where do you want me to go?"

Dan shook his head. "Sit here. You're not supposed to be stressed. I'm not hiding you, Maris. Fuck the department."

"Dan…"

"I know. I don't mean that. I just—" Footsteps pounded up the stairs. Dan rose to meet the officer coming in the door. He stopped at sight of Maris. Dan issued instructions for an immediate search of the area and turned to slip his damp feet into a pair of sneakers. He looked back at Maris. "You're sure you're okay?"

"Yes. Why did someone break into your house? They must have known you were here."

Dan paused in the doorway beside the officer issuing commands through the radio on his shoulder. He took a deep breath. "I don't think he broke in, Maris. I think he's been here since before I came home tonight."

* * * *

"Why would you think that?" Jamie asked when Dan expressed the same suspicion to him.

"He had to unlock the door to get out. Almost didn't do it with his gloves on, but he managed. Besides, these guys have checked every inch of the house. No sign of a break-in."

"So what are you saying? You think that girlfriend of yours let him in?"

Dan's chest tightened. "I do not. What the fuck is wrong with you?"

"Sorry for the confusion. Just seemed to me you were leading up to that. I mean, she was here, you weren't, some guy ends up in your house without forced entry…Have you actually asked her?"

"Why would I? You ask her. For all I know, I might have left to come to the station without locking up, and he walked right in." Dan could barely get the words out. Damn Jamie and his insinuation.

"To what purpose? Why would some random guy walk in? Is anything missing?"

"Not that I've noticed." Dan glanced around the living room, anger seething behind his eyes and making it difficult to see. And yet he knew Jamie was right to ask these questions. It was too coincidental for somebody to show up at the hospital and then here in Dan's house. But that didn't mean Maris had invited him in or had any knowledge of the intruder whatsoever. She'd been sound asleep when Dan went into the guestroom after his dinner with Jamie. There'd been no faking that.

But how long had he been in his room getting ready for bed before she came to the door? Had there been enough time for her to go downstairs and—?

"Enough."

Jamie frowned beside him. "I'm only asking the type of questions you'd ask yourself if your head wasn't locked in a rather uncomfortable position inside your own anatomy."

"Fuck. I know. I *know*."

"It seems too damned fluky to me. Maybe…maybe Maris isn't involved. But if it's that guy from the hospital, the one you believe ran into her with his car, why would he come here into your home? Isn't it more likely she knows your attacker personally?"

Dan said nothing.

"She might have killed her aunt, Dan. Three million's a lot of reason. And she might have had someone help her. And that someone might have been here in your house this evening."

Dan sat on the end of the sofa cushion. He dropped his head onto his palms, pushed his fingers through his hair. Jamie was a methodical man. His arguments usually made sense. They made sense now, but Dan couldn't believe the scenario he was suggesting. The flipside, however, was equally as bad because it meant that Maris had been unprotected while some asshole, with only God knew what on his mind, took his time in Dan's house. Whether he could remember locking the door or not when he left, Dan knew beyond a shadow of a doubt he'd locked it when he came home. He'd locked the guy in with them.

"When do you think Maris might be feeling up to questioning?"

Glancing up, Dan shook his head. "Not right now. You'd have to clear it with her doctor. You could bring the albums by tomorrow, after you and I are done with work."

Jamie studied him for a long moment. "You still want to believe it's somebody else, don't you? Doesn't it usually boil down to family? And she's it, I'll bet on it. She said there's no one else and, about that at least, I'd say she's not lying."

Dan ground his molars together. The remnants of dinner churned in his stomach. Jamie was determined to prove him wrong. Did Jamie think to get his job if Dan failed to find the truth? Of course, Dan had been successfully blocked from the investigation, so finding out anything wasn't likely. Probably much of the Chief's decision to ban him had been based on Jamie's voiced opinions.

Dan shook his head. He and Jamie had been friends, still were. Maris was right. He was too suspicious. "As soon as Maris is up to it," Dan said, "I'll bring her in. I'll question her myself, if necessary—"

"No. You won't. It's not your case, and with good reason."

Did he need that reminder? Dan dropped his hands between his knees, staring toward the kitchen where he'd been fumbling around in the dark with a prowler inches away from him. Where the hell had the guy been hiding when Dan came in? The powder room? The coat closet? Where?

Jamie dropped a hand on his shoulder and shook it. "I think we're through here. Try to get some rest. Where…where is she sleeping?"

"The guestroom."

"Good. Lock your door."

"Oh, fuck you, Rogers."

Jamie straightened. "I'd be pleased as punch to be proven wrong, Dan. You know that. I just don't think it's gonna happen."

Dan didn't get up to see him to the door. He kept his gaze glued on the carpet between his feet as Jamie herded the last two officers outside. They had collected mud from fibers in the rug, although that likely had come from right outside Dan's house. He'd watched one of them measure and photograph the impression of a boot print on the kitchen floor. Other than that, nothing.

For ten minutes, Dan sat on the couch, unmoving. The small mantel clock began to strike the hour with a whirring of gears and the tiny ring of a brass bell. At the eleventh chime, he stood. By the twelfth, he was heading up the stairs, leaving the lights on below. By the time he'd reached his bedroom door, he had made up his mind.

But when he opened it and saw Maris asleep on his bed, all sound reason fled.

Chapter 18

Maris studied the pearly sheen on Dan's skin, the mingling of perspiration and incandescent light from outside the window that had formed a glaze over the musculature of his chest and arms. She wanted to reach out and run a finger along any one of the shadows between his ribs, but she had learned a handful of minutes ago how ticklish he was.

"You're beautiful," she whispered.

"Hush. Don't ruin it with talking." In the silver light, his lips curved, deepening the creases on either side of his mouth. The converse shape of his closed lids hid his eyes, lashes lying in narrow spikes against his skin. "You know your doctor wouldn't approve of what we just did."

"Unless you've got him hidden under the bed, I don't think he's going to find out." At the reminder of the recent intruder, Maris sucked a breath in through her teeth.

Dan moved his hand in blind search across the sheets until he found hers. He squeezed her fingers. "I checked. Jamie stationed one of the officers in a blatant position outside the house. That guy's not coming back tonight."

Maris turned her study to the shape of their fingers together, knots of flesh and bone like lovers in miniature. "What do you think he wanted?"

"I don't know."

"Do you have any idea who he might be?"

Dan released her hand and rolled to a sitting position, feet on the floor. He planted his elbows on his thighs, dropping his head into the grip of his outstretched fingers. He pushed both hands through his hair and rose, his naked body barred by light. "Jamie thinks you might know who it is."

"What?" Maris pulled herself up against the headboard, yanking the sheet to cover herself. "Why on earth would he think that?"

"It can't all be chance, Maris. There's a puzzle here in pieces I can't get to fit together. Jamie thinks he has it, though, the picture in its entirety. He thinks you let the guy in, that he's your accomplice in the murder of your aunt. And yes," he added before she could say a word, "I could get fired for what I've told you. What Jamie says makes sense. It fits, makes the puzzle pieces fall into logical position. Something is missing, though. There's a black, gaping hole he's ignoring and I can't define. Someday soon you're going to be called in for questioning by someone who's not me. Prior to that, Jamie is going to ask you to look through photo albums he took from Alva's attic to try to identify other family members that he might be able to track down. He's giving you a very small benefit of the doubt. If there's another relative who benefited from Alva's Will—"

Maris stretched an arm to the bedside lamp and turned it on. Dan blinked in the flare of light.

"Alva's Will? What are you talking about?"

Dan sat back down on the edge of the mattress. He pulled an edge of the sheet to cover his thigh and groin. "I can't say anything else. If there is a case to be made here, I would be compromising it."

Maris's gaze followed the sweep of Dan's tousled hair, the cowlick stiff with the earlier application of his plowing fingers. "Did they determine what type of poison?"

He shook his head. "I haven't been told."

"What about how—"

"I don't know that either. And even if I did, I...I can't now. I shouldn't. Maris, I know I asked this before, but I'm going to ask again. Did you kill Alva Mabry?"

Maris folded her arms over her breasts, tucking the sheet tightly into the hollow of her armpits. "You would have sex with someone you believed capable of murder?"

"Don't answer a question with a question. God, Maris, please give me a straight answer, in full, with words that speak of innocence, not evasion."

"Or guilt?" she said with undeniable sarcasm.

"Maris!"

She flinched. "I didn't kill Aunt Alva, Dan. I want to know who did. Whatever you need from me, I'll do."

He was still, all of him, as if he'd been converted to stone. He gazed at a place between them without blinking, a trick of the room's illumination giving his eyes the hue and transparency of bottle glass. Abruptly, he stood. "Good." He grabbed his shorts, slipped them on. "Good. We'll figure this out, I promise you." He headed for the door.

"Where are you going?"

"I need a drink. You?"

Maris drew her knees up to her chest. "What are we talking? Vodka? Gin?"

He cocked his head at her. "Are you serious? You're not supposed—"

"No." She lifted the corners of her mouth in a slow smile. "Water would be nice, though, thank you."

He stepped out, leaving the door ajar. She heard the sound of his bare feet whispering on the carpeted steps and then a soft curse as he bumped into an impediment in the dark, a mild expletive only, nothing alarming in content or volume. Maris relaxed against the headboard.

Who was the intruder in Dan's house? She could understand the speculation about her involvement. Jamie was a practical man, and his theory made sense. Dan was such a man, too, except when it came to her. She would be his undoing, no doubt about that. She didn't want to be. Yet her fate and his were as bound together as the twisted strands of a rope, and the darkness clinging to him bore her imprint.

She pressed her face into her hands, whispering Dan's name, longing for answers to the confusion.

"Are you all right, Maris?"

Her head jerked upright. Dan pressed a tumbler of water into her hand. He sat on the bed beside her, drinking his own.

"I'm just thinking about us and how very bad I am for you," she said.

"Why would you say that?"

She sipped the cold water. "Because it's true." Sensing the weight of his gaze, she glanced up from her contemplation of the rippling liquid in the glass. "I am. How many poor decisions have you made since I walked into your life?"

"Believe me, I made plenty of poor decisions before you ever showed up."

"But you're going against your most basic instincts now because of… of what you feel for me."

"My most basic instinct *is* what I feel for you. The rest of it is just a riddle, a challenge that needs sorting out, that's all."

Maris set the water aside. Pulling the covers along with her, she climbed into his lap and burrowed her head against his chest. His heart thumped beneath her ear in steady rhythm. She curled her fingers around the taut muscles in his forearm. "Did you ever have an imaginary friend when you were a kid?"

He pressed his chin against her head. "I think I remember having one, yeah. Don't all kids?"

She toyed with the fine blond hairs on his arm, pulling them up and twisting them between thumb and forefinger. "Probably. They're the friend who is the most constant, who doesn't ridicule or run away. It would make sense to want a companion like that."

He kissed her hair. She perceived the curl of his lips across her scalp. "Yes. And…?"

"My imaginary friend had your eyes. Isn't it strange that I should meet a man after all these years with those eyes and fall in love with him, only to be his ruination?"

Dan tightened his embrace. "You're not my ruination, Maris. In fact, I think you've rescued me from myself."

* * * *

Two days later, seated across the interview table from Jamie Rogers, Maris still experienced a thrill of pure joy at the remembered words. They weren't true, of course, but Dan believed them to be, and that was what mattered.

"You understand why your boyfriend can't be in here with us."

Maris nodded.

"Unfortunately," Jamie added, "he doesn't."

Maris said nothing. Dan had wanted to be present while she looked through the photo albums, but when Jamie refused, Dan had stalked off down the hall to his office. Jamie had opted not to bring the albums to the house, as Dan had suggested, but have her review them at the station prior to further interview.

He slid them across the table to her. He flipped one open. "I thought that was you until I noticed the dress. Even you don't wear something like that."

Maris ignored the "even you" and leaned closer to examine the photo beneath his fingertip. "That's my aunt. That's Alva Mabry. She was about twenty in that photo, I'd guess. My grandmother was still a child then. There was a difference of about ten or twelve years between them."

"Where is she now, your grandmother?"

Maris flipped through to the next page. "There's Grandma. The one on the pony. She died when she was sixty-two. Way too young." Maris lifted her head. "How did Alva die, Detective? I know it was poison, but how did somebody manage it?"

Jamie bridged his fingers, wrists flat on the table. "You tell me, Maris."

Ignoring him, Maris went back to the album, working her way toward the back. She paused, smiling. "There's my father. Look how young he looks. Why do you think he was dressed like that?" She flipped to the next page. "Oh my God. It was his wedding day. Look, there's Mom. Isn't she beautiful?"

Maris flicked her eyes in Jamie's direction to find him stone-faced.

"Other family members?"

Maris moved on to the next album. "Here's Morris. Uncle Morris, my father's youngest brother. He died at sea before we left Alcina Cove. Never married. Like a lot of men around here, I think he was wed to the ocean. He had a girlfriend, though. On again off again relationship for a while. I don't think she was good for him. He didn't seem happy."

"Anybody else?"

Obviously, Jamie held no enjoyment in Maris's trip down memory lane. His voice was clipped with impatience.

"Here's my other uncle. The middle boy, Andrew. He died in an auto accident, and his wife married again a few years later. They had no kids. You see, there were only the two sisters in the older generation. My grandmother, Anne, and her sister, Alva. Anne married and had three sons. Alva never did marry."

Maris considered the loneliness of almost a century without male companionship. She didn't know that was true, however. Alva had been beautiful. She might have had many men in her life, but had chosen not to marry. The only thing Maris knew for certain was there had been none in Maris's childhood years in Alcina Cove.

"So the only living blood relative in that immediate line is you."

Maris closed the album beneath her hand and placed it on top of the pile with the others. "Correct. Will I be allowed to have these?"

"No, not...not yet."

He'd been about to say something else. Maris had caught the tail end of unspoken words like the snap of a whipping branch in the wind. She waited.

"I'm going to record what we say here." He pushed an old-fashioned Dictaphone in her direction so it sat in place between them.

"Don't you need to read me my rights, or something?"

"I'm not arresting you, Maris. I'm only questioning you."

"But if you decide to arrest me later, I've already blown my right to silence, haven't I? And you've recorded it."

He sighed, dropping his hand from the table to his lap. "Don't you want to be helpful?"

"Is that a trick question?"

"No."

"Should I have a lawyer present?"

"Do you need one?"

Maris shook her head. "No." This was why Dan wanted to be here. To keep her from infuriating this man.

Jamie poised his finger above the record button. "May I?"

"Sure."

"Interview of Maris Granger, commencing at"—he glanced at his watch—"one-nineteen on September twenty-eight. Detective Jamie Rogers conducting interview."

He spent the next half hour expounding on the questions Dan had asked her previously, using the notes Dan had scratched on the yellow legal pad for reference. She repeated the information she had given to Dan, but he dug for details. Maris took her time replying, making certain she didn't phrase responses as questions, and maintained her calm. Several times she reached to her ear to caress the feather in an attempt to maintain her equilibrium.

"Why do you do that?"

"What?"

"Mess with that earring of yours?"

"It's a dove feather. I find it keeps me calm."

"And do you need to keep calm? What is it you actually want to be? Angry? Defensive?"

Maris shifted in her seat. "I want to stay calm, that's all. I don't want to be resentful of your questions. I want to remain understanding of your duty. I don't want to think about someone killing my aunt because that upsets me. I want to be able to answer your questions as concisely and completely as possible in order to assist your investigation. Okay?"

He grunted what she assumed was meant to be an affirmative. "Let's return to the stop you made on your way from your home to Alcina Cove. Are you familiar at all with the route you took?"

"Not really. I haven't come back this way in a very long time."

"But perhaps you've visited other towns off the main route and so might be familiar with certain areas."

Maris looked down at a folded map he was pulling from a folder and back up at him. "What, exactly, do you want to ask me?"

"You say you stopped for gas and paid cash, but you don't recall the name of the station and have not yet produced the receipt you told Dan— Detective Stauffer—you would. So let's open this map here and see if you can point out the approximate location of your stop. When you left your house, how much gas did you have in the tank?"

"Why is this so important?" There she went again, answering a question with another.

"To prove you arrived in town when you said you did. We know the approximate time of your aunt's death. Being able to prove definitively the impossibility of your being in town then would clear you of being the physical perpetrator. Understood?"

"Yes, I understand by your wording that it wouldn't clear me of being in possible cahoots with somebody, though. Am I right in assuming that's what you're trying to skirt around?"

"Dan talks too much."

"No, he doesn't. But you, sir, most certainly do."

Jamie's hand shot out to cover the mic. "Don't you dare tell me you can hear what I'm thinking right now."

"I can't. But I can read your intent loud and clear."

He uncovered the microphone end of the machine and resumed spreading the map across the table. "Gas. How much did you have?"

"About a quarter tank."

"Myself, I like to start a trip with a full tank."

"So do I, but I was in a hurry."

"Yes, Detective Stauffer mentioned that. A dream, was it?"

"It was."

"Right." He spun the map around and planted his finger at a point on the far edge. "What kind of mileage do you get?"

"I don't know exactly. Thirty-four, thirty-five miles to the gallon on the open road?"

"And what size tank?"

"Twelve gallons."

"Was the tank on empty when you stopped?"

"I'm not an idiot. I wouldn't take a risk like that in the middle of the night."

He bit back an exclamation. She really was trying his patience. Dan had warned her not to. She took a deep breath. "I think it was on the last line. It's a digital meter."

"Okay, so you'd driven about seventy miles or so. And this was the road you were traveling?"

Maris leaned over the table, looking where he pointed. She nodded.

"Seventy miles puts you about here." He sat back, pulling out his phone.

"What are you doing?"

"Doing a search for gas stations in that vicinity. Most have security cameras these days if we need to check them out." He reached over and clicked off the recorder. "I'll compile a list, and you can let me know if any sound familiar. You might want to head home—well, not home, obviously. To Dan's. You look tired."

"What happened to bad cop-bad cop?"

He tore his gaze from his cell phone. "Don't you mean good cop-bad cop?"

"You're the only one in here, so…"

He jerked his chin toward the door. "I'll be in touch soon. It would be a hell of lot easier if you could find the receipt for your gas that night."

"Got it. I'll look."

"You mean you haven't already?"

"I'll look again. You have any information on the intruder in Dan's house?"

"Not yet."

"Did you put the sketch of the guy in the hospital in the paper?"

He lowered his phone to the tabletop. "Not yet."

Maris rose and went to the door. She grasped the knob. "Because you think it all comes down to a connection with me."

Jamie cleared his throat. "I didn't say that."

Maris returned his look of false innocence with one of challenge. "You didn't need to."

Chapter 19

Maris sat on Felicia's back deck, eyes closed, face lifted to the sun. Dan had dropped her off there and returned to work.

"How are you feeling?"

Maris cracked a peek at Felicia approaching across the weathered boards. "Like a criminal."

"I meant physically." She handed Maris a glass of tea.

"Tired. Still a bit disoriented. I tend to blank on the ability to tell time more than anything else. Isn't that odd, that your brain would pick out one thing to cast away?"

"I'm sure it'll come back. The doctor didn't say any of the damage was permanent, did he?"

"He said as long as I gave the old noggin plenty of rest, it would heal. You know what's odd? The day I was hit is like a shattered mosaic of memories. That, he said, might never fall back into place."

Felicia made a small noise of commiseration. "Which might not be such a bad thing, right?"

Except it was. With all that Jamie believed and Dan's certainty that the man in the hospital might be the one who had been driving the car, if she could remember, she would at least be able to put that mystery to rest. And the gas receipt. She needed to find the blasted receipt for the tank of gas, or at least remember the name of the place where she'd filled the car up.

"You're frowning, Maris. Are you in pain?"

"I'm good. Thinking about things, that's all."

"Well stop. You're not supposed to be doing that, are you?"

"It's pretty darned hard to stop thought altogether. Impossible, really, short of…well, you know. And I'm not there. I survived being struck and count myself damned lucky."

Maris heard the ice clinking in Felicia's glass as she drank, then the bump of the base on the arm of the chair. "I'm aware we don't know each other very well, but I'd like to ask you something personal."

Maris grinned. "Fire away. I've become the queen of premature intimacy."

"Ah, well, I guess I don't need to ask the question then. I was going to ask about you and Dan…"

"Dan and me is one of the scariest things in my life. And one of the best. And I don't know what the hell I'm supposed to do about it."

"Right, then. Want a shot of something in that tea? It'll be dinner time soon."

"Can't. Doctor's orders."

She thought of what else she'd been doing against doctor's orders, none of which involved the brain. Good thing, because she didn't possess the fortitude to turn Dan down.

* * * *

"Working late?"

Dan looked up from the circle of light illuminating papers on his desk to find Sally at his door, peering in at him with a too bright smile.

"What are you doing here at this hour?" he asked, perhaps a little brusquely.

Her smile faded. "Overtime. Could use the money, so I'm not complaining. I thought, um, maybe you'd like to get a drink with me?"

"A drink." She had to be the only person in the entire station who didn't know about him and Maris at this point. Or maybe she did and didn't care. "I have a lot of work to catch up on, but thanks."

She started to back away but returned. "She's trouble. She's no good for you. Everyone knows that. She's got your head turned around backward."

"Sally, you need to leave my office now."

She stepped right inside and took the chair Maris had the night that had begun the transformation of his life. Sally leaned forward, hands together between her knees in a way that caused her arms to push her breasts together and out, the cloth of her blouse stretched tight across them. A couple of weeks ago, he would have viewed the invitation as his due. What an ass he had been.

"You told one of the guys I was pretty."

Dan dropped his pen to his desk and lowered the monitor on his laptop. No need for her to view what he was working on. "I did. I also said you were young. Too young for me."

"I'm twenty-two. Almost twenty-three."

"And I'm thirty-six. In an unfortunate set of circumstances, I could be your father."

"Unfortunate? What they hell do you mean by that?"

"Nothing against you. I meant fathering a child at thirteen—or however that works out age-wise—though not impossible, would have been an unfortunate event. You're too young for me, Sally. Period. And I'm involved."

"Involved. Is that what you call it? That's not what the guys are saying."

Dan swiveled his chair. "I don't care what they're saying."

"You should." She stood. "You really should if you care about your job at all."

Dan turned back to his desk. "Have a good night, Sally. Please shut the door on your way out."

She did, with a slam that made his right ear ring. He picked up his cell and called Maris. He pressed the phone to his left ear, listening for her voice.

"Dan." A sultry simple greeting that rushed blood into places not requiring it at the moment.

"Are you still at Felicia's?"

"She offered to take me back to your place, but we're watching a movie right now. Well, I'm listening with my eyes closed. Are you finished working?"

He glanced at the laptop. "Not yet. Can you stay there a bit longer?" After the other night, he didn't want her at his place alone. She conferred briefly with Felicia before assuring him there would be no problem. "Okay. I'll let you know when I'm heading over. We won't bother Felicia with a ride."

She agreed and hung up. He was about to open his computer again when a knock sounded on the door. "Sally, I told you—"

The door opened. Jamie stuck his head in. "Sally's gone home. In a bit of a hurry."

Dan rolled his eyes. "Thank God."

"Problem?"

"Yeah, she wanted me to go with her for a drink."

"And the problem is?"

"I don't want to."

Jamie pushed the door wide. The knob struck the wall with a small crack. "Crap. Sorry."

Dan shrugged.

Jamie threw himself down into the chair recently vacated by Sally. "You really are into this Maris chick all the way."

"And if I am?"

"It could end badly."

Dan stretched his arms above his head. The chair rocked backward. He shifted his weight to bring it forward again. "Any relationship can end badly. Look at my marriage."

Jamie grunted in agreement. "What are you still doing here?"

"Catching up on some things."

"Like what?"

"Does it matter?"

"Yes," said Jamie, "it does."

Dan ignored him. "How'd your interview with Maris go today? Are you allowed to tell me that?"

"I shouldn't."

"Suit yourself."

"Damn it, Dan!" Jamie's face had gone an apoplectic red. "You're a stupid fucking asshole."

"Thanks. Appreciate the vote of confidence."

Jamie threw up his hands. "We could find both our heads on the block, and though you might not care, I fancy mine right where it is."

"I know you do. I really don't want to endanger your job. But if I'm sacked without any dirt flying your way, my job is yours. That's what you want, isn't it?"

After a moment, Jamie shook his head.

Dan narrowed his eyes. "Look, if there's anything you can tell me…"

Jamie maintained a stubborn silence until he finally released his breath on a long sigh. "I worked with her to narrow down the area where she got gas. I'm compiling a list of stations in the hope she'll remember which one. If not, I'll try to get someone local to check out all the surveillance cameras. For or against her, the timeframe of her travel is the number one priority."

"Understood." Dan picked the pen up from his desk and clicked it twice with the ball of his thumb.

"The hour she bought gas could eliminate Maris being here when Mabry died. It won't, however, fully eliminate her as a person of interest until we find out who did it for certain."

Dan swallowed and nodded. "What about the poison? Any idea how it was administered?"

"I can't answer that. You talk to Maris. I know you do. Hell, I would, too, in your position, but I can't risk that sort of contamination of the case.

It could make the difference between a successful prosecution and having the case thrown out of court. If it comes to that," he added as concession.

"Yeah. If it comes to that." Dan had been locked out of the case file in the computer, but that hadn't stopped him from researching the various types of quick-acting poisons and how they could be administered. Without knowledge of the precise toxin, though, all the research in the world was a futile exercise.

"You should go home, Stauffer. Isn't Maris waiting for you?"

"She's visiting a friend. I'll pick her up in a bit."

"A friend? Good God, that woman works quickly all the way around—" Jamie dropped his head on a release of breath. "Sorry." He looked up. "I'm not trying to be insensitive. Is this someone she knew before?"

"No."

"Huh." Jamie pushed against the chair arms and stood. "Seriously. Go home. Or wherever. Just get out of here."

Dan waited until Jamie had departed before he logged out and shut down. He gathered up his paperwork into a folder, then reached into his drawer to grab a few things he wanted to take home. Forks and a crusty butter knife that needed to be run through the dishwasher, a credit card bill, some notes he'd been making on post-its about a trip he'd considered. In his haste, he scooped up more than he wanted, but he didn't have the time to sort it all out now. He shoved everything into the empty plastic bag from his lunch and then slipped on his coat. Before locking the door, he stood a moment gazing into the darkened office, thinking of how hard he had worked to get to this place in his career. Would it really come down to his job or Maris? He hoped not because he feared he already knew which he would choose.

Twenty minutes later, Dan pulled into Felicia Woodward's driveway. He spotted the flicker of the television through the living room window. A massive shadow shifted across the wall, and his heart leapt into his chest. Quickly, he realized the shadow had been created by Felicia walking in front of a lamp. He got out of the car and strode up to the door where he rang the bell.

The door opened. Felicia greeted him with a grin. "Detective Stauffer."

"Felicia Woodward," he teased. They'd met the year before when she'd befriended another woman he'd known, one every bit as stubborn as Maris who'd been involved with a guy he'd had some professional involvement with out on the coastal highway. Last he'd heard, they were married. He'd doubted the longevity of that relationship, too, given the short time they'd known one another, but it appeared he was wrong.

And now here he was, in the same position, falling hard for someone he barely knew.

"Come in. Your lady has fallen asleep on the couch."

Dan walked into the living room to find Maris curled in a nearly fetal position on the sofa cushions, one of Felicia's many crocheted throws draped over her body. He crouched on the floor and whispered her name. She opened her eyes.

"Dan! I thought you were going to call."

"I forgot."

He studied her sleepy face, feeling his mouth turn up into a stupid, half-grin, not caring that Felicia stood nearby, watching. After a few seconds, the woman walked away, claiming something needed her attention in the kitchen.

Maris sat up, the afghan falling with a thump to the floor at his knees. "What's wrong?"

He stood, restoring the blanket to the couch. "Nothing. Are you ready to go?"

"I—yeah, I think so. Sure." She looked around as if she'd forgotten something. "I have boots here somewhere."

Dan retrieved them for her and helped her put them on. He put his hand against the side of her face, pushing her hair back behind her ear. Leaning toward her, he pressed his lips to her forehead as an overwhelming tenderness rushed through him. "Come on. Let's get you home." He didn't bother with a qualifier. Right now, his home felt like hers, too.

"You're quiet," he said as they drove back toward town.

"Tired. I'm fine. How was your day?"

"Productive." He glanced in the rearview mirror. A pair of headlights shone through the darkness behind him at a distance that had been maintained with precision since he'd pulled back out onto the highway. He recognized the one light blinking with an odd, strobe-like effect whenever the car hit a bump in the road. The same car had been behind him on his way out. "Is your seat belt on?"

"Wha—yes."

"Hold on. I'm taking this next left."

He turned without benefit of signal or application of the brakes. Maris let out a squeak from her side of the car. Yanking beneath the shadow of trees encroaching on the lane, he braked quickly and shoved the car into park, shutting off the lights. Out on the highway, the car slowed down as it neared the side road before speeding up again. The model and make of the car were indistinguishable, the color a darker paint.

"Son of a bitch. Somebody's been following me."

Wheeling the car around, he turned the lights on when he hit the main road, but by that time the other car had gone and several more were approaching behind him. Dan drove home and hustled Maris inside. He secured the front door and made a call to the station asking for frequent checks through the night. More and more, he suspected Jamie was right. These were not separate incidents, but connected somehow. Sure, he pissed off many a criminal with arrest and prosecution, but he had a gut feeling Maris was the catalyst and not him. He refused to believe she was involved in any wrongdoing, so that could only mean one thing. She was a target. That might even explain the hit and run.

The gaping hole in the puzzle seemed to have grown larger, threatening to suck him down.

Chapter 20

The threat to Dan, through her, was closing in. Sometimes she imagined she could push it away, like a blanket from her face. She woke up dreaming about danger and flailing out. Dan would always awaken beside her and whisper soothing words. He thought she was having nightmares about the car hitting her. She couldn't tell him the truth. He had enough to worry about. She needed to keep her senses open to all nuances in the world and beyond if she was going to protect him. And even then, she possessed no guarantee she could. Some things were meant to happen. As viciously cruel as that might appear to people who lived normal lives, it was true.

It had been three days since the car had followed Dan to and from Felicia's home. After permission from the police department to dispose of Alva's body, Maris had her great-aunt cremated. As soon as Maris felt up to the task, she would arrange a service. In the meantime, the mystery of her aunt's demise remained.

Jamie had approached Maris with the names of gas stations. She had picked two that sounded familiar. The detective had contacted a local police department to have someone there check out her story, to review video surveillance, or so Dan told her. She wasn't sure how he knew. He wasn't supposed to be privy to any information. She supposed Jamie allowed him a few select tidbits, enough to keep him satisfied.

Regarding Alva's Will, except for what Dan had let slip, Maris had heard nothing. The attorney had probably been told to hold off on contacting her as long as she remained a suspect. Because that was the gist of the department's motive, wasn't it? Guilt by greed.

Who would kill for a house? Alva Mabry couldn't have owned anything other than the old Victorian. Although if Jamie Rogers suspected Maris had killed Alva for her estate, her aunt must have possessed substantially more.

"God, I'm sick of this!"

Dan looked up from the newspaper. "Sick of what?"

Maris sighed. "A lack of resolution, I guess. Of suspicion and doubt. At some point, do you people—"

"Us people?"

"Police. Law enforcement. At some point, do you accept the fact you must be wrong even if you don't have somebody else to blame?"

He turned the page. "More often than we'd like."

Maris flopped back down on the couch. "I'm sorry I'm grouchy this morning."

"You had a restless night. I'm not surprised you're grouchy. Should we go get some breakfast?"

"Don't you ever cook at home?"

He smiled. "Not if I can help it."

"Doesn't it feel weird to you?"

"What's that?" He flipped another page.

"The two of us and the routine we've fallen into. Like this is our life. I've slipped into yours, yes, but I still have mine, and it's hung up in limbo."

Dan folded the newspaper onto his lap. "Once your doctor clears you medically, you can drive home, return to work. I don't think Jamie has enough to keep you here. At least, he's made no mention of bringing anything before the District Attorney. And he wouldn't. There's absolutely no evidence."

The flat delivery of his words indicated the depth of his hurt. She hadn't meant to offend. If she hadn't been able to read the emotion behind his statements, she would have been wounded herself by what appeared on the surface a brusque dismissal. *Yes, Maris, go home, go back to work as soon as you get the doctor's say-so. I won't miss you, not one little bit.*

She touched his hand. "I don't mean that. I feel like I'm teetering on a fence, and there's something frightening on both sides of it, but I can't see what awaits me in either direction."

"You can't see? The woman with the—what do you call it? The Sight. Why can't you see?"

Maris clasped her hands in her lap, rocking forward once and then back, as if she could rid herself of a tingling premonition with the movement. "I don't know, Dan. I don't know, and I'm frightened."

His expression altered, eyes focusing, jaw set. "What are you frightened of? Tell me."

"Oh, Dan, you care so much."

"Yes." Cautious, his agreement, both wary and defiant.

"People like us, we shouldn't fall in love."

"Why not?"

"Because you have such a concrete sense of duty and I…I have a sense of things I never should. I had half-hoped the injury to my head might rid me of it, but it hasn't."

"Maris."

She shook her head. "No, you're right. Let's go to breakfast. Where shall we go? The Timeless?"

Maris left him on the sofa and went back upstairs to dress. She combed her hair in the bathroom mirror, then fingered the short length of hair growing out where the bandage had been. If not for the scar showing beneath, angry still, raw and shining pink, it might have looked like she had shaved it for fashion.

With a sudden, astonishing clarity, she remembered the moment when she felt death in the hospital emergency room and Alva's voice telling her to hold on, to not give in. That had happened, hadn't it? It hadn't been an illusion created by the building pressure of hemorrhaging blood against her brain. How had she forgotten?

She tapped the mirrored glass with her fingernail. "Because, you idiot, you nearly died. A lot of things have slipped your mind."

Be strong, Maris. Always be strong.

Yes, she was remembering that, too—Alva's voice in life, instructing, molding, urging her to accept what she was and to do right by it.

Dan appeared in the mirror behind her. He slid his arms around her waist and pulled her back against his chest. He kissed the side of her head, the scarred side, with tenderness. "Are you sure you're good?"

She reached up behind and stroked his jaw, resting her hand against his face after. "There may come a time when I will tell you to do something, and you must do it, without question. You will know the moment when it arrives."

His chest rose and fell against her spine with only a small hitch in his respiration. He pressed his mouth into the cup of her palm. "Okay."

Simple. Trusting. Her stomach plummeted.

When they arrived at the Timeless, there was a ten-minute wait for a table due to normal Saturday morning business. Dan gave his name and then suggested a walk in the back garden. Maris readily agreed. She loved gardens. The act of gardening in her own small plot kept her sane and balanced. She noted with delight the plantings had been well thought out, sun-loving blossoms giving way to the hardier blooms of shorter days and cooler nights with no glaring break between. Delicate fragrance perfumed the air, unlike summer's heady scents.

"This place grows less familiar to me each time we come here. I expect it wouldn't have been the same even if your friends hadn't made so many changes. Twenty years is a long time."

She sat on a nearby bench. Instead of joining her, Dan continued down the crushed stone path, idly checking out the flora, hands folded behind his back. He paused beneath the spreading branches of a maple tree large enough to have been original to the yard she'd played in as a child. After a moment, he took a step back, looking from side to side and out toward the street beyond the white, wooden fence. Then his gaze returned to a study of the tree itself. He glanced at her over his shoulder.

Maris rose. "What is it?"

He strode back in her direction. "I think ten minutes is up. We should head back inside. We don't want to lose our table."

Oh, Dan, you're a horribly poor liar. Had he seen someone out in the street to cause alarm? But he didn't appear nervous or on the alert. Besides, wouldn't he have dealt with such a person immediately? Maris tucked her hand into his arm. "A penny for your thoughts."

"Really? Do people still say that?"

"I said it. I'm people."

"I have a lot on my mind, as you can imagine. But I want us to enjoy breakfast, so we won't talk about any of it."

Summarily dismissed, Maris nodded agreement. "Do you like flowers?"

"They're all right."

"Yeah, the yard in front of your townhouse is pretty bland."

"Well, maybe you can remedy—never mind."

Right. Not the time of year and not her job. Springtime was for planting, or bulbs after the first frost of autumn, but with the undefined nature of their relationship and everything hanging over their heads, she certainly wouldn't be around for either. Perhaps she could leave him detailed instructions and come back at some point to see how he'd gotten on. If, however, she ended up in jail...

"I can't be charged without real evidence, can I?"

"Circumstantial cases have been made and even successfully prosecuted—"

"Dan, that's not making me feel any better."

"Sorry."

She shook his arm and released it to follow the hostess's lead to a table. As Dan proceeded to the seat on the opposite side, his cell signaled the receipt of a text with a melodic three-note chime. He pulled the phone from his pocket, glanced at the screen, and tucked the instrument away.

Maris nodded toward his hip. "You can take care of that."

"We're eating. I'll deal with it later."

They were each handed a list of breakfast specials by the hostess before she made her way back to the register. Maris noted a disclaimer on the bottom of her menu. "So, they're only open for breakfast on Saturdays. Doesn't having the restaurant attached ruin the homey bed-and-breakfast feel?"

"There's a dining room for the Inn's guests inside."

He'd withdrawn. Maris began to suspect the recent text wasn't his first, and perhaps he'd received one in the garden she hadn't noticed. As if on cue, the cell rang in his pocket, muffled by denim.

"Damn it. Maris, I'll be right back." Dan pushed away from the table and hurried out of the room. Maris held the menu sheet up as if reading but watched Dan through the wall of windows as he paced back and forth beyond the potted mums, the phone to his ear and his free hand clenched against his thigh.

"Are you ready to order or are you waiting for your husband?"

"He's not—I'm waiting, thank you. Could I have a cup of coffee, though?" The server nodded and went to get the pot. Maris turned the dainty mug upright on the saucer, then returned her gaze to Dan. Spinning on his heel, his eyes searched the glazed reflection in front of him as if he sought her out.

"Oh, shit." Maris glanced quickly around to make sure her voice hadn't carried. When she looked back, Dan had hung up and was making his way at a swift pace toward the door. He arrived at the table together with the waitress, who poured the coffee into Maris's waiting cup.

"And you, sir?"

He nodded absently, taking his seat. Maris reached across and turned his cup over. "Dan?"

"It's all right. We'll eat, and then we have to go to the station."

* * * *

Dan walked Maris down the hall to the interview room where Jamie stood outside the open door. He nodded at Dan and took Maris's arm, leading her inside. The door shut behind them.

The on-duty officers were out of the station, leaving it strangely quiet. He used to like those days, when activity ebbed and waned with the stretches of silence in between. There weren't many of them. Today, however, it made him feel alone.

Dan turned away from the door and headed to his office to await the outcome of this latest interview. Passing Jamie's office door, he noticed a pile of photo albums on the corner of the desk. Following a split second of indecision, he stepped inside and flipped the top one open. Yes, these had come from Alva Mabry's place. With a keen ear to noises in the corridor, Dan began to flip through them. Without Maris beside him to explain, he had no idea who any of these people were with the exception of the younger Alva, due to the remarkable similarity between the woman and her grandniece. Even though nothing he was doing could compromise Jamie's case, his heartbeat raced. He'd been pulled from the investigation. He had no business—

"What the fuck?" Dan whispered.

With a quick check of the hallway, Dan returned to the album and flipped back and forth between several pages. Various photos had been pulled, whether recently or over the years he couldn't tell. But the white squares on yellowed paper were obvious indication that a photo had once rested beneath the plastic. One or two more might not be missed. He couldn't point these out to Jamie until he'd asked some questions, but he didn't want his access to them cut off either. Dan slipped the photos into his breast pocket and restored the albums to their place. The topmost slid off. He caught it on the way down before the photo book hit the floor, pages falling open to a series of children's images. A prickling chill danced between his shoulder blades. He yanked out another photograph from one of these and put the album back.

Out in the corridor, he heard the rattle of a doorknob. He snatched a cup from the water cooler and placed it beneath the tap as an excuse for being outside Jamie's office. The interview room door opened. Maris stepped out, her countenance pale as paper. Quickly Dan filled the cup and held it out to her as she walked stiffly toward him.

"Thanks." Her hand shook as she took the cup.

"What's happened?"

Jamie exited the interview room. His eyes met Dan's in silence and held as he strode along the hall to his office. Without a word, he went inside and closed the door.

"They didn't get anything from either station. The video camera was broken at one, but the clerk didn't remember me there. He was shown a picture. He said 'Her, I would remember,' but he didn't. I turned out my purse on the table in front of Jamie, went through every scrap of paper for the hundredth time. I even ripped the lining to look inside. The receipt's not anywhere, Dan."

Dan yanked her close and held her. Water splashed onto his shirt, cutting cold through the fabric. "It'll be all right."

"No, it won't. Alva has an estate worth three million dollars, and I'm the sole beneficiary. Did you know that? Sufficient motive for murder. Monday, Jamie's going to speak with the District Attorney. At least he gave me notice."

The corridor went red before Dan's eyes. He used to think it was only an expression, "seeing red." Perhaps it was due to blood vessels expanding. Or maybe it was envisioning blood being shed.

"Let's go for a ride along the coast. How's that? Maris, look at me. A ride with the windows down. It's a beautiful day. And after we get back, we'll talk about things like getting you a lawyer."

* * * *

A lawyer. She'd never needed an attorney for anything in her life. She had no idea how much a defense would cost, how broke she would end up in the process of unnecessarily proving her innocence. Maris leaned her head against the headrest, eyes closed against the glare of the sun through the window. Dan had gone into the drugstore on the main street for water for the trip. And chocolate, he'd said. Lots of chocolate.

Hearing footsteps on the sidewalk, Maris peered out between her lashes. Not Dan. At the far end of the street, the sailors' cross rose above the downward curve of the road, dark against the sky. People who looked at the cross and read the names of those they had known, family members going back generations, would feel a sense of connection, of history. She didn't really possess that sense. Her roots hadn't been ripped up and transplanted. They'd been cut off and left behind in the ground to wither and die.

"Here you go."

Maris grabbed the plastic sack through the window and lowered it onto the floor between her feet. Peering at the contents, she removed a candy bar. "Want one?" she asked Dan as he slid behind the wheel.

"In a bit."

Maris broke off pieces of the flat bar and placed them on her tongue to melt while Dan drove. He didn't head straightaway to the coastal road, but took a side street out into the surrounding countryside, climbing hills flanked by scraggly pines and huge boulders. He said little, and Maris was content to leave it that way. After a few minutes, she folded the paper over the remainder of the candy bar and returned it to the drugstore bag.

Dan pulled the car to the side of the road. "Look at that."

Maris followed his gaze to the view of gray sea and blue sky. Terns and gulls rode air currents flaring off the cliff face, while others perched on boulders like a dusting of snow. Pine resin and salt air filled the car. To the left in the distance, the lighthouse stood tall on a spit of rock, waves crashing below. Maris shivered.

"Cold? We can shut the windows."

"Not cold. It's fine. That's a beautiful view."

"I come up here sometimes just to sit and watch the changing light over the water."

"Alone?"

"Always."

"Until now?"

"Until now."

The warmth of his gaze heated her skin. He smiled. Not the smile he threw around like business cards for the ladies he met, but one she'd noted he reserved for her. She didn't deserve it. Not his affection, not his companionship, not his gratitude. In the end, she would let him down. Out there somewhere in the cold dark sea.

"Maris."

"I'm not crying."

"Yes, you are. And you shouldn't. Whatever it takes, we'll work this out."

She knew he meant the possibility of charges, but she wished he meant all of it. Yet these were things beyond his ability to alter. Or hers. She drew a deep breath.

"Maris, would you look at something for me?" He reached into his pocket and pulled out several photos. He shuffled through them and returned one to his shirt.

She held out her hand. "Where did you get these?"

"I, uh, might have come across them on Jamie's desk."

Maris giggled, separating the photos in the sunlight. "They're all of Aunt Alva."

"Who's that?" He pointed to a young boy in all of them. Maris leaned forward for a closer look.

"My dad, I think. Could be one of his brothers, but I don't think so. Yeah, I'd say my dad. Why?"

Dan's shoulders slumped. "I didn't think he looked like the other photos, but then again they might have been taken at a different time. I thought he might be someone else. A relative you don't remember."

Maris tapped the photos into a pile and handed them back. "No. We're not going to be able to go that route. There's no one but me left."

He slipped them back into his pocket, clearly disappointed. "We'll keep driving then?"

"Onward." She squeezed his hand and let go. Jamie had told her the provisions of Alva's Will. If only there were someone else, but even so, would she want suspicion to fall on that person? Why on earth couldn't it be someone with no familial connection whatsoever? Why weren't they checking further into other people in this town? Granted, three million dollars could sway someone to murder, but it didn't have to be that way. Decent people wouldn't care about the money. Unfortunately, Jamie didn't think she was decent. She wasn't sure he even believed she was sane.

Chapter 21

Dan leaned against the hood of his car, arms folded across his chest. Maris sat inside behind him in the passenger's seat, refusing to get out. In front of him, the lighthouse of dark stone loomed high into the brilliant sky, the afternoon sun gilding the back curves. She appeared genuinely afraid. He figured he'd give her a couple of minutes.

The lighthouse was automated now, but for many years it housed the light keeper and, occasionally, his family. Perhaps Maris sensed some long ago tragedy, a spirit or two lingering on the grounds. He felt absolutely nothing except the delightful breeze along his forearms below his rolled-up sleeves.

The passenger door opened and closed again, quietly. Footsteps on gravel heralded Maris's appearance at his side. She leaned her rump against the car hood beside him, mimicking his stance, arms folded over her breast. Her face was as pale as it had been at the station.

"It's a lovely structure."

He nodded. "People are allowed inside up to a point. After that, there's a gate across the steps with a padlock to keep the machinery from being molested."

She didn't move.

"Do you want to go inside?"

"I…"

"We don't have to."

"Okay."

"But I'd like to."

She dropped her arms to her side, straightening. "Fine. We'll go together."

He took her hand and tucked it into his elbow. Her fingers trembled slightly before curving to grip his arm. Could be she was afraid of heights. He couldn't fault her there. A lot of people were.

What had once been a stout wooden door was now another iron gate, less like the fence on the stairs overhead, but more like a true barrier. No lock secured it. He pulled the gate open, the creak of its hinges nearly lost in the pounding of the surf. Inside, the air temperature was cooler by a good twenty degrees. He rolled his sleeves down and buttoned them at the wrist. Somewhere water dripped in a steady, echoing rhythm.

"Hello!" His voice bounced back at him, over and over in diminishing volume.

"Don't," Maris said. Even that small sound whispered in repetition along the walls. He took her hand.

"Do you mind if we climb midway? I'd like you to see the view."

She acquiesced without speaking, stepping forward with a brief nod, and he led the way up the spiraling stone stairway, their steps coming back at them. Her near-panic began to unsettle him, and he found himself listening for other sounds in the echoes.

"Here. Here we are. Look through this casement."

She did, clutching the stone and rising on her tiptoes. She was barely breathing.

"What are you so afraid of?"

"Nothing. I…nothing."

"Do you want go back down?"

"Yes, please."

He took a few seconds to enjoy the view himself before preceding her down the stairs as a barrier to a fall. He ought to have given her recent head injury some consideration before asking her to climb up all those stairs. Outside again, she drew a shuddering breath.

"Better?"

"I didn't mean to ruin your day."

"The day was already ruined. We were just trying to make it a little less so."

Her lips turned up in a weak smile. "Thank you."

If any possibility existed of getting away with it, he would have packed her up and taken her home. Her home, far from Alcina Cove. It wouldn't have done any good. That's what arrest warrants were for. Dragging people back to justice.

"Do you want to sit awhile? Out there on the abutment? I'll get the chocolate out of the car. We'll pretend it's a picnic."

A few minutes later they were seated on the stones, complete with a blanket from the trunk. She ate the rest of her chocolate bar, visibly relaxing as she consumed it. He twisted the cap off her water, then his.

"The scenery is stunning here, I do admit."

Dan took a swig of cool liquid. "What's got you spooked?"

She bit her lip, narrowing her eyes to view the seagulls crying overhead. "I sense danger here. For you, I think, but I'm not sure."

A smattering of his second mouthful went down the wrong way. He coughed the liquid out and wiped his lips with the back of his hand. "What kind of danger?"

"I don't know. Since I've been here, I've been experiencing a kind of sensory overload. It would be hard to explain when you don't fully believe—"

"But I do."

She shook her head, tossing a piece of chocolate to the birds. "That's not bad for them, is it? And you say you do, and a good portion of your good, good heart is all in, but the understandably logical portion of your brain isn't quite so sure, even now."

"Maris, don't doubt me."

"I don't doubt you, Dan. I trust you with my own heart, good or otherwise, and that's never been an easy thing for me to do."

Her face lay in partial shadow. The white feather hanging from her lobe danced madly in the wind. He was glad he'd been able to save that for her, her talisman of peace. It had taken a good bit of cleaning to remove the spattering of blood. Feathers were strong, though. They had to be. They carried birds thousands and thousands of miles in their travels.

Maris reached up and halted the feather's frenzied movements. "In its own way, it's carried me thousands of miles, too."

Dan's lungs deflated. "Maris, how could you believe I doubt you when things like that come out of your mouth?"

"You told me you'd denied something you'd seen with your own eyes. It's not easy, full acceptance. There are times when I question myself." She tipped her head back and closed her eyes. Fine strands of black hair gyrated back and forth around her head like the spokes of a pinwheel.

"We've come an unnaturally long way in two weeks," Dan said quietly. She didn't react. He wondered if she hadn't heard him over the thunder of the waves. "I remember when I first met you I was—"

"Pissed. You thought I was someone else who'd come to the station looking for you." She dropped her head down to study him.

"And now I can't recall what that woman looked like." Clutching his knee cap between two hands, he rocked back. He wondered if he could block his thoughts from her because there was one he wanted desperately to keep hidden. She'd said only some came through. It would be damned inconvenient if this one did. He squeezed his eyes shut and tried to think of something else, the way he might if he was trying to avoid ejaculation. Suddenly, he laughed. "Good God, woman, the gyrations you put me through."

"What are you talking about?"

"I was just…oh, it doesn't matter. Are you ready to head back?"

She clambered to her feet and bent over to gather up their ridiculous feast of chocolate and water. He folded the blanket, still chuckling to himself, the sound dying in his throat at the expression of shocked dismay on Maris's face.

"Dan, I know what happened to the receipt. For the gas. I wrote my number on it that first night and gave it to you. It's probably at the dump by now."

Dan's heart leapt in his ribcage. "No. I think I threw it in my desk drawer at work. We'll swing by the station, and I'll check."

It was all he could do not to peg the accelerator to the floor. Losing his cool wouldn't help anyone. In the past, he'd been a level-headed type of guy, not letting anything get under his skin, always in control. Maybe when some of the attitude went, it all did, like water from a burst dam.

He had Maris wait in the car and went in alone, straight to his office. He turned on the overhead florescent and yanked open the right hand drawer of his desk. Not finding the receipt at first glance, he dumped the contents of the organizer tray on the blotter. Next, he pulled all the files from the drawer beneath, methodically flipping through the papers before spreading them across the floor.

"What the hell are you doing?"

He shot Jamie a butt-the-hell-out look. "Searching for the receipt."

"What receipt?"

"The gas receipt! Maris wrote her number on it that first night and gave it to me."

Jamie came into the room, stepping over a pile of papers. "Let me help."

Dan experienced a surge of gratitude. "Shoot me if I cry, Rogers."

"You're not going to, are you? I don't think I could take it. I know we're modernized men and all that, but yeah, I'd have to put a bullet in your head for that one."

Twenty minutes later, the office looked like a cyclone had struck, but no receipt had been found. Dan smacked an open palm against the metal filing cabinet. "Fuck."

"Where's Maris?"

"In the car."

"And you're sure—"

"Yes."

"Could you have taken it home? Maybe it's stuck in a pair of pants you haven't washed yet."

Dan smacked himself in the forehead hard enough to sting. "I grabbed a bunch of crap from my desk drawer a couple of days ago. The receipt's probably in there." He shoved paperwork back into files, cramming them into the file cabinet. "I'll clean up the rest next time I'm on. Thanks for your help, Jamie. I appreciate it." He reached out and shook Jamie's hand, who hung on a fraction of a second too long.

"I've got to come with you, Stauffer. Chain of evidence."

Dan lowered his hand to his side. He nodded. "I get that. Okay. You following or driving with me?"

"I'll drive myself. It's probably best if I don't appear to be cozying up to that girlfriend of yours."

Snagging his keys and cell from his desk, Dan gave the debris covering the blotter one last look. He indicated Jamie should precede him and then locked the office door on his way out. He didn't need anyone seeing that mess.

Once outside, he found Maris napping like a cat in the sunlight shining through the car window. She awoke with a start at his approach. "Did you find it?"

Dan shook his head. "Jamie's following us back to the house. It's possibly there. I took some stuff home with me the other day. He has to come, Maris," he added at the look on her face. "It's better if he's there when the receipt is found."

Jamie pulled out of the parking lot directly behind them. He followed all the way back to the townhouse at a close distance. Dan parked in the driveway with Jamie right behind, blocking the sidewalk. He was getting the sense Jamie didn't trust him. It wasn't as if he could manufacture a receipt. If the thing was found, it would have to be legit, the real deal. Dan wouldn't argue the point, though. Better to have Jamie's eyes corroborating evidence.

Dan unlocked the front door and held it open for Jamie to enter first, then followed with Maris.

"I'm going upstairs to get out of these boots," she whispered, heading for the steps.

"No," said Jamie. "Not now." He inclined his head toward the sofa. "I'd like you to sit right there."

The color leached from Maris's cheeks, but she didn't protest. She walked with head held high to the sofa and sat, spine rigid, hands in her lap.

Jamie turned to him. "What did you bring home? Where would you have put it?"

"I..." Dan pivoted on his heel, thinking. "I don't know. I had some utensils from the kitchen shoved in the drawer so, yeah, I grabbed those and...put them in the bag my sandwich had come in." Then what? The bag had gone into his jacket pocket. When he got in the door, he'd tossed the utensils into the dishwasher. Had there been anything else in the bag?

Jamie eyed him in mute consideration, not rushing him.

"I recycle."

"What?"

"I recycle the plastic bags, take them back to the grocer's."

"Are you saying you did that with the bag we're looking for?"

"No. Not yet." He pointed generally toward the kitchen. "I have a trash pail in that closet over there where I keep all the canned goods—"

"The pantry?" Maris interjected.

Jamie shot her a look.

Dan brushed past him. He pulled out the pail from the closet in question. "It has to be one of these top few. It hasn't been that long. A white one, the kind they use at the sandwich shop at the corner. No markings on it, I think, except maybe a *thank you*." He started to reach into the container, but Jamie stepped in, grabbing the handle of the can.

"I'll take it from here. Why don't you have a seat next to Maris?"

"Damn it, Rogers, don't treat me like I'm a suspect."

"Why not? You've been holed up with the prime candidate practically since the day she showed up at the station. Maybe I should be checking into exactly how long the two of you have really known each other." Jamie turned his back on him, dumping the plastic bags onto the kitchen floor.

"You fucking—"

"Dan."

Dan spun to find Maris behind him, reaching toward his sleeve. She hooked her pointer finger into the opening at his cuff and tugged once, gently.

"Sit with me," she said.

"I don't—"

"Please." She spoke at the exact instant Jamie uttered the same word. Dan followed her to the couch and sat on the cushion's edge. His head had begun to pound. He would have gone for an aspirin but he wasn't sure Jamie would let him. From Dan's vantage point, he observed Jamie pull on a pair of nitrile gloves and begin to go through each bag, one at a time. Dan's nostrils pinched, and his headache ratcheted up a notch. Maris touched his arm, her middle and ring fingers lying parallel to the veins in his wrist. Checking his pulse, he guessed. Was she concerned about how far his blood pressure had skyrocketed?

Jamie made a neat little pile of crumpled papers pulled from the bottom of several bags. When he recovered the last of them, he returned each plastic sack to the pail and began a methodic check of every receipt, carefully flattening them out and spreading them across the tiles. He pulled an evidence baggie from his pocket.

Dan shifted forward, but he didn't stand. "Did you find it?"

"You got any stronger light in here?"

"Am I allowed to get up now?"

"Yep."

Dan switched on the floor lamp, which had five adjustable LEDs. He carried the lamp closer and pointed all five at the floor where Jamie worked.

"Some of these damn receipts fade before you even get a chance to read 'em," Jamie mumbled.

"Do you have it there?"

"Yes," Jamie said, rising. "I think I do."

Maris gasped. Dan couldn't look at her. Wanting to see for sure, he took a step nearer with his hands behind his back.

Jamie turned the slip of paper for a better view. "It's got the station name, one of those in the area. Not either of the two she told us."

"I wasn't sure which one," Maris said from the couch. "I told you that."

Jamie ignored her. "I might be able to darken this up on the copier."

Maris came to stand beside Dan, the heat of her breath moistening his sleeve as she tipped her face against his bicep. "What are you looking to find?" she asked Jamie.

Jamie slipped the receipt into the baggie and sealed it. He pulled a pen from his pocket and uncapped it with his teeth before writing on the outside. "The date, Maris. The receipt isn't enough. I need to bring up the date and time-stamp to clear you for being in the area at the time of your aunt's murder." It irked Dan that Jamie looked at him, not Maris. "And if it's not the right place, right time, you know what that means, don't you, Stauffer?"

"It will be," Dan said. *It has to be.*

Chapter 22

It has to be. The sentiment of those unspoken words bounced inside the chambers of Maris's heart over and over again as she stared at refracted headlights passing across the ceiling above the bed. Dan lay on his back beside her, shamming sleep, a distance between their bodies as precise as if it had been measured from head to toe with a ruler. He didn't choose to doubt. It was human nature to assume the worst. But guilt over his uncertainty held him apart from her. Counting the chimes on the clock in the living room below as they signaled the hour, she let it be, pretending to believe he slept at her side.

Two. Two in the morning. Why hadn't they heard something from Jamie? Was he not able to darken the receipt? Surely, he couldn't believe her guilty when she had been the one who told Dan about it. Of course, she'd expected the paper to be long gone. The fact it had been found should, under the circumstances, be reason to celebrate.

"Maris."

She jerked on the mattress despite the fact she knew Dan was awake.

"Why did you jump like that?" he said in a tone of bewildered annoyance. "I know you weren't sleeping."

"I didn't expect you to speak. I figured you'd lay there all night, silent."

He grunted, wriggling around until he lay on his right side. "If Jamie couldn't raise a date from the faded ink, he might have to contact the gas station. It'll take time. He's not going to share that information with me until he knows for sure."

"That receipt's going to show what it needs to show. I stopped and got gas on my way here the night my aunt was killed and was nowhere near Alcina Cove."

"I believe you."

Not entirely. Niggling doubt made him flinch in the darkness. She pretended not to see. "Dan, my stomach is in knots. What if Jamie can't get anything from the paper, what if no one remembers me at the gas station, what if their stupid surveillance camera was on the blink or pointed in the wrong direction, or they tape over it every day? What else am I supposed to do?"

He released a weighty breath through his nose. "I don't know. We'll get you a lawyer."

"Not we, Dan. You can't take that stance. You heard Jamie tonight. Fingers are going to start pointing in your direction."

Anger and hopelessness radiated like sweat from his pores. He said nothing, rolling onto his back once more.

"It's just damned frustrating," she whispered. Why had Alva reached out to her, possibly in her final moments, without any hint at what Maris really needed to know?

Dan settled his shoulders into his plumped pillow and then threw his arm over his eyes. "Tomorrow I'll see what I can find out."

"There shouldn't be anything to find out. In a sane world, everything ought to be fine without the need to prove I'm not lying. But I might fail at that, Dan. And I'm sorry if I do. You're going to bear the brunt because of your relationship with me."

He peeked at her from beneath his forearm. "I can deal. And you're not to worry. Understand me?"

She sent a crooked smile in his direction. "Famous last words."

He dropped his arm. "They're not last words. Not between us."

Maris turned toward him, touched his face, ran her finger across his lower lip. "I never would have pegged you for the romantic type, Dan Stauffer."

He kissed her knuckle. "And I never would have pegged you for my type at all."

You may live to regret that, if you don't die first…

"Maris, what's wrong?"

Maris attempted to blink her tears away, but resorted to using both hands to wipe her eyes instead. She sat up. "Ignore me. Just ignore me. It's been a long, rough day. Except for the ride. That was nice. I bet I didn't even thank you for it, did I?"

He struggled onto his knees beside her, snatching up the corner of the sheet to dry her cheeks. "Don't cry. Shit, Maris, please don't cry."

"It's all right. I think I need to. It's cathartic, like watching a movie you know is going to make you bawl your eyes out but you do anyway, because after you recover, you feel a little lighter."

He shook his head. "I don't do movies that make me bawl so please don't ever ask me to. I'd rather set my feet on fire."

A statement like that hinted at a shared future and made her cry harder. Finally, she climbed over him and out of the bed. In the middle of the floor she crossed her arms over the T-shirt she wore. "What if I am guilty?"

His eyes narrowed. "Could you be?"

"Don't answer a question with a question, Dan. Isn't that what you always tell me?"

"Do I?"

"I can see why you find that so annoying." Dan's short snort of humor made her smile through her drying tears. "But I'm serious," she went on. "What if something so devastating occurs tomorrow that you never want to speak to me again?"

He sat up and swung his legs over the edge of the mattress, planting his feet on the carpet. "Then I would need you to tell me now if that's a possibility. I'd want to be prepared. Is it, Maris? Is that what this is all about? Your tears? Your questions? Is there a possibility you've lied to me all along and I've believed you?"

You haven't. Not quite. "No. But the impossible happens sometimes."

He rose. "Maris, I don't understand."

"You know the sensation you get, as if a breath has passed over the fine hairs on your nape and you know something is coming…something that might scare the hell out of you? That's what I feel right now. What I've been feeling. Sometimes I'm sure I shouldn't have returned to Alcina Cove, and yet I was called here. To what end?"

His eyebrows had arched at her last two statements and then lowered into a frown. "I don't know. You tell me."

"Maybe it was for you. And there's danger in that, too."

He exploded into movement, crossing to his desk in swift strides and back to the bed again. "You're talking in circles. My head is already spinning. I can't deal with this. Not tonight. You said you sometimes take sleeping pills. Would you consider taking one now?"

Maris bit her lip and nodded.

"Where are they?"

"Right here in my bag. I'll get one."

"And I'll get you a cup of water."

By the time Dan returned, Maris was back in bed, tucked up against the headboard. She took a pill with water and handed the glass back to him. "Thank you. I'm not meaning to upset you."

"You're actually scaring me, and I don't scare easily."

She slipped two of her fingers into the curve of his hand. "Do you… could we make love, do you think?"

He lowered himself to the bed, expression pained. "I never thought I'd hear myself say this, but I'm not sure I can."

Maris studied his expression, remembering she had called him beautiful. She wanted to smooth away the line between his brows. "Stretch out alongside me then. We both need some sleep."

He did, and she slid down onto the mattress, turning until she had maneuvered herself into a spooning position against him. His breath moved the hair across her crown. "I can't sleep. I don't know what I want. To be close to you—"

"Because if feels like the last time."

"Don't say that." He pressed his lips against the side of her neck. "Why would you say that?"

"Because that's what it feels like to me." She reached back and cupped his face. He turned his mouth into her palm. Yes, the last time, because tomorrow threatened to alter everything in some way beyond her imagining. She couldn't tell him that. She'd frightened him enough already, Dan Stauffer, the man who did not scare easily. Instead, she rolled in his embrace to face him and slid her hand along his belly down into his boxers. He groaned, but not in protest. "I'm ready now," she whispered, "if you're willing."

He said nothing, tossing her onto her back and rising above her. He hiked up her shirt past her belly and slid fingers down between her legs and along flesh slick with arousal. Moaning, she rose to meet him. He leaned his head hard against her collar bone before seeking out her straining nipple, soaking fabric with the ministrations of teeth and tongue while his fingers explored her below. His engorged penis vibrated in the hand she closed around it. Fire surged through her blood. He still had not spoken, but she wanted nothing of words from him. She pushed his hands away and wrapped her legs around his waist, curling her fingers into the taut curve of his buttocks as he slid inside of her.

"Don't slow down," she said. "Tonight is not a night for that."

Arms across his back, she lifted herself to meet him again and again in heated demand, forcing him with selfish disregard to accompany her down into the place where all things are forgotten.

* * * *

Dan sat in his car for nearly ten minutes, swinging the keys in the ignition with his pointer finger. Detectives didn't work Sundays unless some case required it, but there was Jamie's car in its space near the rear entrance of the station. The coffee Dan had grabbed on the way in began to burn in his stomach. He reached into the glove box and removed an open pack of antacids. He popped two into his mouth. He hadn't finished chewing when the back door opened. Jamie stepped out and strode over to the car.

"Good. You're here." He yanked open the door. "Come inside."

Dan closed the window, stripped the key from the ignition, and followed Jamie into the station.

"My office, if you don't mind," Jamie said, without waiting. Dan dogged the junior detective down the hallway. Inside Jamie's office, Dan took a seat, directed to it by a silent nod. Two folders lay on Jamie's blotter. To the right, Alva Mabry's photo albums appeared not to have been moved since Dan rifled through them. He thought about the pictures he'd taken from the pages and shown to Maris. He thought about the one he hadn't. By the look on Jamie's face, Dan had lost the opportunity to do so anytime soon.

Because if feels like the last time.

"If you had something good to tell me, you would have by now, unless you're just that much of a sadistic bastard."

Jamie handed him the folders. "I'm sorry, Dan. I'm taking these to the DA tomorrow. I shouldn't be letting you know because, damn it, if it was me, tangled up like you are, I'd be warning her as soon as I walked out that door. But you won't. You're a good cop. And even if you weren't, you know I'd arrest you, and what could you do for her then?"

"Fuck, Jamie, whatever this is—"

"Open the folders. Top one first."

Dan complied, turning back the manila cover. He stared at the enlarged copy of the gas receipt inside. Every square inch of him went numb except his stomach. Acid burned like fire.

"Look at the date, Stauffer. An entire day before Alva's murder. She lied. If your girlfriend can't account for the time between with a rock-solid alibi, she's done. And I don't think she can. Do you?"

Dan closed his eyes. *What if I am guilty?*

"Oh God," he whispered.

"I hate to say this, buddy, but I think she played you good."

Dan bowed his head, shaking it from side to side. "She's not like that."

"Seriously? How well could you possibly know her in two weeks' time?"

"Better than you think, Jamie."

Jamie made a noise in his throat. "Open the other folder."

"I don't—"

"Open it."

Dan set the first aside. He tapped the file lying across his knee. "What's in it?"

"Open the fucking thing."

Every fiber of Dan's soul screamed in protest. He couldn't breathe, not properly, as if a hand had clamped down on his windpipe. The kernel of doubt he'd been harboring from the beginning started to grow, thrashing in his brain with painful intensity. He didn't want it to. God, he didn't. He wanted to go on believing, trusting, hoping. He snapped open the folder in defiance, while the doubting part of him shouted in vindication, *Look at it, fool. You always knew...*

Papers fluttered to the floor. Jamie reached for them, picked them up, and stuffed them into Dan's hands, making sure Dan could read the letterhead. Dan recognized the hospital name, a well-known institution with a decent reputation for helping people in crisis, for treating those with mental illnesses, who had suffered psychotic breaks and similar life-altering occurrences.

"Makes for interesting reading," Jamie said.

"Where did you get this? There are procedural—"

"Her mother. Maris's mother. She thought she might help her daughter somehow."

The light in Dan's world fragmented and fell away, leaving only darkness.

* * * *

Naturally, Jamie wouldn't let him drive home without following close behind. Jamie sent a car ahead, as well, a marked unit to stand by outside. Although formal charges weren't being levied until after Jamie spoke with a district attorney, he wanted to search the place from top to bottom in an effort to locate more evidence. Not implicating Dan, Jamie had assured him, but on the presumption Maris felt comfortable enough at his home that she might have stashed something there. Dan's stomach turned and speared down into his guts.

Nothing would be found because she wasn't guilty. And even if she was guilty, she wasn't stupid.

He hated himself for thinking that way, for the offhand manner in which he switched from innocence to guilt, as if it didn't matter, as if it might possibly be anything but the former. His fingers tightened around the wheel. At the stop sign, he narrowed his eyes, concentrating hard in warning. Maybe she would receive the message and take whatever steps to get herself away in time.

Like a guilty person. She couldn't do that. She had to stay put and see this whole thing through. And what the hell was he thinking anyway?

She couldn't sense his thoughts, she couldn't see the future, clairvoyance didn't exist, and neither did telepathy. He'd glanced through the doctor's notes, the clinical wording of the report. Maris had been admitted at sixteen following a breakdown of sorts and hadn't left the hospital for nearly a year, at which time she'd been clear about one thing. Her supposed gift wasn't real but only a delusion that had driven her into depression. She'd blamed her aunt for all of it. Familial grudges were the most difficult to overcome and could linger beneath the surface for a lifetime.

"Maris," he whispered, unable to wrap himself around what he'd learned. On the surface, he recognized everything presented to him had been done so in such a light as to make her seem other than who she was. But the cop in him—well, the cop in him was confused as all fucking get-out.

With the exception of her behavior last night, the woman he'd fallen for was bright and funny and loving and—yes, *sane*. Granted, he'd questioned that at first until he had witnessed proof for himself of her abilities and had shared that experience with her at the stone circle. Hell, he'd had his own before they'd ever met. Did that mean he was broken, too?

Dan smacked the steering wheel with his open palm, the impact stinging rounded flesh. "Fucking bullshit. Goddamn it all to hell." He pulled into his driveway, got out of the car, and waited dutifully by the closed door until Jamie had exited his.

"Here's your phone back."

Dan slipped the cell into his pocket. "That was a suck-ass thing to do."

"You would have called her. You wouldn't have been able to help yourself."

Dan said nothing. Jamie was right. At the front door, he inserted the key and pushed the door wide. As soon as he stepped over the threshold, he understood one thing.

Maris was gone.

Chapter 23

Maris squeezed her eyes shut. Closed or open, it was the same. The darkness had come to claim her again, to drag her down into suffering and despair. Lifting her lids, she stared hard, trying to make out outlines, the smallest trace of gray in the blackness, but there was nothing. With a whimper that shamed her, echoing in her head and all around, she rolled onto her side and pulled her knees up to her chest, wrapping her arms around her legs. The floor drummed beneath her body with a constant, pounding rhythm.

Aunt Alva, come take me. Please. I never belonged in this world. I never will.

* * * *

"Are you telling me you didn't notice her car wasn't at the curb?"

"Did you?" Dan shot back. But he had noticed. In his subconscious, Dan had to have been aware of the vehicle's absence. Otherwise, the hollowness he had experienced upon opening the door would have been strange to him. Instead, he had simply known the truth about the state of things inside.

"If I find out you had anything to do with—"

"Don't even go there. Just do your job."

Jamie arched away as if he'd been backhanded. "I am doing my job. Too bad you weren't doing yours."

Dan turned his back on him, going to the kitchen to grab a glass of water. He stopped in front of the refrigerator, fingers around the handle, and leaned his forehead against chilled steel. His insides felt as if they were being whipped by a blender at high speed.

"This her laptop?"

Dan jerked around, looking where Jamie pointed. "Yes."

"Odd that she left that behind."

Yes, it was. Dan didn't understand why she'd bothered to bring it with her. Occasionally, he saw her working on it, but not often. She always made sure she knew where it was, though. Yet she'd taken her bag, all her clothes, her purse, her sleeping pills, the toothbrush she'd set beside his own in the bathroom holder.

"We're confiscating it. Green, snag that will you?"

Dan took a step forward. "She wouldn't leave that here. I know she wouldn't."

"Are you implying she didn't walk out of here voluntarily?" Jamie signaled to Jonathan Green to bag the laptop. "You might want to sit down, Stauffer. You're not looking too good."

"I'm fine."

But he wasn't. The implication here was that she'd run, exactly as he'd tried to will her to do. If so, he hoped she'd gotten far away, but if she really hadn't left until he threw the thought at her, she would have been caught before she reached the corner of the next block. So she left earlier with every intention of slipping the knot before it tightened. A sign of guilt if there ever was one.

Where would she go? He pulled the phone out of his pocket and dialed Maris's cell. The call went straight to voice mail. Next, he tried Felicia, using the number Maris had provided him the day he'd dropped her off.

"Felicia, it's Dan. Dan Stauffer. Is Maris there?" From across the room, Jamie watched him in open speculation.

"I haven't seen her since the other day. Is she not at your house? I thought she wasn't supposed to drive yet."

"She's not." Dan closed his eyes. "Would you have her give me a call if you see her?"

"Sure. And Dan?"

"Yes?"

"Don't close your heart. Now is not the time."

"What do you mean by that?"

"I can tell you're worried, and I hope there's no reason to be. Don't shut down. I know you don't care much for heartache, but you can't always avoid it."

"Thanks." He hung up without saying goodbye.

"Who was that?" Jamie asked.

"Felicia Woodward. Says she hasn't seen her since the other day. If I had Maris's mother's number—"

"I already called it. Got the woman. She hasn't seen or heard from Maris."

Dan nodded. He went back for the water he'd forgotten, drank a full glass down, and then set the tumbler into the sink. Felicia was right about the heartache. He didn't like it and had spent a long time avoiding one. The ache in his heart now, though, wasn't as easily defined as what he'd gone through when he and his ex-wife were in the death throes of their marriage. Perhaps if he could make up his mind that Maris had betrayed him, the pain would be confined into a familiar cage. But somehow, he knew she had not. She hadn't left him. She'd left the situation...or was he deceiving himself again? Jamie would certainly say he was. He'd tell Dan he was an idiot, a sucker, a fool. He'd tell him Maris's flight was proof of her guilt. He'd tell him all the things Dan would have advised another man in his place.

Dan turned on his heel. "I'm going outside."

"Where?"

"I'm going to sit on the step out front until you're done. Okay?"

Jamie waved him off. Dan strode past and out the front door, which no one had bothered to close. He lowered himself onto the porch's concrete edge and stretched his legs out before him. Across the street, down the block, the neighbors were milling about, watching. He ignored them, staring at the laces on his boots. The right one had come untied.

Maris, where are you? Did she need him? Need his help? Was she frightened? Was she thinking, as Jamie suggested, that she'd finished with him, using him while necessary and washing her hands of him? Had she killed her aunt? Was she guilty of cold-blooded murder for the sake of three million dollars? He knew a lot of people who might be tempted, but he didn't think her capable, especially now that he knew her. But how well did he know her? She'd never mentioned her time in the psychiatric hospital. Maybe she would have one day, but it seemed an important piece of information to gloss over when asked about her past, even at this early stage.

"Fuck."

He didn't say the word loudly, but somehow it carried across the street. The woman who lived there covered her child's ears in a dramatic display, like some sitcom out of the fifties. Dan lifted his chin in her direction. "Maybe if you weren't so nosy, you wouldn't be standing close enough with your kid to have heard that."

She huffed away, but only far enough to talk about him in a stage whisper with another neighbor.

"Don't piss off the neighbors. You may need them to alibi you," Jamie said from the doorway. He came forward and sat next to him on the step. "What's this?"

Dan glanced aside at what Jamie held. He stiffened. *Don't touch that card again.* Hadn't that been Maris's instruction to him? He should have returned it that first night. Shit.

He released a short breath. "I took it from the scene when I responded to the call from Green and Whitley. To be honest, I didn't mean to, but I located it in my pocket when I was driving to the station and realized I'd made a serious error."

Jamie turned the Priestess card back and forth in the evidence bag. "I think you're lying to cover for Maris."

Dan threw up his hands and rose. "Think what you want. I'm done with explanations. But when you process that card, I can lay odds you won't find her prints on it. But you'll find mine, and plenty of them."

Jamie shrugged. "We'll see. Where are you going now?"

"To use the bathroom. Am I allowed to do that yet?"

"Be my guest."

He waited until Dan was on the threshold before speaking again. "Do you think she left with her accomplice?"

Dan loosened the hands he'd clenched against his thighs. "The intruder was not with her, he was after her. Instinct, no more, but that's what I think."

"Too much coincidence, Stauffer. That guy in your house was here because of her. She moved way too quickly with you. She was using you. He's the real man in her life. You know it. We all know it."

"Who, exactly, is 'all'?" When Jamie didn't answer, Dan went on. "You're missing a big piece to this puzzle. We both are." Dan stalked away and up the stairs into his bathroom. He locked the door and sat on the shut toilet lid, lowering his head into his hands.

* * * *

Maris had stopped shivering. Not a good sign. She needed to move, force circulation of blood to her limbs. She didn't want to die. Not really. She hadn't all those years ago, either. The incident that had landed her in the psych ward had been more a matter of opportunity, rather than deliberate intent. She wouldn't have harmed herself, she really wouldn't have, but it hadn't looked that way to her parents when they found her. Back then, she had reached the point of not caring. About anything. But she cared now.

With the idea of running in place to get her heart pumping, Maris released her cramped limbs, rolled over, and rose. Her head struck the ceiling before she'd stretched her legs out straight. Skull ringing with the impact, Maris stood with her back arched, running her hands over the wet stone above her. She didn't know where she was, no memory of how she'd gotten here. She remembered sitting in someone's living room reading a magazine that wasn't hers. And then her head hurt. Yes, the same as it was now. There was a reason for the pain in her head, the confusion, but the answer wouldn't formulate in her mind, not enough for her to hold onto it.

She started shuffling across an uneven floor, hands extended before her, looking for...for what? A way out, she supposed. Had she truly come here to die? What an extraordinary choice.

Attempts at remembering anything before the article in the magazine were futile. But the story had been about...prison life. Yes, that was it. The piece had frightened her. Why? Sudden nausea caused her to drop painfully to her knees. She clutched her stomach, fighting the urge to vomit. Terminology entered her mind, a male voice discussing dissociative occurrences, fugue states. The words echoed from a distance of time rather than physical location. Childhood?

She lost her battle against the urge to disgorge the contents of her stomach. Wiping her hand across her mouth, she skirted the bile on the floor and continued her search. If she wanted to live, she had to get out. A simple plan, but impossible, because when she reached the walls and followed them around, she could locate no opening. She sat on the uneven stone, pulling her knees up to her chin. She'd begun shivering again, could feel the cold. For the time being, she'd stopped the process of death. But perhaps she didn't want to, since her only other option in a place from which she could not escape was inexorable starvation. She'd heard that wasn't a pleasant way to go at all.

Chapter 24

Help her.

Dan bolted upright. He stared wide-eyed around the darkened room. After a moment, he scrambled off the bed and ran to the bedroom door, yanking it open. "Hello?" He slammed the door shut and strode to the window, leaning against his once organized desk, strewn now with the contents. No one had bothered to put anything back. Neither had he.

He pushed a hand through his hair, rubbed his neck, dragged his fingers down his shirt. He'd fallen asleep without changing out of his clothes. He hadn't expected to sleep at all.

Spreading the slats of the blinds, Dan peered down to the street below. An unmarked unit was hunkered against the curb opposite his townhouse waiting for Maris's return for reasons contradictory to his own. Not that anyone expected her to come back, but there was always a chance. Maybe it was parked there to see if he ran, too. Dan shrugged in dismissal and turned away. Abruptly, he spun back. The translucent silhouette had appeared beneath the streetlight. Was it Alva Mabry…or this crone Maris spoke of?

"Who are you? What the hell do you want from me?"

Help her.

This time the words were so loud in his head, he staggered back from them. Not a dream, then. Holy Mother, not a dream.

"I don't know how! I don't know where she is."

The apparition faded, drifting away like mist in the wind. At the same time, Dan's cell rang. Dan scrambled in search of it, slapping across the various surfaces in the room. Locating the phone wedged beneath his crumpled pillow, he pulled it out and answered. "Stauffer."

"Dan, it's me," said Jamie. "I know it's late, but I need you at the station. Now."

* * * *

Bleary-eyed, Dan made his way down the corridor to Jamie's office. He hadn't bothered with anything but a shot of mouthwash to rinse his mouth before heading outside and climbing into his car. The officer in the unmarked unit—Wainwright, Dan thought—must have received word of his imminent departure because he hadn't so much as turned his head.

Outside Jamie's office, Dan rapped a knuckle against the open door. The overheads were off. Jamie sat in a puddle of light from the desk lamp, papers spread across his desk. Dan didn't wait for an invitation. He was sick of being treated like a guest in his own house. He took the chair and pulled it closer before sitting in it. "What's going on?"

Recalled from someplace in his head, Jamie looked up, almost as if he hadn't realized Dan was there. "You were right."

"About what?"

"The Tarot card. Maris's prints weren't on it. Just yours and Mabry's and one other."

Dan waited.

"A thumbprint. I ran it through AFIS. Got a hit fairly quickly."

"And?"

"I'll get to that in a minute."

Dan lurched forward. "Shit, don't do that. Just—"

"I looked through Maris's computer myself. Her password was 'password.' One of those. Too trusting."

Yeah, Dan thought, *most definitely.*

"I didn't find anything obvious in her internet history, like a query about poisons. She writes stories. Short stories. Quite the gift with words. Tales her dad told her, and a lot of others I think are based on her experiences. Jumps back and forth between past and present but skilled enough to pull it off. She mentions a diary in one of them. Did she keep a diary, Dan?"

Dan thought a moment. "I have no idea."

"It doesn't matter. She hadn't written about the murder on the computer. Not that I thought she would, but you never know. Something as intimate as a physical diary, however…"

Dan remained silent.

"Anyway, I'm going to remind you now that she said she had no other living blood relatives. But there's a cousin who's been in jail nearly the entirety of her life."

Dan reached into his shirt pocket, pulling out three pictures. "I thought there must be someone else, but since I wasn't allowed to assist I was having difficulty checking. I took these from the albums last time I was in. Maris's uncles have both died. As has Maris's father. Even though

I was off the case, I did some online research and found obits. Maris told me she thought these images all included her father, but that's not accurate, is it?" He shoved the pictures across the desk to Jamie who picked them up, holding the photographs closer to the bulb.

"What makes you think this isn't Maris's father?"

Dan pointed. "Look at the dress Alva is wearing. It's the same as in this other photo with all three of the Granger boys. They seem to have been taken the same day, if you check the background details. The child standing alone with Alva in the first two I handed you is not one of them, but a younger child. I don't believe Maris knew about another boy, if we're right and there really was one."

"If *we* are right? We weren't working together. You were off in some strange fantasy world." Jamie lowered the pictures to the desk. "But there was another. Robert Mabry."

Dan frowned. "Mabry?"

"Yeah, Alva's son. Her illegitimate son. She ended up sending him away to be raised elsewhere. Think of the timeframe. She had him at the end of the fifties without benefit of marriage, and apparently he was a handful. Troubled and in trouble, all the time. His name was never changed, though. He went into prison thirty years ago for manslaughter and served his time. He was released three months ago."

Crossing his arms, Dan sat back. "How'd you find all of that out?"

"Had a talk with a fellow at the FBI."

"So that's his thumbprint on the Priestess card."

"Yep."

"Anything else?"

"There were traces of digoxin on the card."

"Digitalis? The drug used for treatment of heart disorders?"

"Exactly. It can be absorbed through the skin, causing various types of reactions. Alva Mabry, however, was taking the drug for congestive heart failure. She really wasn't doing well at the time she died."

"So, are you saying Alva died of natural causes?" Dan doubted it. After everything that had happened, it couldn't be a case of error on Rankin's part.

Jamie shuffled the photographs into a pile and set them on the desk. "I'm not. It was an overdose of the drug that killed her. Probably over the course of several days. That's what Rankin thinks anyway. Administered topically and absorbed through the raw skin on the old woman's fingertips. Probably applied to the cards themselves. Rankin's running some tests on the others. It wasn't injected. That would have been quick. Rankin doesn't know what that hole was about. The point is, the woman was murdered, and now we know how."

Dan suppressed a sigh of relief he had no desire for Jamie to hear. "Maris is cleared, then?"

"No. This man was a relative of hers. It's conceivable they could have been working together. There's the little issue of her coming to town a day earlier than she claimed. I need to talk to her. Where is she?"

"I haven't any idea. You know I don't. And I need to find her as badly as you do. I'm afraid—" He couldn't tell Jamie about the apparition imploring Dan to help Maris. Despite Jamie's own experience with Maris—an experience he would likely dismiss—he would never believe Dan about something like that. "Maris had this sense of impending danger, of doom. She thought I was the one in peril, but she was wrong about that."

"Stauffer, you're pitiful."

Dan persisted. "Any sign of her car?"

"None."

"I'm going to look for it on my own." Dan rose.

Jamie did, too, closing his hand around Dan's arm. "Don't. We're searching. I've put an all-points bulletin out. You need to stay clear."

Dan shoved Jamie's hand from his arm, reaching past him to the desktop. "You dropped the ball by not putting the sketch of the guy I suspected was the hit and run driver in the papers. This is him. Maris's cousin?" He yanked an enlarged mug shot from the paperwork on Jamie's desk and shook it in Jamie's face. "Age him, and you'll find the guy who was in the hospital. That's why he looked familiar to me. The family resemblance. And to her, too, though she couldn't place the reason." Or had she known him all along, her upset merely the result of him showing up at the hospital and accosting her in the elevator? Dan angrily dismissed the notion. "If he was the driver who tried to run her down, whether they were working together or not, his intention now is to eliminate her. We have to get to her before he does."

"And if the hit and run was a random occurrence, and she left with Robert Mabry?"

Dan waved an arm in rejection. "What was it you kept saying about too much coincidence? This is the missing piece of the puzzle, Jamie. It has to be."

Heart racing, Dan hurried from Jamie's office and back out to his car. Jamie followed, refusing to be left behind, specifically, because he didn't trust Dan's motivations. He sat in the passenger seat, mouth set in a grim line. Dan was grateful for the man's company. Dawn was a long way off, and the dark hours of night could toy with a man's psyche, especially when already troubled. Even though Jamie remained silent, his solid, angry presence was a comfort.

Alcina Cove Nature Preserve had been a bust. Not a single car in the lot, not even the usual late-night parkers. Dan had continued up and down the roads, knowing his efforts were a waste of gas. As Jamie had pointed out before lapsing into silence, Maris could have a damned good head start on her way to Canada.

"She's not running. Not from me. Not even from you and your accusations. She's innocent, Jamie. She's hiding. Or we're too late, and he got to her already."

"She took everything with her. There was no sign of force. Stauffer, you have to face up to reality. You're wasting your time."

"Suppose she's had another mental breakdown?" He didn't like to think that, but the possibility existed, given the stress and her recent injury. "She could be somewhere contemplating the little she might have left of life before she ends it."

"And you want to save her. How the hell could the cool, calm, collected guy I've known for all these years fall in love with a whacko in a matter of days?"

"Don't call her that."

"Sorry."

"And I have fallen in love with her. I make no apologies for that."

Dan continued up the winding road toward the stretch where he'd stopped to show Maris the outstanding view. If her mental state was impaired, she might choose such a spot. The overlook was empty. Dan pulled the car to the side and got out, checking for signs a vehicle had recently been there or gone over the edge. It wasn't a steep drop, but enough. His flashlight cut a swath through the darkness. Soon the light was joined by another. Jamie stood beside him, raising the electric torch above his head and aiming downward for a better angle.

"I get it, Dan. I really do. I'm just doing my job."

"I know." Dan lowered the flashlight to his side, staring toward the ocean flickering in starlight and the constant, rotating beam of the lighthouse, its tall, solid shadow black against the navy sky. "Shit."

"What?"

"I know where she is."

Chapter 25

Maris's stress-induced memory loss had cleared. She sat with her back against the wall, her body jolting forward with every pounding beat of her heart. In the room above, two men argued, voices muffled by the thickness of the iron-bound wood of the trapdoor in the middle of the ceiling. It had taken her some time to locate the door in the dark. Now that she had, she avoided it, stayed in the corners, because she didn't want finding her to be easy. Not this time.

She'd realized in the past—hours, minutes, days?—that she was in the lighthouse. An underground storage cellar, most likely. The beating of the surf against the rocky base in a constant growl beneath her was discernible through the thickness of the stone structure.

She'd fallen a few minutes earlier, trying to ease her position. The uneven stones of the floor, slick with damp, were her undoing. She was wet and cold, disoriented, and now bleeding from a cut on her lip. Through flaring nostrils, the iron scent of blood was strong.

Out of the blackness, a finger traced her ear, touching the feather hanging against her chin. She froze. She'd felt no one come near. The space wasn't large. She knew she was alone.

"Who is that?"

Be strong, child. He is coming. Hold on.

"Aunt Alva? I don't want him to. He'll be killed. At least one of the men up there has a gun. Dan won't know. He won't be prepared."

Maris, I'm so sorry...

What the hell did that mean? "You can't let him come here. Stop him. Please, please stop him."

I am calling him here. It's all I can do.

"No. No!"

The trapdoor lifted. A beam of light shot across the floor but didn't reach her. "Who the fuck are you talking to?"

"Myself." Quickly, she scuttled as noiselessly as possible to a new position before the light found her. As of yet, neither man appeared willing to join her in the cellar. Better to keep it that way.

"Of course you are." The trapdoor slammed shut, plunging her back into darkness.

"Aunt Alva?" she whispered. She received no response.

On hands and knees, Maris made her way once more around the perimeter of the storeroom in search of a weapon. A useless task that kept her mind busy, made her believe she was doing something to save herself. But she would never be able to defend herself against both men. She likely couldn't hold off one.

When the man from the hospital had shown up at Dan's door, she'd been shocked and wary, but willing to listen to him. After all, if he felt as guilty as Dan had hinted, she would accept his apology and exonerate him because she knew very well what guilt could do when it took control. But he hadn't wanted to apologize. And he hadn't only been at the hospital. He freely admitted within minutes that he had been the man in the house who had attacked Dan and fled, assuring her how easily he could have killed him instead. At gunpoint, he'd forced her to gather her things and accompany him out to her car when he made her drive. The other man followed in a car behind them. When they reached the lighthouse, she got her first good look at him. Covered in tattoos, he'd be hard to forget. He was the same man who had come to the door of her room at the motel.

She had learned from eavesdropping on their loud conversation above that the man at Dan's door was the one who had run her down. However, riddled with guilt over the incident he was not. The tattooed man's job had been to watch Maris. From their loud exchange, she understood he'd never been meant to approach her. The first man was angry about the fact he'd knocked on her door. Suddenly hearing Alva's muffled name, Maris gasped and strained to hear more.

"Ouch." A sharp point had jabbed her palm. She felt around until she located what appeared by shape to be an ancient nail, about four inches in length. She placed it in her pocket and continued listening. Without warning, the overhead door opened again. Maris scurried back against the wall.

"I said no!" The first man.

"What does it matter?" The second, bearing the abundance of tattoos. "You're going to kill her anyway. I might as well get a little something out of her beforehand."

Celia Ashley

Maris reached into her pocket and removed the nail, wrapping her fist around it, point sticking out the side by her pinkie for force.

"You fucking idiot. It needs to appear to be a suicide."

Maris sucked in a breath. What the hell?

"Rape will be evident on the body."

A leg swung into the opening, dangling down. The man's body shadowed the room where Maris crouched, ready to fight with all she had in her. "Depends on how long she's in the ocean, doesn't it?"

"I need her to be identifiable."

Suddenly, the man leaned forward, waving a flashlight around, the tattooed tiger on his neck momentarily highlighted until the beam came down and pinned her against the wall. "You hear?" he said. "He needs you to be identifiable. I'm not so sure I care about that."

So saying, he dropped down into the cellar with her.

There was no preamble, no cat and mouse kind of game. He wanted it over, she supposed, before the man upstairs could stop him, and so he lunged at her without any hesitation. His mistake. She plunged the nail into the side of his neck as soon as his body came within striking distance. He jerked upright, struck his head on the ceiling, and collapsed back down, clawing at the rusted iron spike skewering his throat. Not deep enough. Still trying to pull it out, he rose up onto his knees.

"You fucking cu—"

An explosion rent the air, deafening her as she fell backward. The tattooed man sprawled across the stones, clearly dead.

"I told him not to do it," said the man above.

Maris raised her gaze to the man's face outlined grotesquely in the opening by the rolling flashlight of the dead one. She uncovered her ears. "Why did you do that?"

"Would you rather I hadn't? I finished the job you started. Birds of a feather we are, wouldn't you say?"

She rose onto her knees, moving away from the body. "Who are you?"

"Your own flesh and blood, my dear."

Maris stopped. Her stomach coiled. "I'm sorry…what?"

The gun he'd recently used reappeared. "Time for you to climb out of there. Up you go. Any other weapons you might have picked up from the debris down there kindly re-deposit on the floor."

He spoke as if they were discussing a grocery list. Maris made her way to the opening, bowed awkwardly as she crossed the floor. If she stayed down here, she didn't stand a chance. Might not have one above, either, but at least she could pretend. "I don't have anything else." She yanked the pockets of her pajamas inside out as she stood below the man. He rose up, waving the gun in a slow arc to the right.

"Can you pull yourself out? You look strong enough."

She managed, assisted by a fistful of her shirt in his hand, accompanied by a small tearing sound as he tossed her onto the floor above. She feigned a need to catch her breath as she looked around, attempting to assess the situation.

"I couldn't let him do that to you, you know."

"Yes, I know," she said from her position on the floorboards. "It would have been inconvenient to your plan to make my death look like a suicide." He laughed, startling her, the sound loud and familiar. She rolled onto her back, staring up at him. "You sound like...my father?"

"Not your father. Not exactly. Your aunt, my freakish mother. Alva Mabry."

Oh God...

Maris dug in her heels, pushing backward across the floor to increase the distance between them. "Alva didn't have any children. She never married."

The man sat down on a decrepit chair. It appeared they were in the light keeper's living quarters, long abandoned and falling to ruin. "Wrong. And right. Out of wedlock, I believe is the expression." He leaned forward. "You and she weren't the only gifted ones in recent generations. I have it, too. The Sight or whatever people are calling it nowadays. It frightened her because I'm male, or perhaps only made her jealous. Whatever the reason, she couldn't stand to have me around. Got rid of me. While you, she nurtured like a little pet bunny, so soft and sweet and malleable."

Maris managed to gain her feet. He followed her movements with the muzzle of the handgun.

"She used to write me letters. Told me about you. Like it wasn't killing me, bit by bit, receiving letters from my mother while in prison and hearing nothing but enthusiasm over a child who wasn't hers. She'd been oh-so-shocked when I chose to lead the life I did. What the fuck did she think would happen to her little boy? Rubbing you in did nothing to soothe my wounds, believe me." He pulled a battered book from beneath his thigh and waved it at her. "And it wasn't like you weren't damaged goods. Just like me."

Maris stared at her diary in his hand. "You've read it? How much of it?"

"All of it. I took it that night I was in your boyfriend's house."

"But it was in my luggage."

"It was indeed."

"Which was in the room with me."

"Yes."

Maris shuddered at the knowledge this man had been in the guest room with her while she slept. How had she not known, not sensed him there?

"I found the passages from your time in the nuthouse the most interesting. You blamed my mother just as much as I did. There's a lot of time afterward where you didn't write at all. They tell you to do that, those doctors? To keep track of your thoughts, learn to recognize your own instability before it got the better of you? Me, too. It doesn't work, does it? Alva fucked us both up, didn't she?"

Unable to respond, Maris merely shook her head.

"I suppose you think I should take pity on you because of that. But I lost the capacity for sympathy a long time ago."

"Is that…is that why you killed her? Because she turned her back on you? It wasn't the money?"

His head jerked up from a momentary contemplation of the diary. She could see the family resemblance now. No wonder he had unnerved her in the hospital. "What money?"

"In Alva's Will. She left the entirety of her three million dollar estate to be divided between direct descendants of the sisters' bloodline. You and I are it. We're all that's left."

The wheels turned in obvious cogitation behind his eyes. Her father's eyes. Her eyes. Alva's eyes. Except the color. Where theirs were or had been gray as smoke, his were nearly black.

He laughed again, with quick, breathless intensity. "God, why the hell didn't I see that?"

"Would it have made a difference, knowing she meant to take care of you in the end?"

He rocked a little from side to side, his lower lip pushed out. "Nope, probably not."

Maris's gaze darted to the open door behind him and back to his face. "You…you were in her house, weren't you? You laid the cards into a new position on the table. Was there a message in the layout?"

"For who? Alva? She doesn't give a shit anymore. No, I was just fucking with the cops."

"And now? Why do you want me?"

He smiled. "Because it's your turn."

Maris backed against the wall. "Why? You can't mean to kill me because you were resentful as a fully grown man of a little girl who had no idea who you were or that you'd been so hurt."

He shook his head. "Uh-uh. That's not why. I heard her call you in her dying moments. Not out loud. You know the type of calling I mean. And I knew—*knew*, understand?—that you were coming. I have no desire to go back to prison. So I kept an eye on you. That guy downstairs? He helped me a bit. We knew each other in prison. I watched the mistakes you made and tried to figure out a way to lay the blame on you. The cops did that for me. All I had to do was sit back and let it happen. Unfortunately, you saw me fishing on the jetty. I wasn't certain you hadn't recognized something in me—a similarity to family, a kindred gift, something—so I decided not take any chances. Hitting you with my car should have done the job, but I didn't have enough speed."

Maris's chilled body turned colder. She shivered.

"Don't be afraid. It won't take long. You see, wracked with guilt over your aunt's murder, you'll decide to end it all. The three million dollars really makes this an easier decision all around."

"How do you know the police won't suspect you, too? They were looking for family members. If you make an appearance to claim the inheritance when I'm gone, they'll start checking into your whereabouts. You know they will. You said you've been in prison. That's because you got caught. People aren't stupid. Well, I suppose some are."

He rose, quivering with a barely contained wrath, the gun swerving back and forth in a grip that looked too tight for safety. "Don't you say that. Don't you dare say something like that about me."

"What makes you think I'm talking about you?" Maris demanded.

"I don't think. I know. You forgot what I told you already? I'm reading you the way you read that boyfriend of yours. Dan, is it? And a cop, too. Lovely."

Maris swore, lunging past him for the door at his back. He grabbed her arm and yanked her around, the gun against her ribs. "We're going outside. Before it's full light. I don't want you floating around in the tide too long or battered up too badly against those rocks, but I don't want anyone to see me with you either. Don't need witnesses."

With the gun in her side, Maris had no choice but to comply and allowed him to pull her outside to the tall dark stone structure of the lighthouse. He yanked her toward the parapet where she and Dan had eaten their chocolate feast.

"How sweet," he murmured.

"Shut up."

"You haven't even asked me my name."

"Maybe I don't care."

Gunmetal ground into her flesh down to bone. She winced and bit back a yelp of pain.

"It's Robert," he said. "Your dad, his brothers, none of them ever mentioned cousin Bobby to you?"

Maris shook her head. "I'm sorry that they didn't. I'm sorry for the life you had. I—"

"Here we are. Now isn't this perfect?" He spun her around and pushed her forward. Her knees cracked against the stone wall.

"How could you kill your mother?" Maris demanded, clutching the stone for support.

"With poison."

"That's not what I meant."

He went on as if he hadn't heard. "I was with her for a few days. I could tell she wasn't exactly happy to see me, but she didn't kick me out. I made sure she had contact with the same medication I found out she was taking for her heart, increasing it each day in the hope she would just keel over and I could watch when she did, not helping her at all, like she never helped me. She hung on too long, though. I got impatient and put a needle full of air into her neck."

Oh, God. Maris felt the depth of his anger, his years of resentment and pain, his bewilderment and longing. Her stomach twisted. Sorrow filled her. For Alva. For this damaged man who was her son.

He pushed her again. "Climb the fu—"

At the pause in his command, Maris glanced behind and found him staring toward the ocean. She followed his gaze. A golden line burned the length of the horizon, the sky above glowing in gradients of bottle-green to a blue as deep as midnight. Below, the sea reflected the colors beneath an overlay of shimmering silver.

"For thirty years, I've missed this. Even in the time I've been back, I haven't gone out at sunrise. I've been afraid the sight of it would break my heart."

The wistfulness of his voice, the pain of the child he once had been, broke her own heart. Moisture rolled down her cheeks, chilling flesh in the cool morning air.

"Don't weep for me, Maris Granger. I'm a very bad man."

"Robert, please…"

"I can shoot you in places that will prolong your agony and make you beg to go. Do yourself a favor and jump. Now. The water's cold. It won't take long."

Maris bit her lip, tears flowing freely, dripping off her chin. She wanted to save him, from himself, from his long-endured pain.

"You can't save me, Maris. No one can. I understood that long ago."

Maris covered her face with her hands. He jolted her again with the gun. She climbed the stones to the top of the wall. From that height, the fall would be short and swift.

"Drop the gun!"

Struggling for balance, Maris looked back to the sound of Dan's voice. "Dan!" He wasn't alone. Jamie was with him. Beside her, Robert raised his gun higher. Not at her, but at the approaching men.

"Don't do it," Maris implored.

Robert glanced at her, the eyes of the last Mabry awash with agony. He stepped up next to her, his gun still level on Dan and Jamie. "What, death by cop? Keeps me from going back to prison. I'd never come out again. At least I got to see an Alcina Cove sunrise one more time. With family. Pretty fucking strange, huh?"

"Robert, please."

"No." He shoved her. She stumbled back and went over.

Chapter 26

"Son of a fucking bitch!" God the water was like ice, stabbing with needle teeth into Dan's flesh. Ice fish, he couldn't get the image of sharp-toothed ice fish out of his head. Far above, something was taking place. He had no idea what and didn't care. He'd shot Robert Mabry in the right arm, causing the gun to spin out of the man's hand. Dan had been aiming for his freaking head, though. A shot on the fly. He couldn't have hoped for perfection. He was surprised he hadn't missed altogether. Afterward, he'd leapt over the stone wall and followed Maris down into the sea.

They were both probably going to die with the water this cold and waves crashing the surf repeatedly against the rocks. They damned well better die together because he wasn't going to let her die alone.

Had he ever loved anyone this much in his life? He supposed he had, but if he did, they'd been forgotten in the intensity of the moment when he watched Maris tumble off that stone wall forty feet above the waterline.

Bobbing above the waves, he screamed out her name. Fat lot of good that was going to do. Nothing could be heard above the pounding surf. "Maris! Don't you leave me! Damn it all, don't you leave—"

He sucked in a mouthful of salt water and spewed it back out again, floundering to keep his head up, to fight the outgoing current and the incoming breakers. There. There it was again. A glowing ball of silver-white light shooting up and down above the surf.

You find her. That's why I sent her to you. You find my little Maris and save her before I leave.

Dan headed off with strong, sure strokes in the direction of the light.

Chapter 27

Maris smiled up at Jamie. It couldn't have been easy for him to come to her like this, away from the others.

"You're truly cleared now, Maris. The gas station owner said their machine has been printing a day behind for the past six months. They don't seem able to fix the issue. And he remembered you, too, as soon as he saw your photo."

"Thanks, Jamie."

He started to walk away, but turned back. "As for Robert Mabry, if he doesn't plead and goes to trial, the outcome will be the same. He'll never get out of jail again. He'll die there."

Maris nodded. "I'll visit him when I can. And I'll write."

Jamie's eyes went wide. "You'll do what?"

"He never meant to be what he'd become. I'm all the family he has."

The detective stepped forward in awkward haste and threw his arms around her, crushing her against his chest. "You're a strange woman, Maris Granger," he whispered against her ear. "And a wonderful one. No wonder Dan was willing to throw everything away for you."

"I never would have let him."

"I don't think you could have stopped him."

A step sounded on the garden pathway. "Hey! Get your hands off my woman."

Jamie hopped back. Maris spun to look at Dan approaching. "You call me your woman like that again," she said with a smile, "and I'll…I'll… I'll sic Jamie on you."

Jamie arched a brow and snorted. "I'll see you two inside." He strode toward the Timeless Inn's dining room. Dan took her hand and turned it over so the diamond on her finger caught the last of the evening sun. Tonight was a celebration of their engagement. And of life, really, and the abatement of the darkness that had once clung to him. A darkness not of death, of doom, but of emotions he'd kept contained for way too long. He exuded a green light now, of healing and contentment. No one knew the latter part of the celebration except the two of them.

"I have something to show you. I've been saving it for a special moment. I think this is special enough."

She slipped her hand into his and allowed him to lead her back the way he'd come on the path. He brought her to the maple tree, the leaves burgundy and green with autumn's onset. "Stand here," he said, setting her in place on the walkway. He then walked over to the tree and stood in front of it, striking a pose that caused her to frown and laugh at the same time. "I'm sorry, what is it that you're doing?"

"Remember this, where I'm standing and what I'm doing."

"Okay."

He strode back to her side. "And now look at this." He held up a photograph. She gasped.

"That's us. You and me."

"Yeah," he said.

"How old were you? Six? And I was what, about two?"

"Uh-huh, and apparently we were standing there, the best of friends, right here in your backyard. I don't think someone with my eyes was ever your imaginary friend, Maris. I think it's always been me, and you've always been mine."

He kissed her. She slipped her arms behind his back and pulled him close. The word in his heart echoed through hers, over and over.

Always. Always.

About the Author

Celia Ashley lives in rural Lehigh County, Pennsylvania, an area rich in history and beauty and from which she has drawn inspiration for many of her tales. She is the mother of three grown sons, as well as the companion of five cats. When not writing, she is a garden enthusiast and spends time painting in a variety of mediums. Published in historical romance under the pen names Alyssa Deane and Robin Maderich, she has most recently taken to writing spicy contemporary paranormal romance as Celia Ashley, for which she has received enthusiastic reviews. Please visit the author at www.celiaashley.com, find her on Facebook, and follow her on Twitter.

Be sure to read the first book in the series, Dark Tides, followed by Storm Surge. Each gripping tale is set in the fictional coastal town of Alcina Cove and is a standalone novel.

Dark Tides

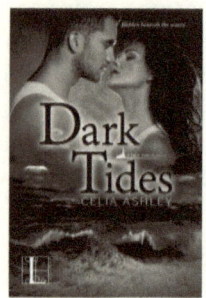

The depths of the ocean hide more secrets than one...

When a man without a memory washes up outside her lonely seaside cottage, Meg can't explain the connection she feels to him. She should be afraid, suspicious, even angry that he would disturb her hard-won peace. But something about Caleb Hunter calls to her. On instinct, Meg asks this stranger into her home, her life—into the place left vacant by her dead husband, who drowned at sea a year to the day before Caleb appeared.

But something isn't right. Half-buried memories begin to haunt Meg's dreams, Caleb seems to know things he can't possibly know, and there are signs that someone else is watching them, someone with a heart as cold as the sea...

Chapter 1

Swiping a handful of sodden hair from his eyes, Caleb Hunter scrambled upright, stepping away from the water purling around his bare feet. An expanse of sand stretched as far as he could see into a soaking fog, although beyond the crest of dune in front of him, a slate-roofed, decrepit white Victorian rose out of the shimmering haze. The house didn't look at all familiar. Neither did the beach. Nothing did, no matter what direction he turned.

With a deep, painful breath, Caleb considered what he did know. His name, for one. Good. He thought he might be thirty-five or thirty-six years old. Somehow, he knew he stood six-foot-one, he had brown eyes, and his nearly black hair badly needed trimming. At this point, it needed a great deal more than that, plastered with salt and sand and a bit of debris hanging in front of his eyes. Yanking a piece of seaweed from above his brow, he tossed the vegetation down, tracking its descent past the length of his naked body. He pivoted in a slow, searching circle. Not a stitch of clothing lay in the sand.

After a moment, he lifted his hands, turning them palm up and finding them well-formed, calloused across the pad of flesh below his fingers. The skin of his fingertips had wrinkled from long immersion, and fine sand had embedded in the bend of each joint. Salt and sand encrusted the hair on his chafed arms. A black, ugly bruise throbbed on his right forearm. When he flexed his hand, the injury burned deep into the muscle. More sand coated his torso and his groin, clumped in the hair on his legs, and grated in places more private. He planted his feet apart and bent to brush the sand away, discovering this only made the situation worse.

Dismayed by his lack of recollection, as well as his lack of garments, Caleb closed his eyes and pushed both hands through his hair. Clasping his fingers behind his neck, he frowned when he located a hard knot of tender flesh at the base of his skull. Something had struck him there. He remembered that.

No, not something. Someone. Someone had tried to kill him.

Shit.

That fragment of recall brought no further revelation, but his skin crawled in reaction to a danger he couldn't fathom, and he checked again to make certain no one else occupied the stretch of beach. Shredding fog revealed a woman approaching him from a short distance. Walking with her head down, she bent every now and then to collect small items from the water's edge. Not knowing what else to do, Caleb sat in the sand once more, pulling his knees up close to his chin and wrapping his arms around his legs. After ascertaining he'd tucked everything neatly out of view, he waited.

She stopped little more than a dozen feet from him, bending to pluck at a polished stone to deposit with the array of minuscule treasures on her palm. The wind fluttered the length of a dark blue shawl from her shoulders, dragging the fringed edge in the sand. Tan trousers, rolled to the knee, exposed the curve of her calf and slender feet washed by the surge of the tide as she crouched. Caleb lifted his gaze again to her face. Even at that distance, he could see her eyes were quite green and staring straight into his.

Clutching her treasure trove against her breast, the woman straightened. Her lips moved in speech, words drowned by the low growl of the tide. Caleb cleared his parched throat, uncertain what to say as the woman continued to stare at him with an unreadable expression. After a moment, she dropped the items from her fingers into a heap on the sand and backed away, placing one bare foot behind the other, gaze never leaving his face until she turned on her heel and started an awkward run across the shifting sand. The blue shawl flew from her shoulders.

Leaping to his feet, Caleb darted forward and snatched up the garment, draping the soft wool around his waist. He tugged the folds to cover as much of his hip area as he could. Scooping the woman's discarded treasure into his hand, he went after her, following her toward the white house. Already a good distance ahead of him, she leaped up the long flight of wooden steps from the beach two at a time, crossing a seaside garden to a porch, where she yanked open the door and disappeared inside. Caleb paused in uncertainty. He hadn't meant to alarm her, and she appeared frightened, not merely startled. Nevertheless, if he didn't speak to her, he had no hope of receiving any answers to his many questions.

Girding his determination, as well as his grip on her shawl, he set his own bare feet to the first step and climbed to a brick pathway that led through the garden. At the porch, he paused again, studying the length of the covered area, the blank face of each window for any sign she peered out at him. He found only the milky reflection on glass of the fogged-in sea.

He walked across the porch and halted in front of the door. "Hello?" he called, listening hard.

She responded in a muffled demand through the solid wood. "Who are you?"

"I'm sorry if I startled you."

Silence.

"My name is Caleb Hunter," he said with a crazy expectation she would throw open the door and announce him welcome, perhaps apologize for not recognizing him in his present state. Instead, he heard nothing. The door remained closed.

"I need help." He waited. "I thought I would return your shawl to you, but…but I have a specific need of it at the moment."

"Keep it," he heard her say. The fact she had spoken again gave him a glimmer of hope.

"I don't know where I am," he persisted. "I don't know who I am," he added, frowning down at the worn boards of the porch floor. Aloud, the statement sounded ludicrous. The brief flare of fear surging through him at his own words held no humor at all.

"What do you mean, you don't know who you are?"

The door creaked open. A security chain stretched taut in the space between frame and door. Her leaf-green eyes regarded him intently from behind a fringe of honey-colored bangs.

"I don't remember much of anything specific," he said. "I believe I was hit on the head and…and maybe I washed up onto the beach from the ocean. I'm not sure. My name is about all I do remember with any certainty. Is the name Caleb Hunter familiar to you?"

"No," she said. "I don't know anyone by that name."

The door shut again. Scoured by the salt winds, the light blue paint had peeled away in places to show the bare, weathered wood beneath. A moment later, the door opened again, enough for her to toss something out at him. He bent and picked up a crumpled pair of pants. Light blue fabric, heavy and faded with wear. Jeans, they were called. He remembered that. They looked like they would fit him.

Turning his back, Caleb dropped the shells, stones, and bits of sea glass onto the lacquered surface of a nearby wicker chair. He set the shawl beside them and hastened into the jeans, grimacing as sand abraded his flesh. If the woman still stood in the doorway watching him struggle with the pants, she gave no indication. He glanced over his shoulder. Through the narrow opening, he saw nothing.

"What was that in your hand?"

At her question, he slowly pivoted to face the door, feeling more naked now than he had in her shawl. Talking to her half-dressed, wearing nothing but a pair of borrowed blue jeans, he contemplated picking up the shawl and draping it across his shoulders. Instead, he seized it from the floor where it had fallen and placed it beside her rescued treasure. The door opened a little more and her face appeared.

"Your things," he said by way of explanation. "I never meant to frighten you, to make you drop what you'd been gathering."

She frowned at the shells and oddments he had placed on the chair before turning her gaze to meet his. Slow to speak, she studied him a moment. "Thank you."

The door closed again.

Caleb moved to another chair and sat down. He leaned forward, elbows on thighs, hands folded together between his knees. The shifting of his body renewed pain in every muscle and tendon. Reaching up, he fingered the back of his head to trace again the contours of the vicious lump. He remembered a flurry of fists, grunting blows, and male voices raised in harsh invective, but he didn't recall the words. Was one of those voices his? Could have been. Yes, it could have been his voice. He remembered...nothing. Nothing else.

Damn it.

Once more, the door opened. The woman stepped onto the porch holding out a T-shirt. Gratefully, he took it, then slipped the garment over his head. It smelled as if it had been left sitting in a drawer. Not that it mattered.

"Your husband's?" he asked, not certain from what part of his brain such a question came.

She nodded.

"Is he here?"

"He's dead," she said.

"Oh." Caleb ran his hand through his salt-encrusted hair. "I'm sorry."

"So am I."

She moved to the chair where her shawl lay and bent to pick up the items he had deposited there. Brushing the sand and crushed shell from the seat into her hand as well, she walked to the porch railing and sprinkled them into the garden below, permitting them to flow through a loose fist. Her eyes closed as she did this, as if something ritualistic existed in the execution of her action. He wondered what had happened to her husband, if maybe she did this in his memory.

"His ship went down in a storm."

He started, meeting her eyes. Her direct gaze made him shiver.

"That's what you were thinking, wasn't it?" she said, brushing her hands clean. "You were wondering how he died."

Caleb shivered again within the confines of a dead man's shirt. "Yes," he admitted, "I was."

She nodded, her longs bangs swinging forward. "A year ago today," she told him quietly.

Today. Caleb said nothing.

She moved back across the porch, stopping before the chair opposite him where she gathered up the shawl and sat, holding the garment balled against her stomach. With her feet tucked around the outside of the legs of the chair, knees angled together, she appeared innocent and vulnerable. Caleb's stomach churned. He shoved a fist against his abdomen in an effort to control the response.

"I dream about him most nights," she confided in a voice barely above a whisper, her eyes intent on his own. "But not always. This morning, though, on the anniversary of his death, I dreamed about someone else. I didn't realize it until I saw you on the beach. I'm fairly certain I dreamed of you."

Stunned by her speech, Caleb sat back hard against the chair frame. His breath exploded as the knot at the base of his skull met wood, causing him to jerk forward again, bright pinpoints of light dancing before his eyes.

He couldn't remember the fundamental particulars about himself and his life, but he knew what dreams were without requiring an explanation. What she said made no sense to him. None at all. Unless—

"What do you mean? Do you know me?" he asked again. Perhaps she didn't know his name, but she might recall having seen him somewhere. Something. Anything.

She raised her eyes from a fierce contemplation of the air between them. After a moment of consideration, she shook her head. He licked his dry, salty lips as he shifted on the seat, frowning at the pain wracking his body. Observing his movements, she reached into her pocket and drew out a narrow black object, holding it on her palm. From somewhere in the recesses of murky recognition, he recognized a cell phone. "What are you doing?"

"Calling the police," she said.

Don't let her. Don't let her. Don't let her.

The force of the voice in his head caused him to gasp, recognizing without understanding that an instinct for preservation spoke to him. "Don't," he said and added "please" more sedately at the widening of her eyes.

She displayed no further consternation at his command, just cocked her head to the side, her gaze turning contemplative as if studying him. Even so, he could see the pulse beating beneath her jaw, the momentary suspension of her respiration.

"Why not?" she asked after a moment, still holding the phone at the ready in her hand.

He tried to dredge up a reply she would find suitable. He couldn't imagine where to begin. "God, I don't know," he answered, lowering his head into his hand, shoving fingers deep into his tangled hair. "I don't. I don't know. I...I don't know."

He heard a short, decisive inhalation and looked up in time to witness her returning the phone to her pocket. Fingers curled loosely, she lowered her right hand into her left across her stomach. "Don't you want to go to the hospital?"

"Why?"

"Aren't you hurt?"

She waited for his reply. Caleb didn't believe he'd ever seen eyes so green, though he couldn't recall for certain. He straightened in the chair, folding his hands in his lap. "What makes you think I'm hurt?"

Blowing out a breath, she stood, tucking the sand-spattered shawl against her abdomen. "You can hardly move," she said. "And the wound to your head—"

"How do you know I have a head wound?"

Her mouth twisted in wry amusement. "I could say I dreamed it, but I didn't. You told me you thought you'd been hit on the head. Even if you hadn't, you wince every time you touch the back of your skull. That and the fact you can't remember who you are are fairly good indicators of some sort of head trauma. Which," she added, "is why you should have a doctor check you out. Even if you don't want the police involved, I could call an ambulance or, well, I suppose I could drive you to the hospital myself."

Possessing a certain amount of defiance in her expression, she did not look away from him. Her stance shifted, and her hand lifted to assist him in rising. He wondered at her trust in a stranger, standing so close to him with her hand extended, as if she had no idea how easily he could overpower her if he had the inclination. He could remember nothing about his past life. For all he knew, he could be a nasty sort of person, a dangerous man. After all, someone had tried to kill him, hadn't they? Somebody must have had good reason for that.

"Not yet," he whispered. His aversion to the possibility of questions, of a need for answers he could not provide, worried him. Was he taking a foolish risk, not getting medical help? Still, he didn't think his injuries were life threatening. He felt no weakness, no disorientation beyond his inability to recall.

"You could be bleeding internally. You could have a skull fracture."

He rubbed his eyes, sand grating across his lids. "Are you suggesting I might die?"

"I don't know," she said. "I'm not a doctor."

Through the slats of the porch railing, he saw the sea, the fog lifting above the waves. Possibly, he'd walked to the beach from somewhere else and collapsed here, but that didn't seem likely. In fact, he knew better. The sensation of plunging into the ocean, tumbling through the cold, salty tides, though not quite memory, had the resonation of truth.

"I know a doctor who will come to the house. I've had him here before. He is…well, discreet. At least he can check you out, and if he feels you need to go to a hospital, you will. If not, well, that's up to you then."

Up to him. What would he do if this doctor pronounced him well enough to avoid treatment? How would he even begin to know what steps to take next? Avoiding thought of all the unimaginable possibilities, he nodded at her. "Fine," he said. "Let him come."

She walked to the far side of the porch, talking into the instrument she'd pulled back out of her pocket, glancing at him over her shoulder as she spoke. After a few minutes, she returned. "He'll be here shortly. You may as well wait inside."

He eyed her with bewilderment. "You're not afraid to have me in your house?"

"Should I be?"

"I don't know."

"I do." She held out her hand again. Swallowing, he slipped his fingers into hers and allowed her to pull him up from his seat with surprising strength. Standing before her, he smelled the sea in her hair, the fresh air, and a faint suffusion of citrus. The top of her head barely came up to his collarbone. A feeling of protectiveness stole over him, making him frown.

"Are you sure you don't know me?" *Because it sure as hell feels like I know you.*

"Positive," she said. "And by the way, my name is Meg. Meg Donovan." Clutching the shawl in her fist, she headed inside, leaving the door standing wide. Confounded, Caleb followed her into the house, the inside of his borrowed pants chafing like sandpaper over thighs and calves and along the tender flesh of his testicles. He trailed her from the back door into the kitchen, where she indicated he should sit in a chair she slid from the table. She pulled back the curtains to allow more light into the room and walked behind him across worn linoleum to take a glass down from a cabinet. Outside the window, he saw the sun had broken through the fog, golden light reflecting in a shimmer on the pale blue ceiling of the porch. She opened the refrigerator and rummaged around inside before returning to stand beside him.

"Here," Meg said, handing him a glass of something orange. Orange juice. Yes, he remembered that. "Drink it slowly. Are you warm enough? I can get you a blanket if you need one. Sometimes shock—"

"I'm fine," he said.

"Hardly."

Circling around the table, she pulled out a chair on the opposite side and sat, folding her hands on the scarred painted surface. "So you know your name."

He nodded.

"Amnesia is a fascinating condition," she went on. "Not to you, I'm sure, but it's odd what the brain might pick and choose in terms of recollection. I'm thinking in the most severe cases, you wouldn't be able to walk or communicate or even pick up that glass, but I could be wrong."

Mulling over her words as he took several sips from the glass, he welcomed the slightly acidic burn in his throat. He set the glass down. "So you're saying I'm not too bad off, even though I can't remember a single goddamn thing except my name?"

"But that's not exactly true, is it?" Her gaze held his until she rose and stepped away from the table, leaving to answer a distant knock on another door. He clutched the glass of juice in both hands on the tabletop, staring past to a series of lines scratched into the table's wooden surface. Not random, but seeming to spell out a word, a word he couldn't focus on as he thought about what she had said. How did she know? How did she know about the jumble of thoughts he held inside this fragile bubble in his mind?

"Caleb Hunter?" a deep voice said. "I'm Dr. Redecker, and I hear you may need my help."

Caleb spun on the chair to face the man standing between him and the interior kitchen door with a vague hope the man's face would be familiar. The gray hair, heavy countenance, and steady blue gaze meant nothing to him. This total lack of recollection made him understand something else, something he hadn't understood earlier. When looking into the eyes of the woman in whose kitchen he sat, he didn't see a stranger.